VIOLENT LEADER

CHICAGO MAFIA DONS

BIANCA COLE

CONTENTS

ROURKE

uty and honor.

Two of the qualities I hold above all else. They've never felt more poignant than they do at this moment. I breathe in the earthy fall air, infused with the scent of rotting leaves as the forest around the cemetery goes into hibernation. A chill breeze flows past me, chilling me to the bone. The breeze brings with it a flutter of amber leaves falling from a nearby tree. My attention lands on one in particular that swirls gently to the ground, landing in the hole waiting for my father.

It's fitting to be here in the cemetery at this time of year, as it serves as a reminder that everything dies in the end. Life will always fade and death will commit us to the earth, although Callaghans seem to go too early. I guess that's the nature of the game when you exist in a world of darkness.

Grief surrounds us as the solemn Gaelic tune fills the air, readying us to lower our father to the ground. The heavyweight of loss presses on my chest as I focus my attention on the casket. It's like deja vu. Only three years ago, we buried our mother right here.

Kieran and Killian stand on either side of me, ready to lower him into the ground. They're both so different. Kieran is the baby of the family and has no shame in showing his emotions as his tears flood down his face. Killian is more like me, staring with a stony, unreadable expression at the casket.

I glance behind me briefly, noticing Maeve standing with tears streaming down her face. Ever since the revelation about Shane, she's been impossible to console, and I wish the trauma had never resurfaced for her, especially at such a difficult time. My sister has always been in touch with her emotions, unlike Killian and me, and it's one thing our father hated about her.

Gael stands with an arm around my sister, supporting her in this time of need. Her support when she needs him, like when our mother died. I know our clan chief has always had eyes for my sister, and with our father dead and buried, I wager it's only a matter of time until he makes a move on her.

I have no objection if it's what Maeve wants. Gael has held her heart for years, and it's plain for anyone to see. The deal with the Volkov bratva is certainly void, meaning I won't stand against them being together. If that's what she wants, then so be it.

I don't agree with selling my flesh and blood for gain like my father, as I will take what I want with brute force. Fuck alliances with other organizations, as we have never needed them before, and we don't need them now. All we need is to stand strong and united, hitting the Russians where it hurts.

Torin finishes saying goodbye to his last surviving sibling. My chaotic thoughts muffle his words as I struggle to comprehend the emotions swirling like a storm inside of me. The task ahead of me isn't daunting. It's exciting. My father always said that I thrive well in chaos, and that's a dangerous quality.

The priest says some bullshit about life and death, but I don't listen. My brothers and I move forward, each grabbing an emerald rope that rests beneath our father's coffin. Torin also helps. It's hard to believe it's only been three years since we stood in this same place, lowering our mother into the ground. A tragedy that haunts me to this day.

My mother's death was my fault.

I had been recklessly dealing with the Morrone family and issued a threat without my father knowing. Their retaliation was to hit my mother on the way to her weekly pilates class. Until my father's dying day, he never knew the truth; he never knew that I started the war.

I swallow the lump in my throat as we take my father's weight and lower him into the hole dug next to Mom. Killian meets my gaze, and for a moment, I detect the grief eating away at him below the surface before he quickly masks it.

The priest clears his throat. "You can say your goodbyes in private." He glances at me. "Rourke, why don't you go first?"

I clench my jaw, knowing that there are no words to say. "Sure." I step forward as everyone gives me space, staring at the coffin lying in the ground, waiting for the soil to cover it forever. All I feel is rage, nothing else. A dark and dangerous rage bubbling beneath the surface.

Father always taught me not to react to emotions, as that is when you make mistakes. Unfortunately, I'm not like him. Rage is a weapon, a powerful weapon if you know how to wield it.

"I'm sorry, Father, but I have to use my anger now to get revenge for your death," I murmur into the wind. "I'll make Spartak pay, I promise." I turn my back on the hole and walk away, allowing everyone else to say their farewells.

My Italian black leather shoes squelch in the mud underfoot as I make my way toward the car, trying to focus my racing thoughts. Ever since he died, I've had one thing on my mind.

Revenge.

I promised Father over his grave that I'd make the Bratva leader pay, and that's what I intend to do. The hardest way to hit a man like Sparktak Volkov is to take something precious from him. He covets his daughter, Viktoria Volkov. There was recent talk of an alliance between the Volkov Bratva and one of the Bratva families in Moscow. Spartak intends to use his untouched princess and marry her off to a powerful oligarch's son.

I'll take her from him and break her, leaving his princess a shell of a woman. Ruining Spartak's intention to strengthen his operations with her marriage and proving to him that the Callaghan Clan aren't to be messed with. Viktoria Volkov will pay for the sins of her father.

MY SISTER truly deserves her happy ending after all the shit she's been through since she was a kid. Our father was always cruel to her, stemming from the trauma she endured. I never understood why he blamed her for something out of her control, but he did.

Our blessing for their pairing has made her happy, and that's all that matters. Father may be gone, but we have to make the best of what we've got. There's no turning back the clock.

Gael turns around and smiles at Maeve. The way he looks at her makes me sure he'd die trying to protect her. An older brother can ask for nothing more.

Killian clears his throat, drawing my attention to him.

"What is it?" I ask when I notice he's glaring daggers at me.

His eyes narrow. "Viktoria Volkov?" He shakes his head. "When the fuck were you going to run it by me?"

I clench my jaw, sensing that our joint leadership will not be easy. Our father never could decide who would take over out of the two of us, stating we had to lead together. "I just ran it by you now, and it's our best option." As the eldest son, I feel responsible for the clan.

He runs a hand across the back of his neck.

"What happened to the two of us leading the clan together?"

"The clan needs strong leadership. As the eldest, I have to make the decisions and stick to them." I take a long swig of whiskey.

My brother is a hard man to read. If he's angry at my declaration that I'm the leader, he doesn't show it. "Aye, that is why I felt I should take Gael's position." He glares at me. "However, you don't want that either."

I'm not sure how he believes that's a good idea. "What message would we send if twenty years of loyal service to the Clan results in a demotion?" I ask. It's ridiculous that he believes it's fine to demote Gael, because he wants a fucking title.

He shakes his head. "Then what do you propose? You're clan captain, and I'm merely the brother?" I can sense the anger building in his tone.

"No, we can restructure the clan." I clench my fists on the table in front of me. "I'll be clan captain, and you can be vice-captain, which stills give you authority over Gael." I raise a brow. "How about it?"

Killian doesn't look thrilled. "It will do." He nods. "Personally, I would've preferred to get rid of Gael."

I sigh heavily. "We can't demote Gael because Father is dead."

Killian grunts. "I've never liked him."

I don't understand Killian's dislike for Gael. "I don't know why. He's practically family."

His eyes narrow. "He's not blood."

"Soon enough, he might be your brother-in-law, so I'd try to get over it, for Maeve's sake."

Killian doesn't comment, lifting his glass and knocking back the rest of the whiskey in his glass.

Kieran has barely said a word tonight. It's unlike him to be so quiet, even with the loss of our father. "What's your opinion on Gael, Kier?" I ask.

He looks startled that I'm asking him anything. "He's alright. Why?"

"Killian isn't a fan." I nod toward our brother. "He thinks we should demote him because Father's dead."

Killian growls softly, shaking his head. "I didn't say that."

"Bullshit. It's exactly what you—"

Torin clears his throat, sitting down at the table. "Don't tell me you are all bickering already, at your father's fucking wake of all places."

I shake my head, and so does Killian. "Of course not," Killian says, standing up. "I'm going to get a drink." He walks away stiffly.

"I can't believe he's gone, lads," Torin says, meeting my gaze. The grief is written all over his face, even if he doesn't allow the tears to fall. It's the

Callaghan way. Most of us are closed off from our emotions, which is how it has to be when brutality is the language of our world.

I don't respond, but Kieran does. "What will we do without him?"

Survive.

It's what the Callaghans are good at. We can't come to a grinding halt because our father is no longer here.

Torin shakes his head. "To my brother and your father." He lifts his pint of Guinness. "May he live on in our memories and the soul of the clan."

Kieran lifts his drink. "Here, here."

The wake is a celebration of life, but it's impossible to celebrate anything. Our father should be here with us, leading the clan as he has always done. Instead, the weight of the empire rests on my shoulders.

I raise my whiskey tumbler and clink it against Torin's glass first and then Kieran's. "To revenge. I will avenge his death if it's that last thing I do."

Torin grimaces. "Careful, lad. I don't want to attend your funeral next." There's concern in his voice. "Revenge is all good and well if you don't wind up dead yourself."

I know the path I'm walking on is dangerous, as it's one I watched my father walk down the moment the Morrone family took our mother too early. The responsibility of which I'll have to carry alone for the rest of my life, as I can't tell anyone what I did. Not only did my actions result in her death, but it resulted in us losing our father, as all that consumed his thoughts was revenge.

However, I intend to go about it entirely differently. Thankfully, I'm not as hot-headed as my father, and I know how to take guidance from my brothers and uncles.

"Aye, don't worry, Uncle. I won't be reckless."

It feels like this is the moment Father has been readying me for all these years, training me to take the lead. It is time to prove that I have what it takes to lead the clan and ensure we keep power over our territory in Chicago. I will not let my father down, no matter how bloody and chaotic this war gets.

2

VIKTORIA

"*A*re you serious?" I ask, glaring at my father. At twenty-one years old, he still won't allow me off his leash. I'm like a dog to him. "I have been planning to go to this party for months, and now you're saying it's not safe?"

My father steps closer to me, towering over me intimidatingly. "Watch yourself Viktoria. You don't understand the danger that has befallen our city." He tilts his head to the side slightly. "We are at war."

"How does that concern me?" I ask. My two best friends, Paige and Alexandra, would never forgive me for bailing on them at the last minute like this.

"You're my heir. Anything that concerns me concerns you too, printessa." He clenches his fists by his side, which should warn me not to push the matter, but I'm not missing this party.

"I have Konstantin, and he will keep me safe." Konstantin is my bodyguard.

My father pinches the bridge of his nose, which means I've really angered him. "Are you questioning me?" His voice is stern, and the sound instills an acute fear inside of me.

I swallow hard. I know better. My father has the last say about everything in my life, and if he says I can't go, then there is no room for discussion. "No."

He narrows his eyes. "Good. I don't want to hear another word about it. Your friends are welcome to come here."

I laugh. "Do you think my friends would come here instead of the party?" I shake my head. "You're delusional."

He growls at that. "Watch your mouth, Viktoria."

I hold back my retort, knowing that he won't be happy if I continue to test him. My only choice now is to sneak out without him knowing. "Fine. I'll be in my room." I turn my back on him, which results in an animal like growl.

"Did I say I'm finished with you?" he asks.

I know that tone of voice all too well. My father is truly angry right now. An emotion I have enticed from him, which means I'll be at the end of his wrath. "No," I mutter, turning back around to look into his dark, rage-filled eyes.

He walks slowly toward me and glares down at me. "I understand you're disappointed, but I won't allow my children to speak to me like that." He grabs my chin between his finger and his thumb. "Two hours in the basement will suffice as punishment."

My stomach dips further. "Right now?" I ask., knowing that two hours in that dank and dark basement will make me late for the party I fully intend to attend.

His dark eyes narrow, and he steps closer. "Yes, and if you say one more word, the time will double."

I bite my lip hard, knowing that he is serious. If he were to double my time in confinement, then I would certainly miss the party.

After a suitable time of silence, he nods in satisfaction. "Follow me."

My father is a harsh disciplinarian who has never allowed us a normal childhood. Maxim, my brother, thrived under his strict and brutal upbringing, groomed to be just like him. After all, he's the Volkov Bratva heir.

The Bratva is a misogynistic construct, and my father has brought me up learning how to be a submissive wife, despite never believing in the role he has groomed me to fill. High school is over, and my friends are moving on, getting jobs, and living their lives. It's what I want too, even though I'm resigned to the fact it isn't in the cards for me. I'd love a life free from crime and my father's warped wars he's constantly fighting, but Father has made it clear I will marry a suitor of his choosing and there is no room for discussion.

Father stops outside of the door and opens it. "Inside," he barks.

I stare into the dark abyss the concrete steps lead into, swallowing hard. It's been a while since Father threw me into the dark basement as punishment.

"Inside now," he barks.

I meet his cold, hard gaze before stepping into the dark abyss. The coldness envelopes me as I descend deeper, jumping at the slam of the door behind me. Father turns the key in the lock, sealing me into the pitch black, chilly space. I shut my eyes, trying to picture my favorite place on this earth.

Our old home back in Russia playing in the waterfall as a child with my mother. The pain cuts through my chest as her smiling face appears in my mind. I fear coming down here so much, as my happy place reminds me of my mother and the gaping hole she left in my heart.

When I was only eleven years old, she died of cancer, only three years after we'd arrived in America. A foreign land where nothing felt right. The only solace was my mother, and when the disease took her so early, it felt like I lived in a world of pure darkness. There isn't a day that goes by that I don't miss her.

"I can't believe your father is such a hard-ass," Paige says, shaking her head as she scrolls through social media in the back of the cab. "Why does he lock you in a basement? It sounds fucking medieval."

My stomach churns as I regret telling her he'd done that. It's not normal behavior, and that's because we're not a normal family. My two best friends don't know who I am or who my father is. "I don't want to talk about it. Let's talk of something else." My brow furrows. "Why didn't Alexandra catch the cab with us?"

Paige finally looks up from her cell phone. "Didn't she tell you? Henry took her for a meal first at some expensive restaurant nearby, so she's going to meet us there."

I swallow hard at the mention of the jackass my best friend is dating. Henry Jacobs was the quarterback at our high school and a complete and utter jerk. The guy was a dick to me throughout school, and when Alexandra told me they'd hooked up at some party a couple of months ago, I couldn't believe it. "She didn't tell me, no."

Paige shrugs. "Maybe she didn't want to bring up Henry." Her brow furrows. "Are you still hung up on that?"

Neither Paige nor Alexandra understand because the jocks and cheerleaders didn't pick on them for being different. My Russian accent was always a cause for amusement amongst the bullies of our school.

I shrug. "I think the guy is an asshole, and it will only end badly."

"He's different from when we were at high school." Paige sighs. "Maybe agree to meet him sometime and see for yourself?"

"Maybe," I murmur, digging my cell phone out of my pocket as a distraction.

Paige continues to scroll through social media.

A message from my brother, Maxim, pops up.

Father is going to kill you if he finds out you snuck out.

Shit.

The last thing I need is my worthless brother ratting me out. I didn't enjoy my two-hour punishment in the basement, but what Father would do to me if he learned I went to the party anyway would be far worse.

Please don't tell him, Maxim.

I send the message, and he types back right away.

Of course not. I'm not a snitch. Be careful. He's right. The city is dangerous for a Volkov right now.

I relax slightly but then wonder if I was a fool to sneak out. If Maxim thinks it's dangerous, then it probably is, as he's rarely shaken by anything.

"You seem tense, Viki. What's up?"

I meet Paige's gaze and shake my head. "Nothing, just family drama." It's hard keeping so many secrets from my two closest friends, but I know I can't reveal my true identity. I trust Paige and Alexandra, but no civilians can know the truth about our family.

The cab pulls up in front of Flux, which has a ridiculously long line outside. "Great, we'll be queuing for ages."

Paige shakes her head. "No, I got us on the VIP guest list last week, as a friend at work owed me."

My stomach churns. "You didn't tell me that."

She smiles. "I wanted it to be a surprise."

Little does she know putting my name on the guest list could attract unwanted attention from the people my father is at war with. Father always taught me to use an alias if I ever have to put my name down for anything, but my friends aren't aware. I push my worries aside and get out of the cab, following Paige to the exclusive VIP line. Alexandra is nowhere to be seen. "Do you think she's running late?" I ask.

Paige shrugs. "Who knows? I'll text her and tell her we've gone in."

I nod, preferring to get inside the club rather than linger on the street. The man at the door asks for our names and finds them, allowing us inside. "That was easy," Paige says, flicking her long, golden blonde hair over her shoulder. Her phone dings, and she pulls it from her purse. "It looks like she's already here." She stuffs her phone back in her purse and grabs my hand, pulling me onto the dancefloor. "Let's dance. We'll bump into her soon enough."

I laugh as Paige forces me to spin around in a pirouette to the music. "You are crazy. What about getting a drink?"

She gives me a skeptical glare. "You know I never buy my drinks, so I need to find a nice man to buy them for me."

I shake my head. "I'll buy them."

Paige is always broke, especially since her parents kicked her out a year ago after flunking out of college. She's been working a job on minimum wage, which barely funds her rent and bills. "Sure, if you don't mind."

"What use is it having a rich dad if you can't spoil your friends?" I ask.

She smiles. "Yeah, let's get your father back for locking you in that basement." Paige grabs my hand and leads me toward the bar when I notice Alexandra. She dances toward us, smiling.

Paige pulls her into a hug first. "This party is awesome."

"Sure is. Thanks for getting us on the guest list." I glance behind her to see Henry leaning against the bar, smirking at us.

"I didn't know your boyfriend was going to be here." I glare at Paige. "Was that another secret?"

Paige holds her hands up. "You need to give him a chance, as he's not so bad."

Alexandra looks guilty. "I thought you said Viki was okay with it?"

It looks like Paige has been up to her games again. I sigh heavily. "Fuck's sake. I hate the guy, and I'm not sure why you have to ambush me with him on a girl's night out."

Alexandra looks hurt by my outburst, but I can't help how I feel.

"Maybe it's because you need to find a hot guy to date yourself, Viki," Paige says.

This fucking subject has to come up whenever we go out together.

Alexandra shakes her head. "Don't start that again, Paige."

"What? All I'm saying is if she got laid, she'd probably finally chill out. Who wants to be so uptight all the time, anyway."

I glare at Paige, wondering at that moment why I'm even friends with her. She can be a real bitch. Out of the three of us, I'm the only one who hasn't lost my virginity yet. I tell her it doesn't bother me, as I'm not interested in hooking up with some random guy at a club, but she won't listen.

My father would probably murder me. He's clarified that he will select my husband when the time comes and that I must be untouched when he does, or there will be hell to pay. I hate obeying him, but there aren't many people alive who have the guts to stand up to him.

"I'm going to the bathroom." I clench my jaw and turn away from her, frustrated by this conversation. I walk away before she can suggest she accompany me.

I'm here to enjoy myself, not be lectured about my choices. As I turn the corner from the dancefloor toward the ladies' room, I slam into something hard. The impact unbalances me, and I stumble onto my ass as my stiletto heels give way.

"Fuck," I murmur, wincing as my ass cheeks throb with pain.

Someone crouches in front of me, drawing my attention. A man with the most mesmerizing crystal blue eyes I've ever seen. He holds my gaze with an intensity that almost has the power to make my toes curl from a stare alone.

For a moment, I wonder if I'm staring at a piece of art, as he's utterly flawless. His high cheekbones and rugged jaw are dusted with a small amount of stubble, affording him a masculine beauty that makes my stomach flutter. His dark hair is medium length and styled impeccably, and he's wearing a blue tailored shirt that is open midway, allowing me a teasing view of his hard, inked chest.

The expensive watch on his wrist, along with a solid gold signet ring, screams this man is wealthy.

It isn't until he speaks I realize I've been staring at him for way too long. "I'm sorry, lass. I didn't see you." He holds out a hand to me. "Are you okay?" His voice is deep and velvety, with a husky tone that makes my cheeks heat. The man's accent is unmistakeably Irish.

I shake my head. "Sorry I wasn't looking where I was going." I take his hand, and the moment I do, it feels like the world stands still. His warm, firm grip sends a need through me I can't quite understand.

The man effortlessly pulls me to my feet. "I hope you aren't hurt?"

I shrug. "Just a sore ass, but I'll survive."

The mention of my ass darkens his gaze, and I feel a shift in the air between us as he moves closer. "Hmm, perhaps I need to kiss it better," he murmurs, his voice sending a thrill through me despite how inappropriate it is for a man I don't know to speak to me like that.

He hasn't let go of my hand as he holds it, keeping me close.

I reclaim my hand and take a step back. "That's a very inappropriate thing to say to someone you don't know."

His piercing blue eyes flash with playfulness as he shrugs. "Sorry, I just like what I see."

This man is hitting on me. The most beautiful man I've ever seen. "Well, I'm not interested."

He smiles, and it's the most painfully stunning thing I've ever seen. My heart skips a beat as butterflies flutter to life in my stomach at the mere look he's giving me. "Perhaps I can make it up to you with a dance?" He suggests, placing a hand on my arm and leaning toward me. "Purely platonic, of course."

Somehow, he makes that sound like a promise to fuck me. His Irish accent is even thicker as his voice deepens, reminding me that my father is currently at war with the Irish Mafia. I take a step back. "Perhaps." I sidestep around him. "Excuse me." I rush down the corridor away from the Irish stranger. Maxim's warning floods into my mind.

The city is dangerous for a Volkov right now.

Once I reach the bathroom door, I glance back to see if he's there. To my relief, there's no sign of him.

My father's insistence I couldn't attend the party has weighed on my mind tonight. Maybe I was foolish to come despite his concern, as I know he doesn't worry for no reason, nor would Maxim.

I walk into the ladies' bathroom, which is empty, and approach a mirror over the sink, turning on the faucet. My fingers dip through the cool water, splashing some on my neck to calm myself down. It's ridiculous how much the random Irishman has got to me.

"Maybe Alexandra's right," I murmur to myself in the mirror. It doesn't matter if she is right. My role as the only daughter of Spartak Volkov is to save myself from marrying a suitor of my father's choosing. It may not be something I look forward to, but I've known it would be my fate since I was very young and a fate my father has brought me up to accept.

Many girls would fight it, but what use is there to fight it when it is inevitable?

3

ROURKE

"*I*'ve found the perfect opportunity," Seamus says, standing in front of me.

It's been three days since my father's funeral, but it's felt like an eternity since I asked Seamus to get me the information I need. "Perfect. When and where?"

He fumbles with the folder in his hands. "Unfortunately, we'll have to act fast."

I raise a brow. "How fast?" I sense his uncertainty about telling me as he shifts his weight from one foot to the other.

"Tonight?"

"Fuck," I growl, running a hand through my hair. It's five o'clock in the afternoon already, which means there won't be much time to plan it. I don't like going into something unprepared. However, I will not wait any longer. "Damn it. Talk me through the opportunity, lad."

Seamus opens the folder and steps forward, placing it on my desk. "This is the guest list for an exclusive party at the club Flux in the city tonight." He points out her name, plain as day.

"Anyone else in attendance that could cause a problem?"

Seamus shakes his head. "Not that I could see."

I run my eyes down the list myself, making sure he's correct. "No, doesn't seem like it." I meet Seamus' gaze. "With the war raging, do you believe she'll attend?" I squint at him. "Spartak will probably have her under lock and key."

Seamus shrugs. "I can't be sure, but it's worth attending to find out, aye?"

I nod in response, glancing down at the mountain of paperwork my father had neglected. He wasn't great at the admin side of things, but I didn't know how out of hand it had gotten. I intended to start it tonight, but getting Viktoria Volkov into the gilded prison cell is more important. "Aye, I'll head there myself."

Seamus clears his throat. "Do you want some backup?"

I meet his questioning gaze and shake my head.

"No, it's Friday night. Spend the time with your family."

He looks uncertain. "Don't you think you'll need help?"

His questioning of my abilities irritates me. "Are you suggesting I can't handle one Russian woman alone, Seamus?"

His eyes widen, and he shakes his head. "Of course not, boss." I can tell the word doesn't come naturally when he's talking to me. After all, the men have seen me as the leader's son rather than as an authoritative figure. Adapting to the change will take time for all the men.

I nod. "Good. Is there anything else?"

Seamus nods, but I can tell he's not keen on telling me.

"Spit it out then," I say.

He runs a hand across the back of his neck. "Volkov hit two more of our drops yesterday. No one understands how they are finding out the locations as we change them every time."

I squint at him. "How much product did we lose?"

The grimace says it all. "One ton."

"Fuck," I growl, running a hand across the back of my neck. "Someone must be tipping them off. Who knows the locations?"

His brow furrows. "Your father and I were the only ones who knew the location of all of them. However, the men charged with the drops on any night would also know."

It sounds like someone working for us as a drug runner is ratting us out to the Russians. "Can you detect a pattern in who is on the drops that get hit?"

Seamus' brow furrows. "Good thinking. I didn't check that. I will do as soon as I'm back in front of my computer."

"Thanks, lad. We need to weed out any potential rats fast." I crack my neck. "The details about Viktoria Volkov remain between us, do you understand?" I meet his gaze.

He nods. "Of course."

I nod toward the door. "Call me once you know more about the potential traitors. We need to tighten control if we're going to survive this war, Seamus."

His Adam's apple bobs as he swallows hard. "Yes, sir." He turns and walks out of my office, shutting the door behind him.

I lean back in the chair my father used to sit in, loosening the tie around my neck. Tonight, I'm going to put in motion my plan for revenge. The Volkov Bratva will wish they never crossed us after I take their princess.

PATIENCE IS important when dealing with a Volkov.

I could sense Viktoria's uncertainty when I bumped into her, no doubt because of my accent. After all, her family is at war with the Irish, even if she doesn't know who I am. The accidental bump into her was a rouse to ensure she didn't know As well as to weigh her up and get a sense of what I'm dealing with. Otherwise, my plan would have had to take a different turn.

I watch her from the shadows, calculating the perfect moment to make my move. It's hard not to be in awe of the Russian Princesses' utter beauty. The way her radiant green eyes almost seem to glow in the lights of the club when she smiles makes my stomach twist in ways I can't quite comprehend.

After setting eyes on her in the flesh up close, I'm sure I'm going to enjoy breaking her more than I expected. She dances with freedom that a girl like her shouldn't have, but soon she will have no freedom at all. To my surprise, she doesn't even have a bodyguard with her, and she's blissfully unaware of the danger lurking in the shadows.

I watch as Viktoria brings her sixth glass of wine to her lips, taking a break from dancing. My cue to make a move. An intoxicated girl will be easier to woo and easier to capture. I'm sure she can't weigh much over one-hundred and fifteen pounds.

I can't understand why this is so intoxicating, waiting and watching like a predator. It's not a job a leader normally takes on, but it was the only option since Seamus' discovery was last minute. Although, one thing I learned over the years shadowing my father is that if you want a job done right, do it yourself. Father didn't agree with me, but I saw countless fuck ups from our men that were avoidable.

I stand from my table in the shadows and casually walk through the dancefloor toward her. Viktoria doesn't notice me. Since she's the daughter of Spartak, I expected her to be more alert. "We meet again," I say once I'm a mere foot from her.

Viktoria's body turns rigid as she spins to face me. "Looks like it."

I tilt my head to the side, smiling. "You don't sound too thrilled about that, princess."

There's a flash in her eyes the moment she hears me calling her princess. Perhaps it rings alarm bells, since I know exactly who she is. "Not particularly, no."

I laugh. "Does that mean the answer to my next question is going to be no?"

She shrugs. "It depends what the question is."

I move closer to her, holding her stunning gaze as

the distance between us shrinks. Her eyes are a mesmerizing emerald green. I've never seen eyes like them before. "How about that dance then, aye?"

There are mere inches between us now. Viktoria's throat bobs softly as she swallows, drawing my attention to her neck. Desire pulses through me at the thought of leaving my mark on her pale, tender skin. I grit my teeth together, trying to focus on the task at hand. "I'm not so sure."

I place my hand on her hip softly, making her tense. "I need to make it up to you for knocking you over earlier," I whisper into her ear before pulling back and searching her eyes. The alcohol she's consumed has dilated her pupils, meaning she's drunk. I can sense she is trying to calculate whether I'm a threat.

Viktoria doesn't move away, leaning into me instead. "Fine, but only one dance."

Big mistake, princess.

I hold out my hand to her, and she takes it. My stomach churns the moment her small hand lands on mine. My cock hardens in my briefs as desire stronger than anything I've felt in a long time kicks me in the gut. It strains against the zipper as I drag her onto the dancefloor.

The song that was playing changes to a slower, more erotic tune that makes my blood boil. With a hard jolt, I pull her body against mine, grabbing her hips.

Viktoria's lips part as she sets her hands on my chest, gazing up at me with those beautiful eyes. I remind myself that she's the enemy, even as my cock continues to push against the zipper of my pants. "I don't normally dance with strangers," she says, an odd innocence in her voice that only heightens my arousal.

I tighten my grasp on her hips and spin her around, molding her back to my chest.

Viktoria gasps softly, only just audible over the music. A sound that draws my mind into the gutter as I imagine how good the Russian princess would feel beneath me, taking my cock hard. An image that merely makes me harder as she sways her hips, grinding her ass into my rock-hard dick. It's a teasing move that drives me wild.

I lean forward and move my lips to her ear, gently caressing the shell with them. "Careful princess, you're playing with fire," I murmur before nipping her earlobe with my teeth.

Viktoria moans softly, a sound that almost makes me forget why I'm here—to capture the woman writhing in my arms. Her unease melts away as we move together on the dancefloor, but something tells me getting her to leave with me will be a challenge. A feat I fear will be far more difficult than getting the dance.

"Come home with me, princess," I murmur into her ear, tightening my hands on her hips and forcing her to face me. "I want you so damn bad."

Viktoria tenses, trying to push me away. "I can't."

I don't release my grasp, knowing that if I let her go now, I might not get another chance. "Okay, but at least dance with me a little longer."

She looks uncertain as she searches my eyes before nodding. "One more dance, and then I'm returning to my friends." She glances over to the table where I found her, and no one is there. "If I can find them."

I pull her against me again, forcing her hips to move to the music. "Don't worry, if you can't find them, you've got me."

She laughs, and it's the most pure sound I've ever heard. She shakes her head. "I'm not sure that's a good thing." She raises a brow. "Is it?"

I don't answer her, spinning her around to the music. "That's for you to find out." It is a terrible thing, but she can't learn that until it's too late. I will have her in the back of my van by the time the night is up. I will imprison Viktoria Volkov tonight, no matter the cost.

She allows me to lead her, swaying to the music as

our bodies writhe together. Her inhibitions are slowly lowering as we dance for more than one song. After five more, she's practically gagging for me as her nipples are hard peaks pointing through the fabric of her thin cream dress. I have to resist the urge to slide my fingers through her panties to see how wet she is for me.

I pull her against me again and lean down, our lips inches away. "How about we get some fresh air?"

I sense her apprehension.

"No funny business, I promise." Not that my promises mean shit. I will bundle her in the back of my van the moment I get her outside this club.

"Okay, but just for a few minutes." She bites her bottom lip, drawing my eyes to them.

I don't understand why I can't resist closing the gap briefly, allowing my lips to tease over hers. "Just a few minutes, and then we can dance more," I murmur before grabbing Viktoria's hand and pulling her through the crowd.

Viktoria doesn't resist, allowing me to pull her to her fate. Within minutes, revenge will be in the palm of my hands.

4

VIKTORIA

lways trust your instincts.

My first impression of the man dragging me forcefully down a dark alleyway was that he was no good. Okay, perhaps not my immediate impression. Before he opened his mouth, my first impression was that he was the most beautiful man I'd ever seen.

I try to open my mouth to scream against the rag against my lips, but it's no use. The man is too strong as he holds me in a vise-like grip. Not to mention, he must have slipped something onto the rag, as I can feel my muscles turning limp. Whatever it is, doesn't knock me out, though. The Irishman, whose name I don't know, is going to kill me.

I'm going to die.

The moment that thought enters my mind, I find

a renewed strength as I try to wrestle out of his grasp. My father always taught me to fight, no matter what.

"Fucking keep still," he growls, tightening his grasp as he moves deeper down the deserted alleyway. There's no way in hell this turns out well. We're at war with the Irish, so if he belongs to the Callaghan Clan, then there will be no mercy.

Liquid ice like dread flows through my veins, forcing me to stop fighting. The reality of my position hits me hard. Father has taught me how to deal with this kind of situation, and I need to stay calm.

The man forces me toward a white van parked there. Panic coils through me as I realize he doesn't intend to kill me, but capture me. I'm not sure which is truly worse, but my father always said it is better to be dead than in our enemy's capture.

Why didn't I listen to him and skip this party?

He keeps one hand over my mouth and uses the other hand to slide open the back of the van. Polythene sheets line the bottom of the van, making me wonder if I was wrong. It looks like it's prepared for a slaughter—my slaughter.

I writhe, trying to overpower him. He's only got one hand on me. It works as I break away from him and get about ten yards, ripping the rag from mouth before his muscular arms wrap around my waist. "Not so fast, princess," he growls, lifting me off my feet.

I scream into the night, hoping someone will hear me.

He's quick to muffle the sound, slamming his hand over my mouth. "Shut it, unless you want me to knock you out."

I feel utter hopelessness sweep over me as he drags me back to the van and slams me onto the polythene sheets, making me groan. "What the hell do you want?"

The man has his back to me as he shuts the van doors, plunging us into semi-darkness. He turns around, and those piercing blue eyes fix on me.

I watch him as he moves toward me, sinking to the floor to crouch next to me. I try to punch him, hoping I can catch him off guard. He grabs hold of my wrist and forces it down hard against the floor of the van before doing the same to the other.

"Who the fuck are you?" I cry, trying desperately to regain control of my arms so I can punch the bastard holding me down with his weight.

He smirks at me, shaking his head. "I thought Daddy would've taught you who your enemies are, Viktoria." The man tilts his head, holding my gaze. "I'm Rourke Callaghan."

Icy terror pierces my heart, wondering if I heard

that right. Rourke Callaghan is the freaking leader of the Callaghan Clan, who are at war with our family. "What do you want?" I ask, remembering my father's lessons if my brother or I were ever to be kidnapped. Never be hostile to your captor initially, and try to bargain for your life.

He narrows his eyes. "Believe me, princess. You don't want to know what I want."

There's a veiled threat in his words. "My father will negotiate for me, I'm sure." I search his bright blue eyes. "Do you want money?"

His laugh is almost cruel. "Money? Do you think your filthy money can make amends for your family killing my father?"

Fuck.

It appears my father left that part out. He told me that an assassin killed Ronan at one of our clubs, and it had nothing to do with the Bratva. He lied to me, and that wouldn't be the first time. I should have known Ronan's death was the catalyst for this war.

"I'm sorry, I didn't know—"

Rourke grabs my throat and squeezes, cutting off my apology. "I don't want to hear it. You'll pay for what your father did to mine."

His words take a moment to sink in, and when they do, the fear I'd felt hits me ten times harder. "I had nothing to do with—"

Rourke tightens his grasp around my throat. "Guilty by association." He moves his face to within an inch of mine. "I'll break you before you see your father again. When you do, he'll know your suffering resulted from his actions against us."

It's hard to believe such a beautiful man can speak such vile words. I don't doubt that he intends to harm me, though. The wars between the criminal organizations in this city are anything but tame, and if my father is right, this is the worst one Chicago has seen in a century.

Rourke's once alluring eyes now appear soulless and dead as he glares at me with hatred. It was all an act. The hot, fiery chemistry between us in the club had nothing to do with attraction. He tilts his head. "You seem disappointed. Perhaps you thought I was going to give you my cock." He moves closer to me, his lips within inches of mine. "I bet your cunt is dripping with desperation for me, isn't it?"

I gasp at his foul language, shaking my head. "No fucking chance," I spit, glaring at the cocky bastard. "I'd rather die a slow and painful death than fuck you."

His eyes narrow. "I'm not sure I believe that." He grabs some rope and slides it around my wrists, binding them together tightly.

"Fuck, that hurts," I say, trying to pull them out of the rope.

He doesn't respond, grabbing my hips and lifting the hem of my dress. I freeze, my body turning to a block of ice so fucking fast. Rourke chuckles softly, the sound almost cruel. "Such a naughty liar you are, Viktoria." He moves his hands to my thighs and grips them hard, making me squirm. "I don't even have to touch you to know how damn wet you are. I can see through your white panties because they are soaked," he growls out the last word like an animal.

"You are sick," I say, trying to wriggle away.

He tightens his grip on my thighs painfully and meets my gaze. "Admit it, Viktoria. You wanted me to fuck you."

I glare at him, knowing that I'll never admit that so long as I'm alive. "Never." say.

He clicks his tongue and moves his hand higher, slipping a finger over my wet panties.

I glare at him, angry that he's touching me without my permission. "Get off me."

Rourke smirks. "What are you going to do about it, princess? You have no power here."

I narrow my eyes, knowing men like him are the men that take what they want, no matter the consequences. Rourke would probably rape me in the back of this van and not think twice about it. Men sicken me, especially men that belong to this underground world my father is so wrapped up in. "I may not have power, but I know my mind." I hold his gaze, feeling rage surge to the surface. "You make me sick, no matter how my body reacts."

Rourke's jaw clenches. "Is that right?" He grabs hold of the waistband of my panties and tears them down my legs, shocking me. "I think that's a fucking lie, and I'm going to prove it by making you come so fast you won't know what hit you."

Rage and shame mix as I try desperately to squirm out of his powerful grasp. "Don't you dare touch me. You're a sick son of a bitch." This is the first time a man has ever seen me so intimately, but he's not a man; he's a fucking monster. I spit in his face, making him growl in anger.

Those bright blue eyes find mine, and his lip turns up in a snarl. "You'll learn to obey by the time I'm through with you, princess. I'll break you, no matter how hard you try to fight." He squints at me. "I can fight harder."

A deep hatred for this man ignites as a result of his cocky attitude. "I doubt that."

He grabs a cloth from behind him and moves back toward me. "Open your mouth."

I glare at him, keeping my jaw closed. There is no

way I'm going to do anything this asshole asks me to do.

Rourke seems to sense that and forces my jaw open, grabbing hold of my chin hard and yanking at it. Despite my attempt to keep it closed, he thrusts the cloth into my mouth and ties it around the back of my head. "Now, you can't spit at me or complain." He smirks, and it makes my insides churn. It's hard to believe that I wanted this man for a moment on the club's dancefloor. For the first time in my life, I truly gave Alexandra's constant pestering to lose my virginity a second thought.

Pathetic.

Rourke spreads my thighs open, making sick dread coil in the pit of my stomach like a viper tightening around its prey. I try to fight him, but it's no use. He's stronger than me. "I'm going to prove how much you want me, princess."

"No," I try to cry against the gag, but it comes out muffled.

Rourke slides a finger through my wet folds, making me shudder with both disgust and arousal. It's impossible not to feel aroused, as it's the first time anyone has ever touched me. He slides a finger inside of me, heightening my sensitivity.

"Stop," I cry behind the gag, wishing I could find some strength to overpower him. The rope burns my skin as I desperately try to free my bound wrists.

Rourke watches me with no emotion or pity. Soulless; that's what he is. A demon with no soul who will not stop, no matter what I say, anyway. "You are practically dripping with need, princess, even if you say you don't want me." He moves his head toward my center, making tears prickle at my eyes. This isn't how I wanted my first sexual experience to occur.

I'm a fool for not trusting my instincts about this man. I gasp as his tongue connects with my clit, lapping at it with a gentleness that makes little sense. Rourke doesn't care that I don't want this because he's doing it, anyway. He groans as his tongue delves into my entrance, tasting me.

I clench my fists, tears prickling at my eyes as pleasure races through me. My thighs shudder despite myself.

What the fuck is he doing to me?

Using my jaw, I ensure the cloth gag rests on my tongue. It allows me to bite my lip as a surge of pleasure hits me the moment Rourke slides a finger inside of me, licking my clit at the same time. There is no way I'm making a sound, as I will not give him that satisfaction.

Never have I felt pleasure like he's giving me. It makes me sick to my stomach. I bite into my lip so hard I break the skin, focusing on the pain rather than the pleasure Rourke is giving me. He's a self-righteous asshole, but I sense things are only going to get worse from here.

If you find yourself in a position where they won't negotiate, fight.

Those were my father's words when he taught us about the risks of a possible kidnap. I'm fighting, but I'm not strong enough to overpower this man. Instead, I have to remain strong mentally.

I will break you, no matter how hard you try to fight.

No. This man won't break me. Rourke Callaghan underestimates how stubborn I can be. I will make his life a living hell before he breaks me. Any chance I get, I'll fight, and I'll hurt him.

Rourke slides his hand around my throat, squeezing hard enough to bring my attention to him. "Stop fighting it, Viktoria." He moves his hand lower down my neck and plays with my hard nipples.

My stomach churns as I continue to bite my lip so hard that blood trickles down my chin.

He smirks at the sight, tilting his head. "You're trying too hard, princess." He moves his face to within inches of my mine.

My stomach churns as I want to punch him, kick him, hurt him in any way possible. However, he's taken that away from me. Instead, all I can do is glare at him with the hatred I feel.

My heart skips a beat as his tongue darts out, licking the blood from my lip and chin. It's sick and twisted. I want to scream at him, gouge his eyes out with my nails, hurt him more than anyone I've ever wanted to hurt.

"Keep looking at me like that. I like the murderous glint in your eye, princess." He slides his fingers back inside of me, making my channel clench around them. "It turns me on." He grabs the back of my neck with his free hand, pumping his other fingers in and out of me with a steady rhythm. "Stop fighting the inevitable. You will come."

I glare back at him, wishing he was wrong. The pleasure he's giving me is more intense than anything I've felt before. "Fuck you," I try to say behind the cloth.

Rourke disappears between my thighs again, thrusting his tongue against my throbbing clit. I bite the gag in my mouth hard with my back teeth, using it to keep quiet as the most intense orgasm hits me. Rourke groans as he laps up my juice, as though he's a starving animal. It's sick that he gets off on forcefully making me come against my will, but I expect nothing less from a Callaghan.

He moves back to crouch in front of me and

moves his lips to within an inch of mine. "You are well on your way to wanting me, princess. In no time, you'll be begging for my cock."

"In your dreams," I spit against the gag, but it's muffled.

Rourke's crystal eyes flash with annoyance as he understands perfectly well. He opens the back of the van and jumps out, glaring at me. "Keep quiet," he orders before slamming the back of the van shut.

Darkness descends around me as the reality of my situation compresses in on me. The enemy has captured me, and my life as I know it is over. There is no way that Rourke Callaghan will let me go alive, and it means I'm destined to spend my last days on this earth being tortured by a man who hates my family.

Panic rises to the surface as my vision turns fuzzy. I know the sensation as unconsciousness takes me in its embrace and everything goes dark.

5

ROURKE

I pull up outside the Callaghan residence, rubbing my face in my hands. It's been a long night. Viktoria's instance she would never want to fuck me broke my resolve. By the time I'm through with her, she will wish I'd fucked her. Viktoria will beg me for it, and when she does, I'll throw her back to her daddy, damaged and desperate for something she can't have.

Her stunning beauty may make it more difficult, though, as she's more beautiful than I remember. I saw Viktoria not so many months ago when my father announced Maxim and Maeve's engagement. She didn't notice me that evening, as there was no recognition.

I can't deny it hurt my ego a little, as I noticed her that night. The princess of the Bratva is stunning, and now she's at my mercy. Deep down, I know a part of me wanted to kidnap her for that reason. Because I knew I'd delight in breaking the beautiful, innocent daughter of Spartak Volkov. She's so polar opposite to the depraved Pakhan that she calls Father.

I slip out of the van and walk around the side, clenching my fists as I prepare myself to drag her out, kicking and screaming. I grab hold of the van door and slide it open, finding her lying in the center of the van, eyes clamped shut. Her skin is unflatteringly pale. As I get into the back of the vehicle, she doesn't move.

I move closer to her. "Get up," I bark.

She remains still, eyes shut. I crouch down next to her and check her pulse, which is there. She's passed out.

Fuck's sake.

This is the last thing I need right now, a fainting diva. I've hardly even started with her, and she can't take a goddamn orgasm. It was non-consensual, but if that makes her faint, she's going to have a serious shock when I start with her. I tighten my grasp around her waist and lift her, hauling her limp body over my shoulder. The restraints remain around her wrists, and the gag is wedged in her mouth.

Carefully, I get out of the van, shouldering the

Volkov princess. One guard notices me and rushes over to offer his help. "Can I give you a hand, sir?"

I shake my head. "I've got it. Open the door."

"Aye, sir," he replies, hurrying ahead of me to open the door to my home.

I keep my hand firmly rested on her bare thigh, feeling my cock harden in my pants. Viktoria Volkov is more tempting than I expected. My sick and twisted urges toward her are almost impossible to quieten, and I have to remind myself who she is. She's a fucking Volkov, related to the people who murdered my father in cold blood.

As I stalk toward the spare room, the image of my father lifeless on the white porcelain floor in a pool of his blood floods my mind. His eyes were still open wide as if he were alive, but his skin had turned a pale gray, proving he was gone.

They slaughtered him and left him like a fucking animal. I have to remember my rage and direct it at Spartak's daughter. It won't be long until he knows she's been taken, and that's when the real fun begins. The city will implode, and I am prepared for it, as are my men.

I open the door to the bedroom next to mine and enter, carrying Viktoria. The large four-poster bed sits pride of place against the back wall, and I carry her to it and lower her onto the bed, untying the restraints around her wrists.

Next, I remove the gag from her mouth.

There's no escape now that she's locked in the gilded cage, so they're no longer necessary.

I discard the rope and gag on the nightstand and rise to my feet, staring down at her.

She looks utterly angelic with her dark brown hair splayed in soft curls over the crisp white pillow. My cock pulses in my boxer briefs as the taste of her sweet arousal still lingers on my tongue. Viktoria Volkov is sweeter than fucking sin. All I want to do right now is taste her again while she's passed out, but I know that doing so wouldn't help my aim.

I need to break her, and my desire for her can't come into the equation. This is strictly business, even if I'll take pleasure from her torture.

She groans, eyes flickering open before shutting again.

I don't intend to be here when she wakes. The Volkov princess needs some time alone for reality to sink in. She's the Callaghan Clan's prisoner now. There is no escape, and by the time I'm through with her, she'll wish she was never born a Volkov.

"Bring the prisoner to me," I order, asking my bodyguard, Aaron, to fetch Viktoria.

"Right away, sir," he replies, leaving me alone.

It's been eight hours since we returned from the club, and it's now morning. I barely slept, unable to quieten my mind.

I sit at the dining table, rapping my fingers impatiently against the solid oak. Our cook, Ally, has put on a spread of french patisseries, fruit, and coffee. My siblings will dine in the kitchen today, allowing me some time alone with Viktoria.

The intention is to send Spartak evidence of us having her. There's no use waiting for him to piece it together, as it packs a more intense punch to deliver the message directly. The Volkov Bratva doesn't scare us, which is the message we need to communicate to Spartak.

The door to the dining room opens. Aaron appears, dragging the prisoner behind him. Viktoria is still wearing the same cream dress as Aaron keeps a firm grasp on her wrist, pulling her closer to the table.

I clench my jaw, feeling an odd sense of possession sweep through me at the sight of him touching her. "That will be all. Leave us."

His brow furrows as he releases her, pushing her toward the table. "But, Sir—"

"I said leave us," I growl, not allowing him to make his case why he needs to stay. If he believe I can't handle Viktoria alone, then I need a new fucking bodyguard.

"Sir," he says as he turns around and leaves us, shutting the door behind him.

I move my gaze to Viktoria, who keeps her attention fixed on the floor rather than looking at me. "Look at me," I order.

She doesn't do as I say, testing what little patience I have left. After practically no sleep, I'm not in the mood to be pushed by a bratty Russian.

I step toward her and grab her throat, squeezing so hard her eyes widen as they meet mine. "I said look at me." I block her airways with my forceful grip. "When I tell you to do something, you do it."

There's that defiance still blazing in her emerald eyes. I fear it'll be difficult to break, but I'm not one for giving up. I release her throat, making her gasp for air. "Take a seat," I order, signaling to the table.

Viktoria narrows her eyes, but she doesn't defy me this time. Instead, she holds her head up high and takes a seat on the left, where the staff set her place. Once she is seated, I take my place on her right. "Eat," I order.

She folds her arms over her chest and meets my gaze. "I'm not hungry."

I grab my fork and grip it so hard I feel the metal bend. "You'll not have another chance to eat for some time." I glare at her. "The smart thing to do would be to take the opportunity." If she doesn't eat, then she'll regret it. This morning is a mere courtesy and a chance to get the evidence to send to her father.

Viktoria sighs and grabs a pain au chocolat from one basket, glaring at me. "Fine."

I ignore her and take a long sip of black coffee, trying to settle my nerves. She's the reason I'm so restless because I could hardly sleep last night. I grab the coffee pot and pour myself another cup. "Coffee?" I ask.

She glares at me with a hatred that matches the hate I feel for her family. "No."

I narrow my eyes and set the pot down on the table.

"Are you going to tell me why you dragged me down to breakfast?" She glares at me. "Or rather your henchman did."

It's as if she has a mission to anger me. I grind my teeth. "So you can eat," I say, not intending to stoop to her level. Another reason I've invited her to breakfast, other than getting photographic evidence, is that I need to get a deeper understanding of the woman I'm trying to break. My father taught me how to get information from people without being too direct.

Viktoria raises a brow as if she doesn't believe me. Perhaps she's too like me to be fooled by this shit. "You're the worst liar I've ever met."

I growl softly. "You'll learn not to speak to me like that, Viktoria."

Her eyes narrow. "Or what?"

Spoiled Volkov brat. I clench the coffee mug so hard the ceramic handle snaps, and the coffee spills. "Fuck." I stand and unbutton my now spoiled white shirt, chucking it off me. The scolding coffee burns my skin as Viktoria watches in surprise.

"Did you break a mug with your bare hands?" She asks.

I glare at her. "Be careful, or I'll break something else in a minute," I snap.

She shudders, the only sign she fears me as she continues to stare. Her eyes roam my chest as she takes in the sight of the tattoos scrolling over my skin. "Why so many tattoos?"

I raise a brow. "I don't have as many as your father and brother." The Bratva are renowned for their obsession with ink, and Spartak is covered in it.

Viktoria stands and walks over to me.

"What are you doing?" I ask, feeling my cock harden as desire pulses to life in the depths of her green eyes.

She moves closer to me and places a finger on

the Celtic knot in the center of my chest. Slowly, she drags her soft finger over it, tracing it. My cock throbs at her touch as I claw myself back from grabbing her hips and fucking her over the table. The Bratva princess is the most alluring woman I've met.

"Careful, princess," I murmur, my voice huskier than before. "You're playing with fire." I grab hold of her hip and pull her close. "Unless you like getting burned."

Viktoria's throat bobs as she tries to take a step back. I hold her, keeping her close. "Let go of me," she says, her voice calm.

I lean into her, smelling her sweet jasmine scent that makes me even harder. "Why did you come so close if you didn't want me to touch you?"

Her nostrils flare. "I said let go of me."

I can't help myself as I tease my hand up her thigh, longing to feel how aroused she is right now.

Viktoria is rigid, and her breathing labors. Suddenly, she slaps me hard in the face.

I grab her wrist and growl, glaring at her. "What the fuck?"

"I told you to let go of me." She yanks her wrist out of my hand and walks away, driving me insane. The image of her hips swaying is enough to turn me into a primal beast. Right now, I'm only thinking with my fucking dick. "You were the one to tease me, princess. What is your problem?"

She spins around, rage blazing in her eyes. "You are my problem." She shakes her head. "Your father deserved what he got, as he didn't raise you right," Viktoria spits.

It feels like she punches me in the gut with her words as intense rage sears through my veins and infects me. I clench my fists by my side and walk closer to her.

Viktoria doesn't know the violence she's stirring inside of me, but if she isn't careful, she will learn how dark my soul truly is.

6

VIKTORIA

*R*ourke glares at me, rage building in his brilliant eyes. Violent power emanates from him in a way I didn't detect at the club, but that's because he was tricking me. His beauty is harsher and even more masculine now, as he's very different in his own home and element.

I know my outburst is foolish, especially as my father always warned us not to anger our captors. Fight, but never make it personal. I made it as personal as it could get by attacking his dead father.

Rourke's chest rises and falls with ragged breaths as his nostrils flare. He clenches his fists tightly by his side, making his knuckles white. Although he doesn't raise them to me, I fear it's only a matter of time.

A shudder starts at the top of my head and spreads through my body, making my knees shake.

Fighting back will land me in more trouble than it is worth. Rourke sees me as this feeble Bratva princess, but that's not how my father raise me. He raised me to be strong, even if he believes a woman's place is by her husband's side. My mother was a powerful woman in her own right.

"Say that again," Rourke says, his voice deadly calm.

I swallow my fear and keep my posture straight, ensuring I don't cower from him. Now that I've said it, it would be weak to backtrack. "I said your father deserved what he got, as he didn't raise you right."

Rourke growls, making me jump. He turns away from me and punches the wall hard, filling the air with a cracking sound. If the impact is painful, he doesn't show it. "You are just like your father and brother, entitled and sick." He paces the floor, keeping his eyes anywhere but on me. "My father didn't raise me right." He shakes his head, coming to a halt and glaring at me. "What about your psycho-pathic brother? He beats women as a hobby, and I'm the one who has been raised wrong?"

I narrow my eyes, wondering what he's talking about. Maxim may be ruthless, but he doesn't beat women. At least, I hope he doesn't. "You don't know my family, and my brother doesn't beat women."

He laughs. "The sheltered princess so ignorant to

the truth about those closest to you." Rourke shakes his head and grabs a folder from the dining table. "What's this then?" He shoves it into my hands.

I glance down at the folder, hesitating.

"Open it," he snaps.

I do as he says, gasping at the police report images of a woman badly beaten. "What is this?"

Rourke narrows his eyes at me. "Read it. The report."

I shuffle the barbaric images to the back, reading through the report.

It has to be a setup, as there is no way my brother is capable of this barbarity. The report says that the woman blames a man for putting her in hospital. She had three broken ribs, internal bleeding, and spent a month recovering in the ICU.

"This is bullshit. If it were true, Maxim would be in jail."

Rourke chuckles, shaking his head. "You're as clueless as you seem."

His comment angers me as I tighten my grasp on the folder. "My brother didn't do this."

"Check the last page," Rourke says.

I shuffle it to find a bank statement, showing a payment into an account for seven hundred thousand dollars from my brother's name.

"He paid her off, and that's how he's not in jail."

He runs a hand across the back of his neck. "Not to mention, your father has enough cops and lawyers in his pocket to get him off, anyway."

"How does this prove anything?" I ask, shaking my head. "My brother made a payment, so what?"

Rourke stalks toward me. "Read her statement." He points at the victim's statement, where she names my brother as the attacker. My stomach twists with sickness as I wonder whether my father is aware of this.

"My father must not know—"

Rourke scoffs. "What planet have you been living on?" His brow furrows. "Your father's the biggest psychopath of them all."

I don't enjoy hearing him talk of my father like that. He's ruthless in his methods that I know, but I won't stand by while he calls my family a bunch of raging psychos. "My father is a better man than you'll ever be, and you know nothing about him or my family."

Rourke growls and moves toward me, making me retreat toward the door. I glance over my shoulder, wanting to run for it.

"Don't even think about it," he warns, stopping still in his tracks.

I don't know if it's his warning the spurs me on, but I act anyway. Twisting away from him fast, I sprint for the door as quickly as my legs can carry me.

A deep, animal-like growl echoes behind me, but I ignore him. All I want is to get as far away as possible from my captor. I don't know where I'm going, but perhaps I can find a room to lock myself inside. Somewhere he can't get to me.

I make it to the door and tear it open, rushing into the corridor. A few yards down the corridor, I see a man standing there with his brow furrowed. "What the fuck is going on, brother?"

His distraction slows me down as Rourke catches me, wrapping his powerful arms around my waist and lifting me off the floor. "Nothing," he growls, carrying me back toward the dining room.

Brother.

The man must be Killian Callaghan, as I met Kieran Callaghan at Maxim and Maeve's engagement announcement.

I go limp in Rourke's arms, accepting that my attempt at an escape has spectacularly failed. "Let me go, and I won't run," I say as he carries me toward the table.

He laughs, but it's a cruel sound that sends a shiver down my spint. "What makes you think I'll trust a damn word you say, lass?" He puts me on my feet and pushes me forward against the table, his chest molded against my back. "It's time I show you what happens when you defy me." He places his palm flat on my back and forces me to bend over the table. "Six should be sufficient."

"Six what?" I ask.

He doesn't answer me, lifting the hem of my dress up. I'm not wearing any panties since he left mine in the back of that van. Rourke makes a groaning sound as he flattens the palm of his hand over my skin. I gasp as he draws back his hand and slams it firmly into my ass with force.

"What the fuck?"

Rourke turns rigid. "Make that seven." His hand gently caresses the skin. "Count." He spanks me again even harder, sending a stinging pain through my flesh.

"Ouch," I cry, feeling tears prickle at my eyes from the pure humiliation of the situation he has me in.

"I said count," he growls, using the same force to hit me again.

"Three," I reply.

He stills. "No, start from one."

My stomach churns at the dark quality of his tone. This man is sick and has a superiority complex if he thinks he's any better than my father or brother. "O—one," I say, feeling despair grip hold of me, wrapping its roots around my heart and squeezing. This treatment is what I will have to endure until Rourke breaks my spirit. It will take a long time. I've always been stubborn.

Rourke flattens his palm and uses even more power, making me yelp. The ache of the impact makes my stomach churn as I long for this to stop. The humiliation of being bent over by him and spanked is far worse than any pain he could inflict on me. "Two," I breathe, knowing that I want this to end as fast as possible.

In reality, I've suffered four strikes but have to accept five more. "You'll learn soon enough to obey me, Viktoria." He brushes his fingertips over my sore skin before spanking me again with more force than before. "In time, you will beg me for the pain."

"Three," I murmur, tears prickling at my eyes at his words. All I want is to scream and shout and fight him, but I know that will only result in more pain. This man is sadistic.

The sting of my ass turns into a burn that filters through my body. I feel a burning need to feel the friction between my thighs as I clench them together, feeling confused by the sudden change.

Rourke chuckles behind me, and it's a dark, evil sound that makes me sick to my stomach. "I'd hoped you might be a masochist, princess." He parts my thighs with his hands, making shame coil through me. "You're so fucking wet," he growls.

I shudder, my knees buckling from a mix of both shame and arousal that shouldn't be there.

Rourke slides a finger through me, hardening my nipples. I hate that my body reacts to his touch, especially when I hate this man more than I've ever hated anyone. My teeth sink into my lip so hard I taste metal as I force myself to fight the sensation.

When I don't make a noise, Rourke spanks me again, but between my thighs with a softer impact. The pain is both excruciating and horrifyingly arousing. It should make me sick. Everything about what he's doing to me here should. "F-four," I gasp before sinking my teeth back into my bottom lip.

By the time he's finally bringing his hand down for the seventh time, I'm panting desperately for oxygen. The desire inside of me sickens me, but it's present, proving to me I'm more broken than I realized. It takes all my willpower not to make any sounds of pleasure; I will not give him the satisfaction.

"Such a stubborn girl, Viktoria." He slides his fingers through my soaking wet entrance, teasing me with the lightest of touches. "You can't stay silent forever." He thrusts three fingers into my pussy, making me gasp.

"What the fuck is wrong with you?" I try to

straighten up, but he has his other hand firm on my back. "Do you get off touching women that tell you to stop?"

Rourke's teeth graze my neck as he runs them down it. "I get off on touching women who clearly deny how badly they want me." His fingers move in slow strokes, in and out of me.

I bite the inside of my cheek, forcing myself to keep quiet. This bastard won't hear me moan for him. Not now. Not ever. "You disgust me."

"Your soaking wet cunt tells a different story, princess." Rourke bites my earlobe, and I have to clench my jaw so tight it feels like my teeth might shatter. "I bet you can't stop thinking about my cock." He pushes his hard erection against my ass, grinding it against me. "It would feel so fucking good buried deep in that virgin cunt of yours."

I tense. How does Rourke know? "I never said I was a virgin."

He chuckles, his warm breath teasing at my neck. "You don't need to. Your father has kept you pure, ready for your arranged marriage to fucking Bratva royalty."

My stomach churns as I realize the power he holds over me.

Rourke knows I'm a virgin, and yet he plays with me. He has no morals, and it means that he could easily take what my father has forced me to preserve in spite. Spoil me so that I am worthless and cast me aside. The Bratva is archaic in their traditions, and men don't want sloppy seconds, as they want their women untouched. "You're a monster," I murmur, feeling the panic clawing at my throat.

"A monster that you want so fucking badly you're dripping." He bumps the pad of his finger over my clit, and stars explode behind my eyes. It's wrong that he can make me come apart so easily.

Rourke knows his way around the female body, which makes me wonder just how many women he's slept with. It's ridiculous that I feel a twinge of jealousy, thinking about him with anyone else.

I bite my lip so hard that blood trickles down my chin, as it's the only way not to scream his name. The climax is mind-blowing as I try to catch my breath.

"You won't stay silent forever," he murmurs, grabbing my hips and forcing me to turn around. "It must have been hard not to scream for me, princess," he murmurs, moving his lips closer to mine. My heart skips a beat as he licks the blood from my chin and then swipes his tongue up and down the self-inflicted wound. My stomach knots together at the unbelievably intimate and erotic act. It takes all my willpower not to moan.

Rourke grabs the back of my neck, kissing me

with a passion that almost robs me of my senses. I keep hold of my mission firmly in my mind, not allowing him to hear how good he makes me feel. When he breaks away, a small smirk spreads onto his lips. "Thank you. I think I have everything I need."

My brow furrows as he holds up his phone, swiping through pictures of me bent over the table and being spanked. "What the fuck is that for?"

"Evidence that we have you." He stows the phone back into his pocket. "I'm sure Daddy won't be thrilled."

Numbness spreads through my entire body. "You better not send those to my father, you sick fuck," I growl, trying to swipe my hand at him.

He captures my wrist and calls to someone. "Aaron." He holds my gaze with those ice-cold eyes, sending shivers down my back.

The guard who brought me in here appears. "Boss?"

"Take the prisoner back to her room."

I glare at Rourke, knowing I've never felt such hatred toward someone before. I want to claw his eyes out.

"Right away." The guard walks toward us, but Rourke doesn't let me go. Only once he reaches my side does he allow Aaron to take my wrist from him.

Rourke's jaw clenches, and he turns his back on the guard and me as if he can't stand watching.

The man is the biggest asshole I've ever met. He's sick if he's going to send those photos to my father, but I know how this world works. Men like Rourke Callaghan will do anything to win.

7

ROURKE

*K*illian pulls his Porsche in front of the house with the windows rolled down. "Get in, or we will be late."

I run a hand across the back of my neck, considering my options. I have no choice but to risk my life in my brother's car, as he's the worst driver I know. When he was eighteen, he borrowed our father's Maserati and smashed it into a lamp post within hours, racing around the city as if it were Dayton racecourse. Killian has always had a need for speed that I don't share, and it's the reason I never get in his car, but my limo is in the shop, meaning I've got no fucking choice.

I slide into the passenger's seat, glancing at him. "You better drive like a normal person, or I'll never get in this fucking car again." I crack my neck, feeling the tension growing, and not because I'm in my brother's death mobile, but because I'm about to attend my first meeting as clan captain.

"You should have thought about that and got out here on time," Killian says, a twinkle of amusement in his dark blue eyes. "Buckle up, Bro."

I put on my safety belt, groaning. "It will be a miracle if we make it to the meeting in one piece."

He revs the engine and speeds around the fountain in front of our home, jerking me in the seat.

I glare at him. "Since you seem to be determined to land us in the same graveyard as our parents."

He laughs, shaking his head. "You need to chill out and stop being so uptight, Rourke."

I allowed Killian to arrange the first sit down with the clan superiors because it's clear that he's still angry I claimed the position as captain. "Where's the sit-down?" I glance at him as his attention remains fixed ahead.

His jaw clenches, and he doesn't look at me. "The Shamrock."

I grimace, knowing that his lack of thought in a location only proves he's not capable of leading this clan. He's too careless. "Was that a good idea?"

Killian rolls his eyes. "What the fuck is wrong with The Shamrock?" He sighs heavily. "It's always been our hub."

"Exactly." And we're at war currently with the Bratva. We've taken the leader's daughter, flaring tensions more than before, and we should stay as far away as possible from locations we'd normally meet. "Which makes it a prime target for Spartak to hit."

Killian's fingers tighten around the steering wheel, turning white at the knuckles. "Where would you have picked?" He spits, clearly angry at my disapproval of his choice.

I run a hand across my chin, feeling the stubble prickling my skin. "The warehouse at the docks." My fingers reach for my cell in my pocket, digging it out as it buzzes against my chest. "Spartak would never expect us to meet there."

It's a text from Kieran.

Where are you guys?

"If you know best, then why don't you plan it?" His jaw is tight set as he gives me an irritated glare. "Why give me the job?"

I don't answer the question, typing a response to Kieran. Next time, I won't be so foolish to give him such an easy yet important task. "Should we divert everyone to the docks?" I suggest.

"No," he snaps, glaring at me with even more rage. "It is happening at The Shamrock. Now drop it."

On the way. ETA ten minutes.

I fire my response to our little brother, stowing my cell phone back in my pocket. Changing the location of the sit-down last minute would undermine his power as vice-captain to the clan, but it's dangerous.

I've a bad feeling about it, but it's futile to argue with Killian. Father's death has strained our relationship, and I know when to choose my battles. "Kieran is taking an active role since Father's death," I say, changing the subject. "I'm not sure he truly has it in him to be a part of the clan, though."

Killian nods. "Yeah, he seems obsessed with taking over the drug operations." His brow pulls together. "As if he's trying to prove himself to us or something."

Our little brother has finally snapped. He's never been enthusiastic about the clan, but Father's death has changed him. Not to mention, he's angry all the time. "I've got Tiernan monitoring him and reporting to me." Tiernan was in charge of my father's security when he died, and since he failed, I've demoted him to tailing my baby brother.

Killian nods. "Best thing, I think."

My cell phone rings, and Seamus' name flashes up. "Why the fuck is Seamus calling me?"

Killian shrugs in response.

I take the call. "What's up, lad?"

There are a few beats of silence as I hear the

wailing of sirens in the distance. "It's The Shamrock." The blood drains from my face. "They fucking blew it to pieces."

"Motherfuckers," I growl, glancing at Killian. "Is anyone hurt?"

"A few injuries, but no one died. At least, not yet." He sighs heavily. "Some staff and men were injured, but they're on the way to the ER as we speak."

I know Kieran was already there. "Kieran?" I ask, detecting the panic in my voice.

"Nah, he's alright. The lad hadn't gone inside, luckily." He clears his throat. "Police are here, though, so best not to make an appearance."

"Fuck." I glare at Killian, wishing I hadn't been right. "Get everyone who is able down to the warehouse at the docks, and be quiet about it. They could be watching."

"Aye, boss," Seamus says.

I cancel the call. "They've blown The Shamrock."

Killian's fingers tighten even more around the steering wheel. "Where is the 'I told you so', then?"

I shrug. "It's a lesson learned, aye, brother?" Heightening the tension between us will achieve nothing. "Route us to the docks."

He nods and mumbles something under his breath, which I don't catch over the purr of the engine. Silence falls between us as he makes the journey toward the docks. "How is your plan for revenge going?" Killian asks, breaking the silence.

The mention of my plan involving Viktoria only worsens my mood. "Fine."

Killian raises a brow. "What's wrong? The Bratva Princess too much of a handful?"

He knows how to wind me up and always has done since we were little. "Don't be an asshole." I glare at him, knowing he saw me wrestling her back into the dining room yesterday morning. "Of course she's not. I will break her." I clench my jaw, knowing that it's going to be more difficult than I'd hoped.

"What did you expect? She's the offspring of a fucking psycho." He slides a hand across the back of his neck. "She was always going to fight."

I clench my jaw and glance out of the window, not answering my brother. My first sit-down is about to take place, and I won't allow him to distract me. I won't allow thoughts of Viktoria to derail me. "Shut it. I need to focus on the meeting." We're in the middle of a war. If the Russians had got their timing correct, they could have caught Killian and me in the blast. Focus is more important than ever.

"Fine," Killian mutters, falling silent as he continues toward the docks.

By the time we get there, most of the men gather

in the old warehouse. We invite fifteen men to the sit-down, all of whom have high-level ranks in the clan. Kieran notices us the moment we enter and walks to join us. "Those motherfuckers blew up The Sham-rock." His eyes are blazing with uncharacteristic rage. "When are we going to retaliate?"

I clap my brother on the shoulder. "Calm down, lad. It took them five days to respond to claims we have Viktoria. We need to be level-headed in our approach."

Kieran's lip curls as he shakes his head. "Fucking bastards almost killed Alex."

Alex is Kieran's closest friend and has been since they were kids. "We'll make them pay, little brother, be patient." I walk to the front of the crowd of men and clap my hands to get their attention.

Killian hangs back, watching with Kieran.

"This sudden change of location is because of the war we're fighting." I scan the men, wondering which one of these fuckers is undermining our operation from the inside. There's a rat amongst us, and we must weed him out before the damage is irreversible. Our contract with the bikers is one of our most lucra-tive, and losing it would be a blow.

At the moment, the Callaghan clan is struggling to keep allies in this shit show. The Italians have been our enemies for as long as I can remember and now so is the Bratva. It only leaves the bikers and the Estrada Cartel family. If I get desperate, we may have to turn to them for help, which I don't want to do.

"Seamus, please come and announce the order of business."

Seamus nods and comes to stand by my side, clearing his throat. "We've got five shipments due this week." He glances at me briefly. "We've reassigned handling the cargo to Kieran and a few of his men."

Our first attempt to eliminate any chance of the Russians hitting our drops is to rely on family. It's all you can do. The men regularly tasked with the cargo handling and drops mutter amongst themselves.

"Any men normally on this will run surveillance on the Bratva's cargo and drops." He runs a hand through his dark hair. "Also, now the Shamrock has been blown apart, we need to select a new hub for meetings." He glances at me. "I will hand that to you, boss."

I crack my neck. "Thanks. Right lads. We need to shake things up because the Russians are gaining on us in this war at the moment." I glance at Killian, knowing he won't like my plan. "All meetings from now on will be at the Callaghan residence, as it's the only fucking place in this city they can't touch us."

"Is that wise, boss?" Tiernan asks, having the audacity to question me in front of everyone, after his failure in protecting my father. He often stepped out of line with my father, too.

"Aye, it's the best option." I move my attention to Gael, who stands next to him. "Don't you think, Gael?"

He nods. "It makes sense to me. The one place in this city the Bratva can't touch is the mansion."

I'm thankful that he supports my decision, just as he would have for my father. With everything that has been going on, I haven't had a meeting with him one on one. He is mine and Killian's right-hand man as the clan chief, even if Killian doesn't like him.

"Great." I meet Killian's gaze and nod. "Come up here, brother."

His brow furrows, moving through the crowd to stand next to me. "As most of you know, my father wanted the two of us to lead together." I meet Kieran's gaze as he watches us, looking left out. He always has been as the youngest child. "For that reason, we've made a new position. While I will be the captain of this clan, Killian is now vice-captain." I meet Gael's gaze, as I haven't run this by him. If he's irritated by the restructuring, he doesn't show it. "Killian has as much authority as me unless we disagree, and then I have the last say."

Our men chuckle at that, and an easiness enters

the air. A lot of the men don't know what to expect from me.

"Are there any other important matters to discuss?" I ask.

Cormac steps forward. "Aye, boss. Cormac is the clan's pursuer, and he handles collecting the cash from our clients. "Go ahead."

"The bikers are a problem." He cracks his knuckles. "They won't pay up for their last shipment, saying we let them down last week with the supply."

I narrow my eyes. "How does that affect the payment for the product they've already received?"

Cormac shakes his head. "Not sure, but I wasn't sure whether you'd want me to shake them down with what is going on with the Russians." He glances at Killian. "I'll need about four men to be sure I get the money."

I nod. "Do it." I crack my knuckles. "We can't let our clients walk over us because of this war. It's business as usual in all areas, no matter what. You get that cash from that son of a bitch, Axel." The bikers think we're too busy to notice their games, but we're not. I won't let them walk all over us.

"Aye, boss. Right away," Cormac says, stepping back into line.

I glance across the room at the men gathered there. "Any other problems?"

Darragh nods. He's one of four generals who each oversees about twenty men. "Aye, my group was handling the drops. You mention a new task. When will you brief us on this?"

I glance at Seamus, who is handling that. "I'll contact you tomorrow with the relevant information," he replies.

I notice the tension in Darragh's shoulders as he nods in reply. Perhaps we have a high-level rat in the management. Seamus can't find a pattern in the drops that got hit and what men were on the job. However, Darragh knows every location for the drops as it's always his men that carry them out.

"That's all." I clap my hands. "Get to work, lads."

The men disperse, leaving me alone with my two brothers, two uncles, and Gael.

Blaine has been staying away, so it is a surprise to see him. "How are you, Blaine?"

"Fine." He runs a hand across the back of his neck. "I thought you'd need a hand since the war is spiraling out of control." His brow furrows. "I can't believe they attacked the Shamrock."

"Aye," Torin says, shaking his head. "My brother loved that pub. They're rubbing salt in the damn wound."

Kieran steps forward. "Don't we need to up our game?"

I raise a brow. "What do you suggest, little bro?"

His jaw clenches in annoyance at me calling him little bro. He hates it when I do that. "Attack them harder."

Killian shakes his head. "We'll attack them, but Rourke is right." He glances at me. "Strategy is important, and acting on impulse is dangerous."

"Exactly," Gael chimes in. "We need to know what will hurt them the most." He tilts his head to the side slightly. "Other than taking Spartak's daughter and doing nothing with her." There's sarcasm in his voice. "What's the end game there?"

I squint at him. "I'm working one out." I glance at my family, who are also looking at me, interested to learn why I captured her. "Spartak wants to marry her off to someone who'll bring him power. Once I work out who that is, I will find any way possible to destroy his plans." I crack my neck. "A source has confirmed that Spartak is pursuing a match for her with more vigor since the war started."

Torin looks confused. "But, he doesn't even have her right now."

"Exactly, which means he's trying to find an ally who will help him retrieve her from us." I clench my fists by my side. "Which we can't let him do."

"Agreed," Killian replies.

Blaine and Gael nod too, but Kieran and Blaine

don't look convinced. Perhaps they can sense I have an ulterior motive behind holding onto her. Viktoria Volkov is quickly becoming a problematic obsession.

IT'S BEEN five days since I bent the Bratva princess over the dining table and spanked her, taking photos to send to her father. Five days since I last allowed myself anywhere near the embodiment of temptation living under my roof. Now that they've retaliated, I need to figure out my next move.

I sit in my home office behind my computer. The surveillance software is already open on my screen. I click into camera twenty-three, sighing the moment I set eyes on her, as watching her helps calm the storm inside of me.

Viktoria Volkov has become my obsession. I watch her more than I should admit. She paces the floor, looking frustrated. I glance at the clock, knowing it's around about now that she showers. I watch as she turns and paces the floor a few more times before tearing off the gown she's wearing.

I groan as she drops it to the floor, her perfect ass swaying as she walks into the adjoining bathroom. My cock is harder than stone as it strains against my pants zipper, forcing me to adjust myself.

The image of having her in that shower, fucking her hard against the wall, floods my mind. I switch to camera twenty-four. A recent addition, which I set up before I captured Viktoria in anticipation of watching her in the shower. After seeing her at Maxim and Maeve's engagement announcement, I knew I'd want her. That's how sick I am.

She washes her hair, gently lathering the soap through the dark raven strands. Every day, she takes a long time in the shower, perhaps because she has nothing better to do. I won't complain, though, as I love watching her.

Viktoria washes her hair painstakingly slowly, running her fingertips through her long locks with such tender strokes. I long to be the one washing her hair, planting soft kisses over every single inch of her body. She goes through the same routine every evening. Showers for about half an hour, touching herself in the cascade of water.

And then she gets out and dries herself off before moving to the bedroom to bring herself to climax. Every single day, I watch and masturbate along with her, feeling like a perverted teenager.

Viktoria finishes with her hair and slowly dips her small hand over her breasts, pinching her hard nipples.

"That's it, princess," I murmur under my breath,

rubbing a hand over my straining cock. "Touch your-self for me." It's impossible to quench the desperate need to be inside of her because it feels almost primal.

My brow furrows as I notice a sound button, which I hadn't seen before. I know security upgraded the software, but I didn't think the camera had audio. I click it, and sure enough, the rush of water echoes through the computer's speakers.

Fuck.

Viktoria moans, and it's the single most exquisite thing I've ever heard before. I rush to unzip my pants, feeling my cock leaking into my boxer briefs. Quickly, I release it and stroke it, sighing in relief as I watch her plunging her fingers into her pretty little pussy.

Her other hand plays with her nipples as she lets her head fall back. "Fuck, yes," she cries, her thighs shaking as she chases her pleasure. "Just like that," she murmurs.

My cock hardens, precum dripping down my shaft and onto my pants. I don't give a damn. All I can focus on is my princess.

She suddenly pulls her fingers from herself and turns off the shower. It's like damn clockwork with her. I continue to stroke my cock, feeling irritated as she leaves my view. I switch back to the camera in her room, waiting for her to enter.

Sure enough, within a couple of minutes, she appears and lies down, her thighs spread wide for me. "That's it, princess, spread them for me."

I click the audio on this camera as she plunges her fingers inside of her tight little cunt.

"Fuck," she moans, thrusting her fingers in and out of herself with violent strokes. Her hips rise off the bed as she mindlessly writhes against her fingers. I fist my cock harder, imagining plunging it deep into her virgin pussy. "Fuck me harder," she murmurs.

I clench my jaw, struggling to stop myself from coming too fast. The mere sound of her sweet voice being so fucking dirty drives me crazy. And then red hot jealously twists through my gut as I wonder who she is imagining.

"Just like that," she moans, throwing her head back against the pillow. "Please, Rourke."

My hand stills on my cock.

"Fuck me," she moans.

I roar as my cock explodes, cum flying onto my desk in violent spurts. "My dirty little virgin," I growl, stuffing my cock back into my pants. There is no stopping me now. Viktoria wants me, and I've heard it from her mouth. I stand and march toward her room, knowing that she has unleashed the monster. She can deny it all she wants, but I know what I heard.

Viktoria Volkov is mine.

8

VIKTORIA

*R*ourke charges into the room, making me gasp.

I pull my fingers out of myself and quickly scramble under the bedsheets, feeling mortified that he just caught me touching myself. The mortifying thing is, I was thinking of him and the way he made me come in the back of that van and then again bent over the dining table.

Talk about unfortunate timing. It's been four or five days since I saw Rourke, but I'm not sure which. I've lost count as the days and nights seem to merge with boredom. Something tells me that it isn't a coincidence that he had barged in here after I'd showered while I was touching myself.

I move my gaze to the ceiling, squinting. Sure

enough, there is a tiny surveillance camera in the corner, with a perfect view of the bed.

"What the fuck do you want?" I ask, feeling sickened by the realization that he's been watching me. "And why the fuck have you been spying on me?"

Rourke follows my gaze to the camera. "Smart. When did you notice it?" His eyes narrow, and I realize he thinks I was putting on a show for him.

"Just now. It was too much of a coincidence that you walk in the first time I touch myself."

A smirk flits onto his lips. "Don't lie, Viktoria. It's not the first time."

My stomach dips. Does this bastard have cameras fitted in the bathroom? If he does, that's a sick invasion of privacy. "Where else do you have cameras?"

He slams the door behind him and flicks the lock, making awareness prickle over my skin. "In the shower, princess. I know you can't stop fucking touching yourself and screaming my name." He takes each step with deliberate slowness, holding my gaze with those piercing, icy blue eyes. "There's no point denying it. I heard you begging me to fuck you." He stops at the foot of the bed. "I know how badly you want me."

I narrow my eyes, feeling anger blazing to life. "Bullshit. I don't want you in reality." I shift uncomfortably under his gaze. "Sure, you're hot to fantasize about, but I'd never actually want to fuck you."

He tilts his head. "We'll see about that." He grabs the duvet and yanks it off me, exposing my body to his hungry gaze.

"Give that back," I say, trying to reach for it before he pulls it entirely out of my grasp.

I grab a corner, which he attempts to yank from my hands. I hold on with all my strength, although my naked body is entirely visible to him right now.

"Let go," he growls, the sound of his voice sending unwanted desire to my core.

I don't let go because it will give him power over me to do what he wants. "You let it go."

The rage heightens in his eyes as he yanks it so hard I fall forward, tumbling off the bed along with it. I land at his feet, naked and ashamed. The moment I try to scramble away from him, he grabs a handful of hair to stop me.

I freeze, knowing that I've stumbled into the hands of a devil. I should have known this sick son of a bitch was watching me.

How the fuck did I forget to check for cameras?

I know my father would be ashamed of me, as he taught me better.

Rourke forces me to my feet in front of him,

tugging me painfully with my hair. "It's time I teach you a real lesson, princess," he purrs.

I hate that my knees buckle at the velvety sound of his voice. Not to mention, my stomach clenches with need. After all, I was just fantasizing about the beautiful yet irritating man standing in front of me.

Is it possible to hate someone as badly as you desire them?

It doesn't make logical sense, and yet that is exactly how I feel. "Let go of me, you psycho," I demand, glaring into Rourke's eyes. "Do you enjoy watching unsuspecting women naked?"

He smirks at me. "Very much." He pulls me closer and spins me around, molding my back to his rock-hard chest. "Especially when the woman is so fucking beautiful," he murmurs, his lip grazing the shell of my ear.

I hate hearing him call me beautiful makes me feel special. My stomach dips when I feel the hard press of his cock against my lower back. Angry and throbbing and ready to fuck me senseless. I tense at that, knowing that if he goes too far, my life is over. My father isn't a forgiving man, and despite me being in an impossible position, he would blame me if Rourke took my virginity. "Please don't," I say, hating how insignificant my voice sounds.

Rourke digs his fingertips into my hips and moves

his lips against the shell of my ear. "Don't what, princess?"

I shudder, feeling tears prickling in my eyes. "Don't defile me, or I will be dead."

His body tenses against mine. "Dead?" He questions.

"My father wouldn't hesitate to kill me if he found out I sullied the family's name." I feel the fear of facing my father growing with every second that passes if Rourke takes this too far. This man wants to hurt my family and me, so why the fuck am I telling him this? "I would be worthless to him."

Rourke's lips move to my neck, and he kisses me there. "I won't go that far," he whispers, his voice less aggressive and tender. His touch turns softer as he runs his palm over the curves of my hips, enticing goosebumps to prickle over my skin. It makes little sense why he would preserve my virginity. Surely, he wants to hurt my family as much as possible.

Why else is he holding me here?

"Rourke," I murmur his name, but I'm not sure why.

"Yes, princess?"

My throat bobs as I swallow hard. "Why are you doing this?"

His hands still for a moment, and I think he's

going to answer, but he slides his finger through my soaking wet lips.

"Fuck," I hiss, feeling unbelievably sensitive to his touch. "Stop this."

He forces me to face him, yanking me hard against his powerful body. "I can still make you feel good without fucking you, princess." His lips clash with mine, and he takes what he wants, sliding his into my mouth with a violent passion.

When he breaks away, my lips feel swollen, and my body is highly strung. Rourke's hands move softly down the curve of my body, feeling me as if he's trying to memorize how I feel. "Lie on your back for me."

I meet his gaze, feeling uncertain about doing anything he says. The memory of the way he made me feel bent over that table and in the back of the van come rushing back, forcing me to submit to him. I need him to make me feel like that again. "Why would I do that?"

He pulls my bottom lip between his teeth, biting softly. "Because you want me to make you feel good, like I did when I spanked you."

I narrow my eyes at him, hating that he knows how weak I am. "No, I don't." I cross my arms over my chest. "Fuck you."

He growls softly. "Very well, sounds like you need to be punished." He tilts his head. "Five should do."

"Punish me all you want. I won't be your puppet."

"That's six." His eyes narrow. "The count keeps rising until you do as I say."

I fix him with a defiant stare, knowing that he can count to a million if he wants. I won't bow to his will.

"Seven," he murmurs, eyes narrowing.

My stomach churns as the rage in his eyes grows with each second. "Keep counting," I say.

He growls softly and turns away, walking toward the closet in the far corner of the room. He disappears inside, and when he returns, he's holding handcuffs and a rather painful-looking instrument.

Terror arcs through my body as I turn stiff, realizing that this will not be like last time.

"You gave me no choice, Viktoria," he says, moving toward me.

I sideways glance at the bathroom door, which is cracked open.

"Don't even think about it."

I meet his gaze as he moves toward me faster, knowing I probably won't make it. I decide to try. It beats being humiliated by this man again. I run as fast as I can toward the bathroom door.

A deep growl followed by Rourke dropping the handcuffs to the floor echoes toward me.

I swallow hard, knowing he's closing in on me fast. As I grab the door, ready to slam it shut in his face. Rourke is there, blocking the doorway with his immense body. My stomach churns as he grabs my wrist forcefully, yanking me out of the bathroom with one tug.

I stumble into him.

"You know how to push my buttons, princess," he says, his voice husky and deep. "We're up to fifteen."

He drags me over to the handcuffs, which he grabs and slaps around my wrists. Then, he grabs the riding crop. My stomach churns at the thought of him hitting me with that.

Rourke drags me by the chain of the handcuffs and practically flings me onto the bed. I try to move, but he is over me before I can. He grabs my hips and forces me onto all fours, teasing the tip of the riding crop through my soaking wet lips.

I shudder. My body was primed and on the edge of climax before Rourke burst in here, which gives him more power over me.

"Count," he barks.

The crop hits my right ass cheek with such force my mind short-circuits. The stinging pain is far more intense than his hand. I cry out, feeling angry with myself the moment the sound escapes me. I bite my lip hard, opening the wound I'd inflicted on myself the first day.

"Princess," he says it as a warning, and then I realize I haven't counted.

"One," I say before sinking my teeth back into my lip.

Rourke moves the tip of the crop through my entrance again, making my body react sickeningly. The pain he inflicts heightens the pleasure. He does the same on my left ass cheek, but this time I'm prepared, sinking my teeth into my lip before he hits me.

"T-Two," I say, feeling tears prickle at my eyes.

The arousal between my thighs heightens as I feel the wetness gush down my leg. It's sick that this bad treatment is making me wetter. Rourke follows the same pattern, bumping the crop over my clit each time before spanking me again. By the time he reaches ten, I'm ready to combust.

"It looks like the Bratva princess is a masochist," he muses.

I hate him now more than before. He's a fucking sick son of a bitch. "It looks like the Callaghan leader is a sick pervert who enjoys hitting women."

Rourke growls and yanks my hair, forcing my neck up as he looms over me. "You know that this is what you craved when you were plunging your fingers into your cunt, and you are too fucking stubborn to admit it."

He forces me back down and gives me two hits with the crop in quick succession.

"Eleven, twelve," I cry before biting my lip so hard I taste blood.

He moves the crop to my pussy again and teases it over my lips before giving me a gentle spank against the sensitive area.

My body tenses as pleasure and pain collide most erotically. I feel myself coming undone from that soft impact. "Fuck," I shout, as Rourke does it again two more times, sending me free-falling off the edge of a cliff. "Oh my God," I cry, forgetting about keeping silent.

My entire body shatters for him. Liquid gushing from my pussy all over the bedsheets as I turn to jelly, collapsing onto my front on the bed from the force of the most extreme orgasm I've ever experienced. I bite down on the pillow, knowing that if I don't, I won't stop moaning.

Rourke grabs my hips and forces me onto my back. He holds my gaze before moving between my thighs and spreading them wide. "You come so well, princess," he murmurs before burying his mouth between my legs.

He finally breaks me as my mind blanks. I moan loud, enjoying the feel of this man's tongue against my clit. I'm not even sure my orgasm has ended as he pushes me toward another so fast, I don't know if I'll survive it.

9

ROURKE

*H*er moans are like music. I've broken her resolve as she rests her head back on the pillow, letting go as I drive her toward another orgasm.

Viktoria loves the pain. A masochist at heart, which suits my sadistic tendencies. It is an irresistible sound as she arches her back, demanding more from me, and I give it to her, thrusting four fingers inside her tight virgin entrance.

She groans, her body tensing. "Fuck, Rourke," she cries.

I could spend the rest of my life listening to her scream my name and be a happy man. Slowly, I drag the flat of my tongue over her clit. Viktoria jolts, her eyes clamping shut as the pleasure overwhelms her.

I dig my fingertips into her hips hard, forcing

them open. "Watch me, princess." I lap at her clit with the tip of my tongue. "Watch while I feast on your perfect little cunt."

Her eyes roll in her head and she moans deeply, enjoying hearing me talk so filthy to her. "Rourke, please," she begs.

I smirk up at her. "Please, what?"

She groans. "I need to come."

"That's very greedy, princess. I've already made you come once." I lick my lips as my cock throbs against the zipper of my pants. "First, how about you make me feel good?"

Her eyes dilate with desire as her gaze drops to the hard bulge in my pants. "I've never done it before."

Fuck.

The mere thought of being the only man to be in her hot little mouth drives me wild. "Good." I stand at the edge of the bed and unzip my pants. "I want to be all of your firsts."

Viktoria watches as if mesmerized, waiting in anticipation to see me.

Slowly, I drag my cock out, and she gasps. Her eyes widen. "I'm not sure that'll fit in my mouth, Rourke."

I smirk at her. "Don't worry. I'll make it fit."

A flash of defiance enters her emerald eyes. As if

she is just now remembering that she hates my guts. "You better not choke me with it."

I grab the chain of the cuffs and force her forward onto all fours in front of me. "Put it in your mouth." That's what I want, the Volkov princess choking on my dick.

Her eyes blaze with a mix of lust and anger. "There's no need to be fucking rude about it." She tries to move away from me despite being cuffed. "On second thought, I think I'd rather not."

I growl and grab her hair, holding her in place. "Suck it, princess," I order, thrusting my hips toward her lips.

"Suck it yourself, asshole," she spits, trying to fight against me.

It only turns me on more as I force open her mouth with the head of my cock. Her eyes widen as I grab the back of her head, and my cock rests on her tongue as she remains still, glaring at me.

"You look like a work of art with my cock in your mouth." I thrust a little, making her gag. "I've been thinking about this for so fucking long."

The desire wins out as I talk dirty to her, and she opens wide enough for my dick to sink inside. She pulls back and teases the tip of my cock with her tongue. I groan, feeling at a loss at the way this woman makes me feel.

Viktoria hums around my cock, taking me deeper into her throat as she bobs up and down.

Little does she know she is playing with fire. The all-consuming desire I have for her longs for me to grab her hair and force every inch down her throat. I want to hear her gag on my cock, see her saliva spill down my length and down her chin. The mere vision in my mind spurs me on as I slide every inch into the back of her throat.

Her eyes widen, and nostrils flare as she gags, saliva spilling onto my cock and balls.

I groan. "That's it, choke on my dick," I rasp.

She panics, trying to lift her cuffed hands and push me away, but she only falls deeper onto my cock.

I remain still in the back of her throat. "Relax and breathe through your nose."

Viktoria relaxes and does as I say, tears gathering in her eyes.

Slowly, I pull my cock all the way out before slamming back in.

"Fuck, your mouth is heaven, princess," I growl, tightening my grasp on her hair as I wrap it around my knuckles. "I could spend the rest of my life fucking your little throat."

Her eyes dilate as I continue to chase my pleasure,

using her like I've longed to ever since I set eyes on her in the Shamrock months ago.

"Get ready, princess." I wrap her hair tighter around my fist. "I want you to swallow every drop."

She groans around me; the vibrations pushing me closer to the edge. I pump two more times into her mouth before unleashing my seed.

I roar, my cock hardening as I explode in her throat.

Viktoria's eyes widen as she swallows the first two loads before choking a little as more cum floods her mouth. A few droplets spill from her lips, and it's the sexiest thing I've ever seen.

I pull my cock out. "Lick every drop," I order.

She does as I say, licking my cock clean. Then, I slip it back into my pants and do up the zipper.

"Good girl," I murmur, yanking her by her hair and lifting her mouth to mine. I slide my tongue into her mouth. "Such a good girl. I think you deserve to come now."

I push her down, kissing a path down her body toward the apex of her thighs.

Viktoria watches me with a far-off expression. She's no longer fighting but lost to the visceral need for each other. I slide the flat of my tongue through her soaking wet entrance, groaning at her taste.

"Fuck, Rourke," she cries, her wrists clenched

above her head as she remains restrained for me. "It feels so good."

I suck on her clit before grazing the tips of my teeth over it.

Her eyes go wide, and her breathing labors.

I know it won't take long for her to reach her climax, but I don't want this to end. It's clear that the Bratva Princess is becoming my sordid obsession, and I'm not sure I'll ever get enough of her.

"Come for me," I murmur before continuing to finger fuck her and lick her most sensitive spot.

My command is all it takes as she shudders, her body falling over the edge as her pussy gushes with her delicious nectar.

"Rourke, yes, oh fuck, yes."

I slide my fingers out of her, holding her gaze. Slowly, I slip them into my mouth and suck them clean, making her moan.

I reach for the handcuffs key I placed on the nightstand and unlock them, pulling them from her wrists. The skin beneath them is sore and red as I stroke my fingers over the welts.

She winces slightly, and I let go. Without a word, I turn away from her and leave the room, knowing that I'm in too deep. I close the door and lock it before resting my back against it.

What the hell have I gotten myself into?

I SIT in the office of Callaghan enterprises. It's my first appearance at the headquarters since Father died. The mahogany desk I remember watching him sit behind as a kid. It's hard to believe that I'm now in his position, at the helm of it all.

"Sir, there is a Cormack O'Leary to see you." My secretary's voice sounds over the intercom.

I press the reply button. "Send him in."

Cormac opens the door and enters, looking totally out of place for the HQ of Callaghan Enterprises. He's wearing a pair of jeans and a polo shirt.

"Word of advice, lad. Next time you visit, wear your best suit."

Cormac's face falls, and then he nods. "Of course, sorry, boss." He shuffles on his feet. "I didn't think. Your father never asked me to meet him here."

My father didn't like to use his legitimate business for meetings, but it seems like one of the best places to meet while we're at war.

"Aye, not to worry." I sit up straighter in my office chair. "What have you got for me?"

He looks concerned. "I went to Axel and demanded the cash he owed." He steps forward and pulls out a wedge of cash, but it's nowhere near what he owes. "He said that he hasn't got it all for us because business is slow since we aren't supplying him enough product."

"Bullshit," I say, grabbing the cash and weighing it in my hand. "That's not even half Axel owes, and he had the product two weeks ago. If he's sold it, he should have our money." I stand and pace the length of the office next to the floor-to-ceiling window that looks out over Chicago. "Set up a meeting with him, as I'm going to visit him myself."

"Is that wise, boss?" Cormac asks.

I raise a brow. "What else do you advise I do?"

He shakes his head. "I'm not sure. While I was there, I noticed a few Morrone men hanging around." His brow furrows. "I'm not sure what he's up to, but I've got a bad feeling, boss."

Perhaps the bikers think they can make a power play now that our clan is at war with the Russians. "Set up the meeting for this afternoon." I run a hand across the back of my neck. "In the meantime, I'll have someone investigate why Axel has Morrone men lurking around his facility."

Cormac nods. "Right away, I'll text you the time."

"Thanks."

Cormac leaves my office, leaving me with my chaotic thoughts. If anything else goes wrong, I'm worried we will not survive this war. At the moment, the Russians are always one step ahead of us. If we have to add the Morrone family into the mix, we're going to have serious problems.

I pick up the phone on my desk and dial Seamus' number.

"Boss?" He answers after the second dial tone.

"I've got a problem. Can you investigate why Axel has Morrone men lurking around his bar?" I ask.

"Shit." There's a few moments of silence. "Of course. Do you think they're going to break the contract and switch to the Italians?"

"Fuck knows. That's what I need you to find out." I hate pointless fucking questions, and Seamus likes to ask them.

"Okay, I'm on it," he says.

"Seamus, I need answers fast. We have to act before they can cross us."

"Aye, I've got it, boss." There's a roar of a car engine as he's driving. "I'll get onto it now and call you as soon as I know."

"Thanks." I put down the phone, leaning back in my father's old chair.

"What the fuck did you leave me with this shit for?" I murmur into the air, feeling instantly stupid as I know the fucker can't hear me as he's dead and buried.

My father's absence has never felt more poignant

than it does right now. I shut my eyes, feeling an ache in my chest, wishing he was here. The weight of the empire he left me in charge of it heavier than I expected, even with my family to share the burden.

———

I PULL into the biker's bar on the outskirts of the city the next day, feeling the heaviness of my rage churning beneath the surface. It would be dangerous for Axel to disrespect me to my face, as I fear I won't be able to subdue the violent stirring inside of me if he says the wrong thing.

"Ready?" I ask Seamus, glancing at him.

He nods. "Aye, boss."

Axel agreed to a meeting. I don't think he has the balls to stand up to me in person, which means we'll get our money, and I'll promise to deliver his next shipment.

We've got product coming into the docks tonight.

I get out of my car and lock it, attracting a few curious stares from some members as I walk toward the bar. Seamus follows close behind. I enter the dive and walk toward the bar.

"Where is Axel?" I ask the bartender.

He meets my gaze, eyes narrowing. "Who wants to know?"

"Rourke Callaghan," I announce.

The man pales and nods toward the back. "He's waiting for you out back."

A sense of unease prickles over my neck as I glance down the dark corridor. "I'll wait for Axel out here, thanks."

Seamus nods. "Good call."

I narrow my eyes and wait for the bartender to go and get him.

He hurries away from the bar and out the back. There is no way I'm heading back there with no idea what is waiting for me.

Axel appears, holding his hands out. "Rourke, what is with the lack of trust?" He asks.

I shake my head. "No lack of trust, but it's too busy in here. Let's talk in the parking lot."

Axel's eyes narrow, but he follows me out with a few of his men flanking him. "To what do I owe this pleasure?" He asks.

"Cut the crap. You know why I'm here."

He smirks. "The money?"

"Aye. Pay up." I cross my arms over my chest. "You've sold the product, so stop this bullshit about us not delivering your order." I tilt my head to the side. "We've had a few hiccups, but you'll get your order tomorrow."

"Is that a guarantee?" He asks.

I glance at Seamus, knowing that the drop going smoothly isn't guaranteed. "You have my word."

He regards me for a few moments before turning to one of his guys. "Pay him, Ink."

Ink steps forward and slides a hand into his pocket, pulling out two wedges of cash the same size as the one he already sent Cormac back with.

I snatch them from him, weighing them in my hand. "Do I need to count it?"

Axel spits on the floor. "It's all there. What the fuck happened to trust?"

I don't trust this man at all, but I pass it to Seamus, who stows it in his pocket. "I trust it's all there, but don't mess with me again, Axel." I fix him with a sharp glare. "Just because my father isn't here doesn't mean you can fuck with us."

Axel holds his hands up. "Clearly." The sarcastic tone of his voice irritates me as I turn my back on him. "Darragh will be in touch with a drop location for your order."

He nods. "Great. I better have product tomorrow."

I don't bother responding, knowing he's trying to flare tensions. If this asshole goes to the Morrone Family for his product, there'll be hell to pay. I won't stand by why a load of worthless bikers tries to take advantage of us when we're fighting a war.

"Good talking to you," I say, infusing my tone with sarcasm. "Next time my pursuer asks for money, pay, or there will be harsher consequences." I crack my knuckles. "I don't have time for this shit." I turn to walk away from him, and Seamus follows.

Axel doesn't have the balls to challenge me in person. I need to find out why Morrone men hang around here. If he's going to break our contract, there will be hell to pay.

10

VIKTORIA

*T*he door to the bedroom swings open, and a guard enters.

"Good afternoon. My boss instructed me to take you on a short walk around the grounds."

My brow furrows. "Why?"

His jaw tightens. "It's my orders. He doesn't give me a reason." He turns away from me. "Get dressed. I'll wait outside for you." He slams the door behind him.

Rude.

I get up from the bed and walk toward the closet. It's been days since I bothered to dress out of my gown since I don't even leave this room. Rourke is allowing me out of my cage for a walk, like a fucking dog.

Yesterday evening was confusing. My desire for

my captor makes little sense because I hate the man. He's a cocky, self-righteous pain in my ass, as well as being a gorgeous sex god.

His touch turns me into liquid fire. His words are damn filthy, but addictive. I've never felt such a physical magnetic pull to someone before, but I felt it in that club as well as here, which means it wasn't all an act. Our chemistry exists, even if it makes no sense.

I pull on a shirt and pants before walking toward the door.

Why would he allow me out of the cage?

My heart pounds hard as I reach for the handle. The guard is there, towering over me. "Ready?"

I nod. "Yes."

"Follow me." He leads me down the corridor toward a set of stairs. It's the first time I've seen anything outside that room since I was unconscious when Rourke brought me here.

I can hear my father's voice.

If you get a chance, scout out the surroundings for any weak spots. The moment you get an opening to escape, take it.

Maxim and I trained for this kind of situation our entire lives. I observe my surroundings, noting the emerald green wallpaper that lines the walls of the corridor. It has an emblem in it, which I can only assume is the Callaghan coat of arms.

I shake my head, trying to focus, as that will not

help me escape. I take a mental note of each turn before making it to the main stairwell descending into a large entryway.

A large painting sits pride of place at the top of the stairs. It's a family portrait of Rourke's siblings and his parents, as I recognize him instantly. Even as a child, he had those same piercing blue eyes that the artist has captured perfectly. "Is that the Callaghan family?" I ask, trying to make small talk.

The guard stops, glaring at me. "No questions."

I sigh as he leads the way down the stairs and out the front door. There are three cars parked on the driveway. A Porsche, Range Rover, and a Mustang. None of them would be easy to hot-wire; another skill my father ensured I learned.

"We will take a walk around the perimeter. Stay in front of me," the guard orders.

"Aye, sir," I say, giving him a salute.

The guy doesn't even crack a smile.

"Jeez, would it kill you to smile?" I ask.

His eyes narrow. "I'm not paid to smile."

This guy is more uptight than the guards who work for my father. That is saying something since Russians aren't exactly renowned for their bubbly personality, but this guy takes first prize for the grumpy guard of the year awards.

The grounds around the house are ridiculous. We

have a small yard out the back of our townhouse which doesn't compare to this, but we live in central Chicago.

"How much land has this place got?" I ask, glancing back at the grump.

He huffs. "Two acres, I think."

I'm surprised he even answers, but thankful that perhaps he's not opposed to a little small talk. "Wow, that's a lot."

He doesn't respond as I continue to walk around the vast mansion. A bird swoops down right in front of me, startling me a little. I watch as the bird flies off into the distance, joining another bird in a tree as they chirp happily. The Callaghans have an idyllic place, considering it's still officially in Chicago.

"How long has this home belonged to the Callaghan family?" I ask, glancing back at him.

His jaw clenches, but he answers. "About one-hundred years since it was first built." He shrugs. "It's not me you should ask."

I continue my walk in silence, admiring the natural beauty surrounding Rourke's home. Once we get back to the front door, the guard opens it.

"Time to return to your room."

I sigh. "Do I have to?"

He gives me an irritated glare. "In, now," he barks.

I do as he says and allow him to lead me back to my room. On my first excursion, I didn't see any obvious weakness I could exploit to escape.

The guard unlocks the door, and I walk into my room, which is nothing more than a cage. He doesn't say a word before shutting it and locking me inside.

I flop onto my back on the bed, feeling more resigned than ever that I'll never leave this place. It's like a fortress surrounded by two acres of land, meaning I've got no chance in hell of finding an escape route.

THIS GILDED CAGE is driving me insane.

Why did he give me a taste of freedom only to rip it away?

It feels like it was all part of his torture. Rourke hasn't been to my room in at least five days, I think. The days seem to merge. The last time I saw Rourke, he punished me, made me come, and then forced his cock down my throat.

The guard took me around the grounds the day after, but I've only seen the maid who brings my food since then. I've asked her if I can go for another walk, but she won't talk to me. It's driving me crazy, not to mention I can't even touch myself since I found out the sick fuck is watching me.

Even though I'm going out of my mind with boredom and the need to satiate my desire. All I can think about is how he made me feel. The man is a sex god, even if he is a bastard.

The cocky son of a bitch knows how to anger me in ways no one else does. Not to mention, he has no regard for consent. It's hard to believe that a man like him regards himself as any better than my brother or father.

I pace the width of the bedroom bare-foot, sinking into the thick carpets as I walk. Walking and sleeping is the only entertainment I can find in this room. No television, books, music, computer, and I'm going fucking mad with nothing to do. Somehow, I need to escape.

I sit on the window seat and gaze out of it, wincing as the bruises on my ass still ache. They remind me of the degradation I endured and will continue to endure if I don't find a way out of here.

It could have been worse since Father always prepared us for far worse situations when he spoke about us being kidnapped. Rourke could have locked me in a dark basement and tortured me by now, or I could have been dead.

My brow furrows as the catch of the window captures my attention.

It's unlocked.

How have I spent this long locked in here and not noticed? I try the window, and sure enough, it opens with ease. Hope blooms in the pit of my stomach as I glance out of the window, knowing it's about a twelve-foot drop. Heights aren't exactly my forte. Not to mention, I'll need something to abseil down the wall.

I turn my attention back to the room, which I turned upside down already. There was nothing I found that was that long or strong enough to take my weight.

Shit.

The hope dies, but then I realize I haven't searched the closet. It's full of clothes, but there might be something in there I could use.

I walk into it and start by searching the built-in drawers for something. My hope is waning as I get to the last drawer. When I open it, I can't quite believe what I'm seeing. The drawer is full of sex toys, including a long length of strong rope. Hopefully, there is enough to reach the ground.

I grab it and rush back into the bedroom, loosening the knots in it. I drop the rope down out of the window, keeping the other end at the foot of the bed.

I lean over to see how far it goes before tying it to the bed. It reaches about ten feet, leaving just a two-foot drop at the end.

Easy.

I swallow hard, ever since my father threw me off a clifftop when I refused to do a bungee jump. Thankfully, the bungee was in place when he did it ever since I fear heights worse than before that day.

My father isn't a patient man, and he hates weakness. I remember how angry my mom was with him when we returned that day, and Maxim explained what happened. I was a mess of nerves, and she couldn't believe he'd done such a thing. She was undergoing chemotherapy and was weak, which my father used as an excuse not to argue about it.

I grip hold of the window edge and peer over again, shutting my eyes and imagining myself climbing out and using the rope to power down to the ground. In my mind, it is easy, but in reality, it is something else entirely.

Once I open my eyes, I feel no more ready to tackle my escape.

"Fuck," I breathe.

I glance around the gilded prison cell, knowing I can't put this off. Escape is within my grasp, and my fears can't impede that. My fate, if I remain trapped in this cage, is grim. I grab a shirt and rip it apart, wrapping each piece around my palms and tying them.

"Come on, Viki," I murmur, trying to encourage myself to climb out of the window. I climb onto the sill and try not to look down, knowing that if I do, I'll probably chicken out.

I lower myself down and grab hold of the rope, using it to dangle out of the window.

Shit.

There's no going back now.

The door to the bedroom flings open as I cling onto the rope. My heart stills in my chest as I meet the wide-eyed stare of the man who has held me captive. The same man I longed for with every part of my body only days ago. Sexual chemistry isn't worth staying in this hell-hole, no matter how earth-shattering it is.

I'm so close to freedom I can taste it. It's not over until Rourke has caught me.

"Viktoria, don't even—"

I don't allow him to finish the sentence, wrapping the shirt around my hands and then loosening them around the rope to drop to the ground.

The rope jerks as it takes my weight, forcing me into the wall hard. I grunt, gently dropping lower and lower as Rourke appears above me.

I drop to the floor, letting go of the rope and

dropping the shirt. My heart pounds frantically in my chest as I push into a sprint, racing for my freedom. There's no way Rourke will let me get away that easily, as he'll be close behind, but I have to get out of here before he can catch me.

It shouldn't be too hard.

I know that is wishful thinking. Rourke knows these grounds, and I don't. Other than my brief tour four or five days ago, I don't know the grounds, and it's dark. I don't like my chances of escaping.

He's going to catch me, but I'll make it as hard as fucking possible for him.

11

ROURKE

y stomach churns as I reach the window.

Viktoria slips down onto the ground the moment I make it there.

"Viktoria," I growl, watching as she runs into the darkness. Grabbing hold of the rope, I swing out of the window and use my gloves to glide down it fast, tightening my grip to slow myself down before hitting the ground. I take off, running toward the Bratva princess.

She can't escape.

I will not allow her to leave these grounds.

How the fuck did I forget to check the windows?

It's clear that since I captured her, I've not been thinking straight. After the shit day I've had, the last thing I need is this. Problems are cropping up all over the place as the Russians hit another one of our drops. Not to mention, some of our low-level drug runners were murdered and left for dead on the street. Five of them, leaving us with no fucking product and fewer dealers. The Russians are winning this war, and we'll lose if we don't work out how we're hemorrhaging product.

My footsteps speed up as I hear her heavy breathing in the distance as she makes good ground, but she's not as fast as I am.

"Give up now," I shout, pushing my muscles harder as I sprint toward her.

"Never," she shouts back, somehow speeding up.

The girl can run better than I'd expect a princess to run. She's not your typical mafia princess, as her father has brought her up to be strong and fearless. Viktoria is a fighter, but that could work out badly for her in the end.

I push my legs harder, chasing after her in the darkness. The sick thing is, my cock is hardening as I chase her. It's a primal sensation, chasing a woman I desire through my grounds, and the thrill of the chase is unlike anything I've experienced.

The ground between us shortens as she gets tired. I'm not sure where she thinks she can escape to. Six-foot walls surround the grounds. "There's nowhere for you to go," I call.

Viktoria doesn't give up, her labored breaths echoing through the air.

"I'm gaining on you. Quit now," I call, watching as the ground between us shortens. All Viki is doing is putting off the inevitable and turning me on.

My breathing labors as the adrenaline heightens. My senses feel more acute as I run harder again, pushing myself to the max to catch her.

Once she's mere feet from me, I launch at her. Viktoria groans as I wrap my arms around her waist, pulling her to the ground with a thud. She lands on top of me, her firm ass nestled perfectly against my straining crotch.

"Fucking let go of me," she cries, attempting to elbow me in the ribs.

I clench my jaw and hold firm. "Hold still," I order.

She turns limp in my arms.

It's a depraved fact that when she fights, I want her more. I roll her over onto the ground, covering her with my body. "Where the fuck do you think you are going, princess?"

Her nostrils flare, and she takes me by surprise, bringing her fist up and landing a well-aimed punch to my jaw. I groan the moment her knuckles connect with my face, but she practically cries.

"What the fuck is your face made of? Steel?" Her face twists in agony as she clutches onto her busted hand.

"I guess you don't punch people often." I grab her two wrists and force them over her head against the muddy ground. "But I have something that is as hard as steel for you," I murmur, grinding my cock into her stomach.

Viktoria freezes, and her eyes widen. "Don't be a fucking pig."

Even when she's in such a powerless position, she doesn't back down. It has an undesirable effect on me because I want her more than ever.

I kiss her neck and then move lower, pulling apart the shirt she is wearing, making the buttons shoot off of it, scattering them across the ground. She's wearing no bra, which means I have unrestricted access to her beautiful, pert nipples.

She gasps as I suck on them, making her buck her hips upward. "What are you—"

I cover her mouth with mine, kissing her deeply. My tongue strokes against hers as I pour all my desire into it. "Quiet, princess. All I want to hear coming from your pretty little mouth is moans of pleasure." I kiss a path down her stomach toward her pussy. She's wearing a skirt, making it easy for me to get access to her most intimate region.

No panties either.

I run the length of my tongue down her dripping wet entrance, groaning as I taste her sweetness. She's fucking addictive.

Viktoria sinks her teeth into her lip, opening the barely healed wound. She always tries to deny me her moans of pleasure, which both angers and spurs me on. In the end, she'll break as she did before. When the pleasure gets too much to handle, she can't help herself.

I grab her hips, and her hands move to push me away, but she doesn't have the strength.

"Stop this, now," she breathes, her voice laced with desire.

I suck her sensitive clit into my mouth, rolling my tongue over it.

"Shit," she hisses, sinking her fingernails into my scalp.

It stings, but I welcome the pain. I want to feel her reaction to me. "That's it, princess. I want you to moan for me."

She glares at me. "No."

I growl softly and grab her hips, forcing her onto

BIANCA COLE

all fours in the dirt. "We'll see." I bury my tongue against her asshole, making her freeze.

"What the fuck?" She says, but the arousal in her voice is unmistakable.

I lick her ass, making her shudder. Slowly, I plunge two fingers into her dripping pussy, making her muscles spasm instantly. I smirk against her skin as she comes undone, her body shaking from the force. My dirty virgin princess enjoys having her ass licked.

"Fuck," she cries.

"I think that may be a record." I plunge my fingers into her wet heat over and over, licking her tight ring of muscles while she continues to ride her orgasm.

"Rourke," she hisses my name.

"Yes, princess?"

"Stop this, now," she says, her voice breaking at the end as I thrust four thick fingers inside of her.

"Are you sure that's what you want?" I pull my fingers from her for a moment, and she whimpers. "I need to hear you say it."

When she remains silent, I shove them back inside of her and move my tongue in a circle around her tight sphincter. This time, she moans deeply, and it makes the rest of my blood race south. My hard cock pulses against the zipper of my pants, longing to be buried in my princess.

I remove my fingers again, which results in a frustrated cry.

"I can't get enough of you," I murmur, kissing a path up her back. I bite her shoulder and grab a fistful of her hair, forcing her neck upwards. "Open your mouth."

She does as I command, and I slide my fingers covered in her juice into it.

"Taste yourself and lick my fingers clean," I order.

She moans around my fingers, sucking at them as if her life depends on it. It's so hot. I grind the length of my cock in my pants against her bare ass, making her shudder.

I pull my fingers from her mouth. The burning need to feel my skin against hers is almost impossible to satiate as I pull at my shirt, popping the buttons. "I need to feel your skin against mine," I murmur, discarding it in the mud. I remove her torn open shirt and chuck it on top.

I force her onto her back and move my body to cover hers. Viktoria's eyes dip down my body, and I watch her as they observe every tattoo and scar on my chest. Her green eyes are merely a rim around such dilated pupils, signaling she's beyond turned on right now.

She reaches her busted hand toward me, and I tense, wondering if she's going to punch me again. Slowly, she traces the Callaghan clan coat of arms on my left pectoral with her dainty finger. "This is on the wall of your home," she murmurs, her eyes moving to meet mine.

I like her like this. As much as I enjoy her fighting, she's just as beautiful when calm and turned on. I take her hand in mine and move it to my lips, kissing it. "Aye, it's our family's coat of arms."

A whisper of a beautiful smile twists onto her lips. One I have seen little of since the night I danced with her in the club.

"You're so beautiful," I murmur.

My declaration seems to surprise her as her eyes widen for a second. "You aren't too bad yourself for an asshole."

I growl, irritated that she feels she can get away with calling me names. "Drop the act, princess." I narrow my eyes. "We both know that you want me."

My words merely seem to bring her back to reality as her body tenses beneath me. I'd hoped we were past fighting, but the look in her eyes tells me we're far from it. "Why on earth would I want the most annoying person I've ever met?" She moves her hand to my chest, trying to push me off her.

I don't move, pinning her to the ground with all my strength. My heart pounds hard in my chest as if it is trying to escape my rib cage. The primal desire I have for this beautiful girl beneath me is impossible to overcome, and I need to fuck her out of my system.

I move my lips to her ear and bite the shell. "Because you can't stop fantasizing about me fucking you when you touch yourself." I lick her neck, feeling that all-consuming desire rise to the surface. "Because I'm exactly the type of man you want, even if you keep denying it to yourself."

Viki shudders beneath me, her body relaxing. She doesn't say a word in response because she knows it's true.

"Because deep down you can't stop thinking about me fucking that pretty virgin pussy," I murmur, moving my lips lower to her breasts. Slowly, I tease the tip of my tongue around her pink, pert nipples.

My princess moans as her eyes roll back in her head.

I can't help but smile at the vision of her sprawled on her back in the mud. Her dark hair splayed over the floor and her bare shoulders. It's the most beautiful thing I've ever seen. My heavy cock throbs between my thighs, making the need to enter her even more pressing.

I want to hear her tell me she wants me. Strike that. I need to hear her say she wants me.

"Beg me for it, princess," I say.

She turns rigid and shakes her head. "Never."

I groan as it seems Viki needs a little more coaxing, but I can't wait any longer. Viktoria Volkov is mine, and I intend to stake my claim tonight.

12

VIKTORIA

"You're infuriating," he murmurs, lips mere inches from mine.

"And you are a cocky asshole," I reply, feeling an odd sensation pulling at my gut. The push and pull between us excite me, which is so messed up. Rourke is one of the most attractive men I've ever met, but he's also depraved, and I'm not sure what that says for me since I just came all over his face in the mud like some sex-crazed animal.

His eyes dip to my lips and then move back to meet my gaze. "Admit it, princess. You want my cock inside of you."

I glare at the man pinning me to the muddy ground with his weight. "I'll never admit that."

He clenches his jaw and forces more of his weight on me. "Never is very definitive, isn't it?"

"Yes, because I know for definite, I'll never want your cock inside of me," I lie, holding his gaze and not backing down. The fact is, it's all I want right now.

A slight smirk twists onto his lips. He tilts his head to the side. "If that's true, why did you moan my name while I ate your pretty little cunt in the bedroom?"

Heat flares through my body, burning my cheeks. I have no answer to that because, despite my shame, I moaned Rourke's name.

Rourke shakes his head. "Before you deny it, I think I'll have to make you moan for me now, princess."

A thrill of excitement coils through me, which is so wrong.

He moves his lips to my neck and plants an opened mouth kiss against my skin, making goose-bumps rise over my flesh. "I'm going to make you beg me."

This man is the most arrogant person I've ever met. "In your dreams."

He bites my cut bottom lip into his mouth and slides his tongue over it softly, sending an unwanted shiver down my spine. "I'm going to make you scream."

My stomach flutters as I try to ignore the heat

flaring between us. The crackle of electricity flooding the air makes my heart skip a beat. I feel that undeniable chemistry igniting, just as it did in the club when we danced. Just like it does every damn time this man goes near me. "Don't you dare touch me again," I warn, knowing that I don't just fear how far this man would push this, but how my body might react if he fucks me.

He smirks at me. "Or what?"

I swallow hard, knowing that I have no power. Rourke has me pinned to the ground, and I've got nowhere to go. My escape plan has backfired spectacularly. "Or I'll kill you the first chance I get."

He moves his weight off of me, allowing me to scramble to my feet. "Believe me. You'd never get the chance." Before I can think, he wraps his powerful arms around my waist and yanks me against his hard, muscular body. "I know you want it, princess." He moves his lips close to mine again, staring into my eyes with a sudden tender desire that makes no sense. The electric tension swirls through the air, sending a shiver down my spine.

There is no tenderness between us, but how can there be when I'm his prisoner? And yet, his touch holds a promise of something more profound.

I swallow my fear, feeling heat spiral through me as his hand moves to cup my breasts.

"Deep down, princess, you want this." He ghosts his lips over mine with a gentleness that makes me shudder. "You want me," he murmurs.

"How can I want you when you kidnapped me?" I breathe. I know it's a question that even I don't have the answer to.

He smirks against my lips, still not kissing me. "Not a denial, though, is it?"

Before I can open my mouth to speak, Rourke covers it with his. Out of instinct, I wrap my hands around the back of his neck, feeling a visceral need to draw him closer to me. It's as if he's got me under his spell.

Rourke's mouth opens, and he parts my lips with his tongue. I feel it swipe against my own in hungry, demanding strokes. It stokes to life that all-consuming need for him that, for some sick reason, lives deep within me.

I allow him to kiss me, touch me. Our bodies writhe together as our need for one another heightens. The fight escapes me, as all I can think about is satisfying that deep craving. Despite him already making me come, I want—no, I need, more.

When our lips part, I can't help myself. "I need you," I murmur.

The smirk on his lips reminds me of my dislike for his

personality. My words only inflate his ego, but my desire is impossible to tame. "As you wish." The zipper of his pants sends both terror and excitement through me. I can't fight it anymore. The pure chemistry that draws our bodies together, no matter how much I try to fight.

Rourke releases his beautiful cock, hard and heavy and perfectly thick. A tinge of fear pierces me at the thought of his stretching me open. He lifts me from the mud, carrying me toward a dry patch of grass beneath a large tree. "You are mine, princess," he murmurs, biting my ear hard enough to hurt. "All mine." The pain only tightens the excitement in my guy.

I can't understand why the declaration only heightens my need for him. The possessive tone of his voice is addictive. "Yours," I murmur against his lips. "Fuck me," I breathe.

He smiles. "You don't need to ask me twice." The hard, thick head of his cock rests at my entrance. I want it despite the consequences. Right now, everything else has faded into the distance, and all I can think about is our bodies joining.

Rourke forces his hips forward, groaning the moment he enters me.

I hiss at the burning pain of his cock, stretching me open for the first time. "Shit," I cry, tensing as the pain is unbelievable. It feels like he's trying to split me in half.

Rourke stills, kissing me softly. "Relax, princess," he murmurs against my lips. "The pain will subside, and pure pleasure will replace it." He slides his tongue into my mouth, forcing that inexplicable need to sink into my bone, making me want to be joined to him in a primal way. The pressure inside of me builds again as he pushes forward, sinking inch after agonizing inch inside of my tight channel. He breaks through my innocence with a painful thrust and buries himself deeper.

I groan, clawing at his back as my body struggles with the pain. I bite my lip, forcing open the cut on it again as metallic blood coats my teeth. The pain is both irresistible and excruciating.

"Good girl," he murmurs into my ear, nipping it with his teeth. "Open up and take my cock, princess." A rumble echoes through his chest as the last inch slides inside of me, filling me in a way I never knew possible. "You've taken every inch inside," he breathes, his voice exasperated.

"Fuck me," I hiss, needing to feel him move, despite the burning pain of his cock stretching me open.

He chuckles softly, a sound that reminds me of *who* I'm currently writhing beneath. A monster of a man who cares about no one but himself. "So demanding," he mutters, his teeth nibbling at the sensitive flesh where my neck meets my shoulder.

I glare at him as he moves to hold my gaze, electricity and fire blazing between us uncontrollably every single time we meet each other's gaze.

"Whatever you command, princess," he says before pulling his cock out of me.

I whine, feeling so empty at the hole he leaves inside of me. It's almost as painful to lose his cock as it was for him to enter, but the emptiness doesn't last long.

Rourke slams inside of me with one hard stroke.

"Oh, God," I cry, my eyes rolling back in my head as the burning pain return with more intensity. Despite how wet I am between my thighs, the friction and burn are intense.

"Such a tight little cunt," Rourke wheezes, his breath coming sharp and uneven.

I moan unashamedly, feeling the heat in my body spread as he talks dirty to me. "You have a filthy mouth, Rourke Callaghan," I breathe.

He smirks at me. "And you love it." He pulls out of me and back in with deliberate slowness, allowing me to feel every inch as he moves. "You feel so good," he growls.

The burning sensation slowly turns to something

deeper, pleasure and pain morphing into one as he ravages me. The wetness between my thighs slides down my legs as he plows into me on the muddy ground.

The moment is so visceral and savage like wild animals mating. As if we've been playing a game leading up to this moment for the past few weeks.

"You're such a good little virgin for taking my cock so well," he murmurs, before moving his mouth over mine.

I groan as his tongue prizes my lips open with force and drives inside my mouth with as much violence as he fucks me with, taking everything from me with each swipe of his tongue and stroke of his cock. And yet I'm giving it all to him willingly, enjoying it even.

Rourke digs his fingertips into my hips harder and holds my gaze, darkness swirling in the air between us. "So fucking good," he spits, fucking me harder with each pump of his hips. I can see Rourke is trying desperately to keep hold of his control, but it's waning. The muscles in his shoulders are bunched and tense, and his jaw clenched so hard it looks like he's trying to break it and his eyes blazing with conflict as he tries to hold himself together. He doesn't want to snap and show me the real Rourke Callaghan.

I'm a glutton for pain and punishment and darkness, so I do something crazy. "Harder," I breathe, the tone of my voice quiet as fear of the unknown holds me back. Any sensible person would know not to push a man as dark as Rourke when you're at his mercy, but it's clear I'm not sensible. I'm reckless and needy for pain, which Rourke has made me realize can be as addicting as pleasure.

Rourke's nostrils flare as his chest tenses, turning him rigid above me. His movements stop for a moment while his eyes flash with a burning need. "Be careful what you wish for, Viki."

Viki.

Only my friends call me that, but it sounds right hearing it from him. I hold his gaze. "Or what?"

His eyes narrow. "You might regret it." He continues to fuck me with the same slow and soft strokes, hitting my g-spot every single time. "You don't want to unleash the monster within."

I lick my bottom lip. "Perhaps that is what I want."

He growls and moves his hand to my neck, gripping me so hard it hurts. "Stop pushing me," he snarls, plowing into me with so much strength it feels like he is trying to break me in half. "An innocent thing like you can't take the darkness inside of me."

"Try me," I spit out, grinding my teeth into my

lip and breaking the skin. "I'm not as innocent as you think."

He laughs, a manic sound as he pounds into me with such force. "Says the pretty little virgin. You're the fucking epitome of innocence."

I grit my teeth together as he's wrong. "I may be a virgin, but it doesn't mean I'm innocent."

He holds my gaze as he continues to fuck me, eyes blazing with untamed power, which I'm becoming to believe is my addiction. "Believe what you want, but you are not built to experience the darkest side of me."

I reach for him, digging my fingernails into his back so hard I know they will leave marks, perhaps even break the skin.

Rourke's eyes darken, and he stops, pulling his cock from me. I feel emptier than I've ever felt for a moment, lost without him inside of me. He flips me onto all fours and grabs my wrists behind my back.

I feel the tip of his hard cock against my entrance.

Rourke's breathing is labored, and the rasp of it makes me long for him even more. Suddenly, he slams his cock into me. My body allows him in. This time, he isn't holding himself back. His body weight crushes me as he unleashes the monster inside of him. He thrusts his hips violently, plowing into me as deep as possible.

"Fuck, yes," I cry, wondering if I'm broken for enjoying such harsh, painful treatment.

There's always been darkness inside me I can't comprehend. Rourke thinks I'm this innocent virgin Bratva princess, shielded from the terror of our world, but that's a lie. My father has never tried to shield me from it, and he's molded me in his image along with my brother, making sure we had the strength to survive such a ruthless existence. I may have been a virgin when we met, but I lost my innocence many years ago.

"Take it," he growls, his teeth grazing my earlobe. "My filthy princess."

His body weight presses me against the ground as he continues to move in and out. Rourke keeps one hand wrapped around my wrists forcefully behind my back with his other hand tightly locked on the back of my neck, grabbing me hard enough to leave bruises.

The earthy scent of rotting fall leaves beneath me, and the mud only heightens the archaic, almost primal way we're fucking like animals in the mud, forgetting everything other than the basic need to mate with each other.

"Oh, God," I cry out, my clit grinding into the

grass. My body feels numb and sensitive as Rourke violently breaks me in, pushing me toward the edge of oblivion. "Fuck, yes," I shout.

"Come for me," he roars, his body weighing me down harder into the ground. My arms ache as I try to keep my face off the ground. My hard nipples graze against the grass as he thrusts with power and speed and savagery. White-hot tendrils wrap around my body as I crash over the edge, pleasure bursting in my veins and turning me into a trembling mess. "Fuck," I scream.

Rourke growls, his cock swelling inside of me as he thrusts one, two, three more times in jerky motions, releasing inside of me.

My body continues to spasm and shake beneath him long after we've both come apart. We rest for what feels like an eternity, trapped in the same position until I feel the cold infecting my bones. "Rourke, I'm freezing here."

He grumbles, pulling his cock from me and releasing me from his heavyweight.

I struggle to scramble to my feet, brushing off the damp leaves all over my dress. When I glance at Rourke, he's zipping his cock back inside his pants.

The man won't look in my direction. "Follow me," he orders.

I set my hands on my hips, glaring at him. "Or what?"

His pale blue eyes sparkle in the starlight as he glares at me coldly, moving closer. "Don't make me carry you inside, Viktoria."

I hold Rourke's gaze, despite feeling smaller than I've ever felt. This man took the one thing that made me worth a damn to my family, to my father, and now he's acting like it was nothing.

My stomach churns as I realize the grave mistake I made, allowing him to worm his way under my skin, infecting my blood, taking hold of my bones, and sinking his claws into my heart.

13

ROURKE

Killian marches into my office. "Brother, we have a problem."

Great.

Another one to add to the ever-growing list. I minimize the surveillance screen on my computer, which I watch Viktoria on. A dirty secret that I'm unable to stop.

I've had to claw myself back from going anywhere near her after I took Viki's virginity like an animal rolling around in the dirt. That was five days ago.

Instead, I watch her like a sick pervert, stroking myself while I think of our hot, primal sex. I shouldn't be sitting here watching a woman while we're at war. The only way to win is to remain focused, yet the Volkov princess has derailed my focus entirely.

I clench my jaw. "What is it?"

Killian runs a hand through his hair. "The bikers are getting seriously restless since you promised we'd deliver that shipment, and we didn't."

It was a stupid thing to promise, since I couldn't have been sure our drop would go ahead without a hitch. "Yeah, bad move, I know." I sigh heavily.

He shakes his head. "Seamus spotted Axel meeting with Massimo at one of Massimo's restaurants in the city."

"What?" I growl, wondering if I heard that right. We've had so much of our attention on the Russians we forgot to watch the Italians. "Do you think they'll steal the contract from us?"

Killian shrugs. "I reckon the bastards will try."

It's been just under two weeks since the Russians blew up The Shamrock. We've been lying in wait, searching for the perfect opportunity to strike, but the constant attacks on our shipments are causing us problems. If we don't have the drugs, we can't supply our customers."

"Fuck." I pace the floor of the library, contemplating my next move. This game just became far more complicated. It doesn't just involve the Bratva. Before long, all the underworld will be enthralled in the war. "This war is costing us more than it's costing the Russians at the moment." An idea hits me. "I'm too focused on the Bratva to even look at the Italians." I narrow my eyes. "Why don't we split our efforts? You monitor the Morrone Family while I handle the Russians."

Killian nods. "Sounds like a plan."

I walk to the dresser in my office and pour myself a glass of whiskey. "Do you want one?"

Killian checks his watch, raising an eyebrow. "You realize it's ten in the morning?"

"What is your point?" I loosen my tie as his judgment only irritates me.

He shakes his head, holding his hands up. "No point. I'll pass, though, thanks."

I knock back the whiskey, sighing as it burns through my chest. The pain is welcome as I dig my cell phone out of my pocket. "I'll get Seamus to investigate the Bratva supply chain, as we need to strike back hard and soon."

Killian moves closer to me. "Brother, don't you think we need to send a harsher message."

I square my jaw. "Like what?" I pace the office floor again. "We need to hurt them financially, and a hit on their supply would be a good start." I raise a brow. "Do you have any other suggestions?"

Killian looks thoughtful. "Why don't we give the girl back?"

My brow furrows. "What the fuck would we do that for?"

A dark smirk flickers onto his lips, making me dread his next words. "I don't mean alive, of course, but we can send Viktoria back in pieces to him and make Spartak squirm."

The cold severity in my brother's tone makes me shudder as I glare at him, knowing he's sicker than me. My father would consider it too, and perhaps I would if I weren't so obsessed with the Bratva princess. There is no world in which I'd ever consider carving her up or allowing anyone else to do it. "No," I snap. I will allow no one to lay a hand on her, even if it seems contrary to the ultimate goal; to punish Spartak for murdering our father.

He raises a brow at my outburst. "Calm down. It was a suggestion." His brow furrows. "I'm not sure what good it is keeping her if you don't intend to use the girl unless you have a thing for her."

Killian knows me better than anyone, so lying to him will be hard. I grind my teeth and glare at him. "Do you think I'd be into a Volkov?"

"Fuck knows." He shrugs. "She's fucking hot, though, isn't she?"

I sense he's trying to push my buttons, but the fact

he's noticed her beauty angers me. It's been five days since I fucked her roughly. Since then, I've kept my distance from her, only watching the surveillance because my quest for revenge is twisting and warping into an obsession.

No matter how badly I want to go into her room, I must resist. Her body attracts mine like a fucking magnet, even when she fights the chemistry between us. It's becoming painfully clear to me that one taste of her will never be enough.

"Hadn't noticed," I reply, turning my back on him. "Have you spoken to Hernandez Estrada?" I ask, changing the subject.

We have to find an ally in this war if we're going to survive. The bikers can't be trusted, meaning our only option is the Estrada Cartel.

"He's being difficult to pin down." Killian runs a hand through his hair. "They offered a meeting with his son, but not him."

I raise a brow. "Which son?"

"Thiago."

I clench my jaw. "Not even the eldest son, aye?" I don't appreciate Hernandez refusing to meet with us, but offensively, even Mattias isn't willing to make an appearance. It makes it appear as if he doesn't believe the Callaghan Clan is worth his time, but we are desperate. "Fine, arrange it."

Killian nods. "I will do." He glances at his watch. "Torin said he was on his way here to meet us."

"What for?"

Killian shakes his head. "Not entirely sure, but he said he had an important matter to discuss with the both of us."

I sigh heavily. It is one thing after another. Father may have prepared me for leadership, but he didn't prepare me for dealing with a war. "Great, probably more problems." I stand and walk to the dresser in the office's corner, selecting one of Father's vintage whiskeys. "A toast?" I ask.

Killian raises a brow. "A toast to what? Problems?"

I shake my head. "No, to our father."

Killian's jaw clenches, and he nods. "You seem determined to make me drink in the morning." He walks over to join me, and I pour each of us a glass, passing him one. "Fine, just this once."

"To making the Volkov Bratva pay for taking him too fucking early."

"Here, here," Killian replies, sipping the whiskey and turning to take a seat. He sets the glass down on the coffee table and sits back, shutting his eyes. "We aren't prepared for this shit, are we?"

I raise a brow. "What shit?"

"Leading the clan during a war." He opens his

eyes and looks at me. "Father never had to deal with this kind of chaos. At least, not since we've been alive."

I nod, knowing that Father didn't equip us to be in charge during such an unstable time, but thankfully, we have our uncles. Torin has been by my father's side through it all. "It's a crazy time to be in charge." I sip my whiskey, enjoying the warm burn as it slides down my throat.

A knock echoes. "Come in," I call.

Torin enters with a look on his face that tells me my instinct was correct. We have another problem.

"Lads, I'm afraid I've got bad news."

The last thing I need to hear today is anymore bad news. "What is it?"

Torin marches in and slumps down in a seat opposite Killian. "Spartak hit our delivery at the docks last night." He cracks his neck. "Three tons gone."

"Motherfuckers," I growl, throwing my whiskey tumbler against the wall, shattering it into pieces. When I turn around, Torin and Killian are staring at me as if I'm a psychopath who needs locking in a psych ward. "How did they get to us at the docks? We run the territory." I glare at Torin.

Torin clears his throat. "No idea, but we need to root out our weak spots if we are going to survive this war." The tension in his voice is clear, which means the hit at the docks has rattled him. Torin is rarely rattled. "It's been a shit show for the clan up to now." He loosens his tie around his neck, letting out a shaky breath. "We need to hit the Russians hard and fast."

"That's what I've been saying," Killian counters, trying to suck up to our uncle. He's always been a suck-up. "We need to use the Volkov girl for something productive and start carving her up and shipping her to Spartak."

Torin's eyebrows hitch up, hearing the extent of my brother's depravity. Out of all of us, he's always been the sick one. "That's one angle, I guess." He sits up straighter, leaning forward and clasping his hands on his legs. "I feel we need to hit them financially. Take out a huge shipment." His eyes narrow. "They use the airstrips for drug drops. We need to take some of their shipments in return."

I nod in response, agreeing with my uncle's logic. "It's a good plan, but how are we going to find out where a shipment is coming in?"

Torin cracks his knuckles. "Leave it to me, as I have a way of getting that information."

"Perfect." I clap my hands. "The Mexicans will still want payment for the shipment, though. We're hemorrhaging cash faster than an alcoholic with a gambling problem. If this keeps up, we won't be able to afford it, and then we'll be in real shit. You know the Vasquez Cartel doesn't take any shit."

Torin grimaces. "I know." He glances at the clock on the wall. "I'll get to work now and sort out the hit. Do you want me to arrange it all or run it by you first?"

I stand and walk over to my uncle. "Arrange it. I trust you." I glance at Killian. "If we've got any shot at winning this war, then we have to work together."

Killian runs a hand across the back of his neck. "Yeah, otherwise, we'll end up in a grave next to our parents in no time."

Torin stands. "I'll die before I see anything to you." He gives us both a nod. "Don't worry about it. We'll hit them hard, and I'll keep you both updated."

Without another word, he walks out, leaving Killian and me alone. Killian sighs, shaking his head. "If it isn't one thing, it's another." His brow furrows. "Should we ask Kieran to monitor the bikers?"

I wouldn't say I like the idea of involving our baby brother in any of this. He isn't ready. Father never trained him the way he trained the two of us. It was never his calling to be a leader in the clan, even if he's trying hard now to fit in. "Let's leave Kier out of this." I shrug. "Blaine would be a better option."

"Kieran's twenty-one now. It is time you stop seeing him as a helpless child." Killian walks toward the door. "He's getting fed up with it if you hadn't noticed. All he wants is to prove himself to you."

I narrow my eyes as I watch Killian's back. "It's too dangerous for an inexperienced kid like him."

Killian stops at the doorway and glances back, raising an eyebrow. "How the fuck do you think we learned? On the job. Give it a thought." He walks out of the room.

I pour myself another glass of whiskey, knocking it back. This world isn't built for people like Kieran, as he's too emotional and doesn't have what it takes to be a clan member, even if he's part of the family. I ignore my brother's musings and sit down in front of my computer, waking it up.

My heart skips a beat as I hover over the surveillance software a moment before clicking it and accessing it. Viktoria Volkov appears on my screen, her thighs spread wide open, angled at the camera, and her fingers dipping in and out of her wet pussy.

She's getting desperate.

I watch as her eyes focus on the camera, taunting me. Desire shakes me to the bone as I clench my fists on the desk, knowing that I can't take the bait, no matter how badly I want to. Viktoria Volkov is becoming a problem I don't know how to handle. My brother's right that maybe I need to let her go.

The moment the thought enters my mind, I hear a voice in my head.

Never. She's mine.

I know it to be true. Viki Volkov isn't going anywhere. She belongs to me, and nothing can change that. Not my brothers, not my uncles, not Spartak or his Bratva. No one is going to stand in our way.

I WALK toward my room but find my feet carrying me the opposite way. Straight to my princess. A deep, rasping moan echoes from the other side of the door.

She can't be at it again.

I watched her in my office, thrusting her fingers into her greedy little pussy until she climaxed. I came along with her all over my desk before shutting my computer down, feeling disgusted.

I lean my forehead against the door, breathing a deep breath as my body shudders with a palpable need. "What am I doing?" I whisper to myself.

My cock thickens as the need to take her heightens, wrapping vines around my free will and forcing me to reach for the key in my pocket.

It's been a week since I fucked her, and it's only polite to service her again. Even though she has been at it herself constantly for the last few days. I place the key in the door and turn it in the lock, forcing it open and stepping inside.

The image in front of me nearly breaks any self-control I have left. Viktoria is bent over the bed with her ass toward me and her dripping pussy on display. She thrusts a thick dildo into herself and her ass is plugged with an anal plug. She must have found it in the same drawer as the rope she tried to escape with.

"Beautiful," I murmur behind her.

She freezes and lets go of the dildo, dropping it to the bed and making a mess. "Rourke," she croaks, scrambling under the sheets of the bed. "What are you doing?"

I smirk at her. "I could ask you the same question, princess."

Her cheeks turn a Scarlett red as I step closer to the bed, unable to get the image of her bent over out of my mind.

"Insatiable, aren't you?"

She shakes her head. "I don't know what you mean."

I stop a foot from the bed. "I've been watching you, princess. You can't stop touching yourself."

Her eyes narrow. "Maybe I wouldn't have to touch myself if you paid me a visit once in a while."

My brow furrows as I wonder if she expects me to

repeat what happened the other night. "And why would I do that, Viki? You're my captive."

Her expression hardens. "Right, get out then," she barks.

"I won't take orders from a woman who is my prisoner." I reach for her, but she dodges away from me, jumping out of the bed buck naked.

My eyes dip down her exquisite body, taking in every dip and curve. Her wide hips and thick thighs are female perfection. "Aingeal," I murmur, which means angel in Gaelic.

Her elegant eyebrows pull together in the middle. "What?"

I move toward her, my dick thickening with every step I take. "Bend over for me. You need to be taught a lesson, princess."

Her eyes flare with such rage it only increases my lust. "No chance."

"The count started at five and will go up the longer you disobey me."

I notice her frame stiffen. "Go to hell."

I smirk. "Been there and done that. Six." I walk around the bed, closing the gap between us. "Bend over."

Her lip quivers as she takes steps backward, trying to escape me. "Leave me alone."

"Seven," I breathe, moving closer to her.

She keeps moving backward until her spine collides with the wall. Viktoria's eyes widen, fear flashing in her eyes.

"Eight," I murmur, now only a few feet from her. "Don't make me drag you back to the bed."

Her body shudders as I reach for her hips, digging my fingertips into them hard enough to leave bruises. "Rourke," she breathes my name, and it sounds as dirty as a curse from her lips.

"Be a good girl and bend over the bed for me."

She shakes, her body thrumming with desire as she nods in response.

I let go of her, and she walks to the bed. At the last moment, she glances over her shoulder and says, "Fuck you." She rushes for the bathroom so fast that I can't stop her. The door slams and the lock clicks, shutting me out of the room.

I growl and stride toward the shut door, banging my fist on it. "Count went up to fifteen," I shout, feeling angered by Viki's stubbornness that won't quit.

Viktoria has been trying to get my attention, finger fucking her tight little cunt in front of the camera. Now I'm here, and she is acting like a spoiled brat. I reach into my pocket and pull out the key, which also fits the bathroom door. "I'm going to count to three. If you don't open the door, I will."

I hear soft footsteps as she paces on the other side.

"One," I say, listening as she moves closer. "Two."

The click of the lock sounds, and she swings the door open, wearing a robe to hide her body.

Viki is playing a dangerous game with me. If she keeps pushing me, I'll snap. My princess doesn't want to see the true monster behind the man.

14

VIKTORIA

*H*e holds my gaze, electricity swirling in the air between us and zapping all the oxygen from it.

I'm angry with the man in front of me, and I know it's not only because he hasn't visited me since he took my virginity. A part of my rage isn't only because of Rourke, but I'm angry with myself. For allowing this beautiful creature to get under my skin.

It's been five days since he fucked me. It stings knowing that I let him take my virginity, and he doesn't care about me. All he wants is to hurt my family and me.

What stings more is that he admitted he has been watching me, but only now has he broken and come to my room. It's taken this long for him to snap. All I can think about day and night is his touch, locked and bored in a room with no escape.

Now, I've earned myself a punishment from this man. Fifteen spanks. I shudder at the mere thought, gazing into his angry blue eyes.

"Good decision," he murmurs darkly, stepping forward and grabbing my wrist with harsh force.

I wince as he drags me into the bedroom and positions me in front of the bed, my back to him.

"Robe off," Rourke barks.

Coldness seeps into my bones as I reach for the tie around my waist, pulling it open. I drop the robe to the floor, and Rourke kicks it out of the way. "Bend over," he orders.

I swallow hard, feeling a mix of fear and arousal taking over my body. Slowly, I bend at the waist and place my forearms on the bed, giving Rourke unrestricted access to the most intimate part of my body. The anal plug is still in my ass. When I found it the other day, along with some lube, I wanted to try it.

Rourke groans as he slides his finger through me, feeling how wet I am. My nipples tighten against the fabric of the comforter. "Fifteen is the number, princess. Count for me."

I shudder, my eyes clamping shut in anticipation of the pain, which makes me wetter than anything else. I wait for the first impact, holding my breath.

Rourke flattens his palm and spanks my left ass cheek hard.

My stomach churns, and my nipples harden. "One," I count, keeping my voice even. How am I going to endure fourteen more of those?

The next four spanks come in fast succession.

"Two, three, four, five," I cry, my body coiling with tension as every touch serves to magnify my arousal.

Rourke chuckles softly. "Such a masochist," he muses, gently teasing his finger through my dripping wet center. "I've never seen a woman get so wet from being spanked."

I tense, my body turning to ice. A flood of green envy hits me and the mere mention of other women. At that moment, I wonder how many women he's been with, as he's the furthest thing from a virgin.

The next spank connects with my already stinging ass, but I'm too wrapped up in my thoughts.

"Count," he roars.

I swallow hard. "Six," I murmur.

He spanks my pussy next, making me shriek in both pleasure and pain. "S-seven," I say, tears prickling my eyes as I realize I'm not even halfway yet. It's not the pain that I fear but the mounting pressure deep inside of me, warning me I might come undone from the punishment alone. It's sick and twisted and so fucking wrong.

I bite my lip, forcing my teeth into the skin and breaking the healing flesh once again. The metallic tang of blood infuses my mouth as Rourke spanks me four more times.

"E-eight, N-n-nine, ten, E-eleven," I cry, my thighs shaking from the pressure building deep inside of me.

He gives me a break from the impact but moves his fingers between my thighs again. "So fucking wet," he murmurs. I'm shaking like a leaf in the strong fall breeze, threatening to be blown to the ground and reduced to nothing.

"Rourke," I rasp his name, my body so highly strung I can hardly think anymore.

He growls softly. "Count." His firm palm lands on my ass cheeks in a pair this time.

"Twelve, thirteen-n," I stammer, my entire body shaking as I try hard not to come apart from Rourke's violent treatment.

"Just let go," he purrs. I can tell he's enjoying this, watching me squirm.

He's bruising my ass, and yet I'm practically falling apart from the pain, enjoying every second.

He spanks my pussy once, and that's all it takes. I

don't feel the next spank, and I'm not even sure if he doles it out. My entire body turns rigid as the most world-shaking orgasm ever grabs hold of my soul, threatening destroy me.

I moan out loud, a deep, guttural sound that doesn't even sound like it comes from me. My pussy gushes, and my juice runs down my thigh. "Fuck, fuck," I cry, fisting the comforter beneath me as my body turns into jelly for the man who spanked me.

"My little masochist," he purrs, finger dipping into my pussy as he plays me right through it, building that need inside of me like a master musician. "Are you ready for my cock?" He taps the base of the plug gently, making my body react.

Internally, my brain screams *yes*. As it's all I've thought about since that night, but I've too much self-respect to answer him.

He grabs the back of my neck forcefully. "I asked you a question," he says.

"No, I'll never be."

He growls in frustration as I hear the zip of his pants come down. Within seconds, he thrusts forward and buries every inch of cock deep inside of me.

I cry out, my body accepting his sudden, violent invasion. His heavy erection fills that deep cavernous hole that I've felt gnawing at me since he fucked me the first time. "Fuck," I say, feeling my mind lost to the sensation. The pressure of his cock stretching my channel against the plug in my ass is overwhelming.

Rourke's possessive grip tightens on my hips, dragging me against him to meet the thrusts, plowing into me with all his power. I feel so weak and yet so wanted as he loses control. The darkness inside of him comes to the forefront.

"You are so dirty, Viki," he murmurs against my ear, his warm breath teasing at my flesh. "I bet you'd love to feel my cock in that tight little ass, wouldn't you?"

I tense, my body turning to ice.

He wouldn't.

I know as that thought crosses my mind that he would. The idea of his heavy erection lodged deep inside my ass frightens me. It hurt enough the first time he entered my pussy, and putting the relatively small buttplug in took a lot of work.

"No," I murmur, the fear clear in my voice.

He licks a path down the column of my neck. "Are you sure?" He taps the plug in my ass, holding his thick cock deep inside of me. "What were you thinking about when you put this buttplug in your ass, then?"

A shiver starts at the top of my head and races

down my spine, making me prickle with anticipation. "I was curious how it would feel, that's all."

"I'm going to claim your ass for myself one of these days," he bites my earlobe forcefully, making me yelp. "But, not today." He moves his hand slowly down the front of my body, holding himself deep inside of me.

"You're an arrogant, self-serving asshole," I reply, despite the pleasure he's giving me.

He chuckles, the rumble sending tremors through my body. My clit throbs and aches for friction as he holds himself still inside of me, keeping his large hand flat against my stomach. "That's not a nice way to talk to the man inside of you, is it?"

I hold still, feeling weak and vulnerable. Rourke has so much power over me it should scare me. A man whose darkness runs deep in his bones. He kidnapped me without a second thought, an innocent in his father's demise, and yet he saw an opportunity and snatched it. I've given him everything and allowed him to bleed me dry, tear me apart from the inside out.

No matter how much I try to keep up this front that I hate him, it's as if he knows it is a lie. He knows he has me in the palm of his hand.

"Shut up and fuck me," I respond, knowing that fighting only delays what I want.

He smiles against my back, sinking his teeth into the flesh between my shoulder blades, which makes me cry out in both pain and pleasure. "You don't have the manners of a princess, Viki," he murmurs before sinking his teeth into the sensitive flesh where my shoulder meets my neck.

I grind my teeth, clenching my jaw. "Please fuck me," I bite out.

He remains still inside of me, his cock as deep as possible in my body. I focus on the pain his teeth inflict on my shoulder, biting me like a savage. He still doesn't move.

Frustration heightens as I fist the comforter beneath me, needing to feel him fuck me so badly. I've wanted nothing as deeply as I want him.

"Please, Rourke," I moan, forgetting that I have any self-respect at all. "I need to feel you."

He groans against my skin, his teeth leaving the flesh between my shoulder blades. "Good girl," he murmurs as his fingers return to my hips, digging into them with exactly the right amount of pressure.

Tomorrow I'll be bruised and unable to sit after his violent assault on my ass, but right now, all it does is elevate my craving for this monster. A man who delights in providing me pain, abusing me to get himself off. He's right. I'm a woman who takes satisfaction from pain, a masochist, and he's a man who takes satisfaction from giving it to me.

It's as if God made us to satisfy one another, as we'd be a perfect match if we hadn't been from two opposing sides in a war.

Rourke allows the beast off the leash, plowing his cock so deep into me with each stroke. My body bends to his will in submission. I can't hold myself up anymore, as my arms give way under his crushing weight. My stomach presses firmly into the soft mattress as he fucks me with such force it feels like his sole aim is to break me apart.

I struggle to draw in oxygen, drowning in the violent intensity of our relations. "Fuck," I scream into the pillow beneath my face, knowing the fabric will muffle it. The pressure between my thighs becomes intense as his cock stretches me open further with each thrust, bottoming out as deep as possible inside of me. "Yes," I cry, tears biting at the edges of my eyes as the commotion inside of me comes to a head.

Every nerve ending in my body blisters with white-hot pleasure. My thighs shake as I come undone. I claw into the comforter with my nails so hard I'm sure I'll tear the expensive silk, screaming so loud I know that the whole of Chicago can probably hear me being ravaged by my family's number one enemy.

Rourke growls, his teeth sinking into my shoulder hard. I feel his release deep inside of me, filling me with his seed as our bodies convulse together in a state of unadulterated bliss.

My breathing is uneven as I try to draw oxygen into my lungs. Rourke's heavyweight still pins me against the mattress.

Suddenly, the weight disappears, and his cock slides out of me, leaving me feeling empty. His warmth escapes me along with it as I hear the zip of his pants, followed by brisk footsteps away from me.

I turnover in time to see him leave through the door without a glance backward, walking away from me without a word.

Heartache pulls at my chest, threatening to drown me in its pain. I hate how bad it stings. The pain of his indifference burns more than a raging fire consuming me from the inside out. It's a deep, wounding pain that only deepens the longer this sick and twisted dance continues. The most painful part of it all is that I have no escape.

I'M surprised when it isn't the maid who enters at seven o'clock the next evening, but the bad-tempered guard who took me on a tour of the grounds. "Get dressed in that," the guard says, flinging a dress bag at me. "You have twenty minutes."

I catch it, only just. The bag is heavier than I expected as I stare at it in confusion, wondering why I'm being given an outfit.

The guard doesn't wait for my response, walking out of the room and slamming the door behind him.

I unzip the bag, and my heart skips a beat. The Callaghan colors in rich silk fabric are what I see first, but as I remove the dress from the bag, I reveal an exquisite evening gown that looks tailor made. "What's this for?" I murmur to myself, running my hands through the satin pleated skirt.

I remove the black bag around it and step back, wondering why I'm being supplied a dress. Besides the first morning breakfast, which Rourke used to get sick photos of me and one lousy walk in the grounds, I've not left this room since he captured me, so I can't see why I'd need a dress.

I drop my robe to the floor and pull the dress out, unzipping it and stepping in. It fits like a glove, but I can't zip it up, which is problematic. I glance at the door, wondering if the guard is hanging around. Slowly, I walk toward the door and listen before knocking. "Anyone out there, I need help with the zip of my dress."

I hear an irritated huff, which is the guard. He still hasn't told me his name.

"Please," I say.

There are a few moments of silence before the lock in the door clicks open. "Stand back," the guard orders. This guy could use a personality replacement, or he needs to take a chill pill. Either would work.

I take a few steps back, waiting for him to enter.

The door swings open, and he appears, glaring at me in his usual manner. "What's the problem?"

I spin around to show him the zip back of the dress. "Can't reach to do it up, I'm afraid." I glance over my shoulder, smiling at him. "Could you help a girl out?"

The guard looks uncomfortable, glancing down the corridor as if he's worried he might get caught. "Fine," he huffs, stepping into the room. "This isn't part of my job description," he mumbles, grabbing the zip.

His rough hands graze against my skin as he pulls the zip up, and once it's almost done, I hear an animal-like growl. A growl that makes the both of us jump out of our skin.

"What the fuck are you doing?" Rourke barks, sounding angrier than I've ever heard him.

Rage is written all over his beautiful, angelic face when I turn around to look at him. I don't think he liked the guard touching me, and now he looks like he wants to murder him. A shudder races down my spine as I wonder if he'd hurt him when it was my fault he was touching me.

15

ROURKE

*E*very muscle in my body coils with tension as I stand at the door, watching as my guard slides the zip of her dress up her back. The mere proximity between them makes me ready to chop his hands off so he can never touch her again.

"What the fuck are you doing?" I growl.

He jumps back at the sound of my voice, moving his hands away. "Sir, the prisoner couldn't do up her dress." He doesn't meet my gaze. "She asked me to help."

I glare at him, possessive jealousy coiling through my gut. My fists are clenched, and I am ready for blood. "Did I say you could touch the prisoner?" I snarl, realizing how crazy I sound.

The guard, I think his name is Arthur, shakes his head. "Sorry, boss."

"Sorry, will not cut it." I crack my knuckles and move toward him, ready to fuck this idiot up for touching what's mine. "I'll make you pay for touching her."

The guard turns pale, eyes shooting up to meet mine. Viktoria leaps in front of him, crossing her arms over her chest. "I asked him to help, so punish me."

I stop in my tracks, glaring at her. "Move out of the way, princess."

She straightens her back, trying to look taller. "No." Her eyes are blazing with purpose. The complimenting green of the dress I made him bring to her highlights them. My princess looks more majestic than ever. A true gem who I intend to cherish and protect with my life.

I move my gaze to the guard. "You, out now. I'll deal with you later," I order.

He moves past Viktoria, leaving me alone with her. Exactly how I like it.

"I told you. I asked for the guard's help, so if you want someone to punish. It should be me." This Russian princess is testing my last nerve.

I tilt my head slightly. "Difficult when you practically orgasm every time I spank you."

Her cheeks flush, but she doesn't back down.

"Change it up then. Give me a different punishment."

I narrow my eyes at her. "You don't tell me what to do, Viki." I glance at my watch. "Come on, we're going to be late."

"Late for what?"

I move toward her and grab her wrist, pulling her toward the door. "A charity event which you're attending as my date."

Her brow pulls together in confusion, but she doesn't ask another question. I pull her to the driveway and open the door to the limousine. "Get in," I order.

Viktoria does as I say, sliding as far as possible from the door. If she hopes I'll keep my distance from her, then she's mistaken.

I slide in, settling next to her. My hand lands on her thigh, making her glare at me. "You look stunning."

She grabs my hand and forces it off her leg. "Keep your hands to yourself."

Viktoria won't let go of this childish need to fight the palpable chemistry between us. "Since when do you order me about?" I ask, forcing my hand higher on her thigh and squeezing it. "You'll behave tonight unless you want me to bend you over in front of the two-hundred people and spank your ass raw." I smirk at her. "I'm sure daddy would be so proud seeing the tabloids the next morning."

Her nose wrinkles in disgust as she sighs heavily, moving her attention away from me and out of the window. "You make me sick."

I grab her throat. "We both know that's a lie." I yank her over me, forcing her to lie across my lap. "Why don't I prove it right now."

"Rourke," she says my name in warning, anger lacing the syllables. "Let go of me."

I ignore her protest, pushing the skirt of her dress up her thighs. My cock is heavy against her abdomen as I reveal her black thong. The bruises I inflicted on her ass last night mark her beautiful soft skin in deep purples and blacks, stirring something inside me. A discomfort at seeing what I've done to her coupled with satisfaction. Both sensations feel at odds with each other.

A mark of ownership is what it is, but I can't work out how I feel about seeing them after the event. I dip my finger lazily into her pussy, feeling how wet she is. "Hmm, I thought so."

She squirms over my lap, which does nothing to help her other than harden my cock. "Let go."

"As I thought, your pussy is dripping wet." I drag my finger from her pussy and slowly circle her clit with it, making her legs shudder. "I don't make you sick, princess. You want me to fuck you every time I'm near you. Why don't you admit it?"

She's silent and still in my lap, trying her best to control her reactions to me.

I sigh heavily and thrust my fingers inside of her, making her jolt. "This hard-to-get act is getting old." I play with her lazily, teasing her orgasm out of her slowly.

Viki stays quiet, no doubt sinking her teeth into her plump bottom lip as she always does.

"I'd think twice about busting that lip. Otherwise, everyone will know what we were up to in the limo," I warn.

She whimpers, listening to my advice.

"Good girl," I praise, which only turns her on more.

She writhes against my legs, trying to find the friction she craves.

I hold her still, controlling her pleasure. "You're insatiable, princess. Admit you want me."

Viki tenses, her body becoming as stiff as a board over my lap. She doesn't say a word, but I can sense she is still fighting the truth. "I don't."

"You are a terrible liar, Viki." I plunge four fingers inside of her at once, making her gasp. "At some point, you need to admit it."

Viktoria groans. Her body reacts to my sudden invasion. "Why?" She asks.

"Because I want to hear you tell me you want me," I purr, knowing that it is only a matter of time until she does. The chemistry neither of us can deny. A force that is so magnetic I couldn't stay away from her if my life depended on it.

The vehicle comes to a stop, warning me I don't have time to finish. Instead, I pull my finger out of her and lick it clean. "Look sharp, princess," I say, lifting her off my lap and into the seat next to me. "We're here."

Viki opens her mouth to speak, but before she can say a word, the driver opens the door, and we're met with the flashing lights of the paparazzi. She looks utterly star-struck, not moving. "Get out of the car, Viki," I breathe into her ear.

My voice snaps her out of it as she does as I say, moving to stand on the sidewalk. I join her, placing a hand on the small of her back to lead her through the crowd of vultures fighting for the best photo. Once we're out of earshot of the media, Viktoria leans toward me. "What the fuck was that about?" She hisses.

I smirk at her. "It's a high-profile event and one that I want your father to see you attending with me, as it will cause a stir."

Her face falls as she shakes her head. "Do you realize how dangerous that is?" Her eyes dart from side to side, checking our surroundings as if she's expecting an attack at any moment. "My father could be here."

I feel offended she thinks I'm amateur enough not to check the guest list. "He's not on the guest list because I checked."

She raises a brow. "My father attends these parties under aliases."

The revelation knocks me off guard, as that's information none of my men have brought to me. Maybe she's right, and coming here will be a grave mistake.

I push the concern out of my mind. "Come on." I lead her inside to the main events hall, instantly spotting Hernandez Estrada. The only man who is yet to play his hand against us in this war. Killian has a meeting set with his son next week.

Viktoria tugs at my jacket, trying to get my attention.

"Cut that out," I hiss, keeping my attention on Hernandez, who is speaking to some high-flying politician.

"Rourke," she snarls my name, getting my attention.

"What is it?" I snap before noticing how pale her face is as she stares into the distance.

I follow her gaze to find her father making his way through the crowd toward us. "Shit, keep calm. Don't say a fucking word, do you hear me?"

Her delicate throat bobs as she nods in agreement. "My father is going to kill us both," she mutters.

"I said not a word," I spit, keeping my attention fixed on my enemy. The man who killed my father, maybe not with his own hands, but he was responsible.

Spartak dares to walk straight up to me. "Callaghan," he says, eyes narrowing as they move between his daughter, who clings to my side, and me. "Have you come to your senses and decided to deliver my daughter back to me?"

"Volkov, what an unpleasant surprise." I squint at him. "No, I didn't know you were attending since your name isn't on the guest list."

An evil smirk spreads onto his lips, and he tilts his head. "Ah, that explains it. You thought you could use this event to rub the fact you have my daughter in my face." He cracks his knuckles as if preparing for a fight. "Bad move, Callaghan."

I stand taller, squaring my shoulders. We're about

the same height, but there's something in the way Viki's father holds himself that makes me feel smaller. It doesn't help that I've heard the rumors of what this man is capable of. "You wouldn't make a scene here. Too much bad press." I smirk at him. "You can spend the entire night watching me with your daughter, knowing there's nothing you can do about it." I tighten my grasp on Viki's hip and try to steer her away.

Spartak grabs my wrist and yanks me close. "Don't push me, Rourke. If you think you can prance around here with my daughter all night, you're wrong." His lips turn up in a snarl. "I will rip you apart with my bare hands in front of these people and not bat an eyelid. Let her go now."

Viktoria remains silent, trembling against me in fear.

I reclaim my wrist from him and meet his gaze, smirking. "I'd love to see you try, old man."

I tighten my grasp on Viktoria's hip, steering her away from him at a fast pace, knowing the danger we're in. Fleeing the event would admit I fear him, but staying means I could lose Viktoria. Any chance he gets, he'll try to steal her back from me.

After not seeing her for weeks, he didn't say a word to his daughter, proving this has nothing to do with her and more to do with his wounded ego.

"He's going to kill us both," Viki hisses the moment we're away from him.

I roll my eyes and yank her into a quiet corner of the room. "Would you stop being so dramatic? He won't touch us here at such a public event."

She stares at me as if I've told her I've seen pigs flying. "You don't know my father, Rourke. He would kill everyone at this event if he had to, to get what he wants."

I pause a moment, searching Viki's deep green eyes. "You honestly believe he'll try to harm us here?"

She looks at me like I'm insane. "Don't you? My father is not a sane man, Rourke. You've bought me here to rub it in his face with the media and over-looked the fact he's attending. What would you do in his position?"

Viki has a good point. I would go through heaven and hell to get my daughter back if it were me. "Fine, we're leaving now." I yank her toward a fire exit at the back, knowing that staying might lead to our deaths.

My heart turns to ice the moment I step out of the door, crashing into Adrik, one of Spartak's men. He foresaw me trying to run. "Not so fast, pretty boy."

"Adrik," Viktoria says his name, his eyes darting to her.

"Don't worry, printessa. We're going to save you."

Viki's eyes narrow. "I don't need saving. Step aside."

Adrik's brow furrows. "What do you mean? You can't want to be with this Irish scum." He shakes his head. "He kidnapped you."

I take the opportunity while he's distracted to knock him over the head with the butt of my Glock. The Russian slumps to the ground like a sack of potatoes.

Viki gasps in shock, eyes wide as they move to me. "What did you do that for?" She shakes her head. "He would have let us go."

I shake my head. "There's no guarantee. I don't take risks, princess." I grab her hand and yank her down the alleyway toward the limousine parked in the parking lot.

I freeze when I hear the fire exit swing open and a gun cock behind me.

"Give it up, Callaghan. Hand her over before I put a bullet in your worthless skull," Spartak calls.

I turn around slowly, holding my hands up.

Viktoria launches herself in front of me. "If you want to kill him, kill me first," she counters.

Spartak's lip turns up in disgust as he glares at his daughter. "Don't tempt me, Viktoria." His eyes are dead and soulless as he stares at his daughter. "It's what you deserve for disobeying me and attending that party."

I place a hand on Viki's hip, leaning toward her to whisper into her ear. "We need to run for it. Only two hundred yards." Both of us can make it, and I'm still betting on Spartak not having the balls to shoot his daughter.

She nods. "I'll follow you."

I squeeze her hand and turn around, dashing down the alleyway and dragging his daughter with me.

She is fast, matching my pace with no trouble.

A shot sounds, and we both duck as the bullet whizzes past our heads.

"Fuck," Viki shouts, eyes wide as she pushes harder, moving further in front of me as we make it out of the alleyway and onto the main road. "Where's the limo?"

My brow pulls together, as it isn't where it was supposed to stay. "Shit. They've had it moved on." I run a hand across the back of my neck, glancing at the alleyway and then left and right. "Come on. We're safest amongst a crowd." I pull her along the street, weaving in and out of people. I slide my hand into my pocket and pull out my cell, dialing Jack's number.

"Boss?"

"Where the fuck are you?" I hiss.

There's a beat of silence. "A couple of guys from the event told me not to park near the building, so I'm a block away. Is there a problem?"

"Aye, Spartak is after me. I'm on——" I glance around, looking for the street name. "Summer Street walking east. Get here quickly." I cancel the call and glance over my shoulder, searching for any sign of Spartak following us.

"I told you he would try to kill us," Viki says, concern blazing in her beautiful green eyes. "Now that I've taken your side, I'm sure he will kill me if he ever gets me back." She trembles violently. "Unless maybe I can reason with him somehow."

I ignore her words, despite knowing that she's right. Spartak would have shot her without a second thought back there, and I don't think he will listen to reason. We were running, and he fired a couple of near-misses at Viktoria. It means Viki Volkov just became my responsibility, as I would never let her die at the hands of her father.

The limousine pulls up at the curb as Jack spots us. He is quick to jump out of the car, opening the door. "Sorry, sir," he says as I march toward him.

I help Viki in and then follow her inside, glancing up at him. "Get us the hell out of here, fast."

He nods and shuts the door.

I focus my attention out of the window, as I can't trust myself to look at Viktoria. I don't know how I'm going to figure this one out, but Viktoria Volkov has become a permanent problem in my life that I didn't need.

"IT'S DONE," Torin says, walking into the dining room the next morning.

"What is?" I ask.

"My guys stole three tons of cocaine from the Volkov Bratva last night."

I smile and stand, walking to my uncle and clapping him on the shoulder. "Well done, uncle. Good work." I run a hand across the back of my neck. "How fast do you think they'll retaliate?"

He shrugs. "Not sure, but I have another opportunity to hit them again next week." He tilts his head. "Should I take it?"

"Aye, we need to mount the pressure." I pull my cell phone out of my pocket. "I need to find out if Seamus has had any luck weeding out the rat in our ranks."

Torin growls softly. "I have my money on

Darragh. That piece of shit has been gunning for more power for as long as I can remember."

I sit back down at the head of the dining table and type a text to him.

Any news on the rat?

I tap my fingers on the table, taking a sip of coffee and watching my phone as it lights up, signaling a text has come back.

Yes. Best to tell you in person. When can we meet?

I glance up, and Torin is watching me. "Anything?" .

"He wants to meet, so hopefully, he has some news." I down the rest of my coffee, wishing it was whiskey. "Do you want to tag along?"

Torin shakes his head. "Wish I could, but I've got to meet with my guys." Torin is the most authoritative of the clan's generals and the only family member to take such a position. He runs a group of twenty-five men.

"No worries." I fire a text back to Seamus.

My office. Callaghan Enterprise HQ. One hour.

"Keep me informed about the hit on the next shipment. Hopefully, we will recover everything the Russians took from us and more." I pop my knuckles as a text comes through from Seamus.

See you there.

"You got it. When is the next sitdown?"

"Next week. Seamus will send you the details." I set my empty mug down and stand. "I need to get going."

Torin walks with me as we both head out of the house. I can sense the tension as if he wants to say something. When we get to the door, he places a hand on my shoulder. "Rourke, what is the endgame with Viktoria Volkov?" He asks, his brows pulling together.

I feel a flicker of irritation pulse through me at my uncle's question. "Haven't thought about it much. Why?"

He hardens his jaw, squaring his shoulders. "It may have been hasty, snatching his daughter so fast, as it's only escalated tensions, and we're falling behind in the war. Can we use her to get ahead or not?" He asks.

To get ahead.

I've been so wrapped up in the pretty Bratva princess that I've paid no mind to how I can use her to make Spartak squirm. It was the reason for kidnapping her.

"I'm working on an angle. Seamus is helping." I clench my jaw, knowing my uncle is one of the best people at identifying bullshit when he hears it. "I'll ask for an update at our meeting. We don't want to act too fast."

I've no intention of harming my princess to get what I want. It didn't take long for her to worm her way into my affections.

He nods in response. "Okay, we need to use the girl soon, though. Spartak is winning, and if we don't act, we'll be too far behind to make a comeback."

I know my uncle is right. Spartak has the upper hand, and even my botched PR stunt with his daughter hasn't slowed him down. He's ramped up his efforts and started hitting us daily.

"Agreed. I'll let you know what Seamus says." I stand. "I've got to get to Callaghan Enterprises HQ."

Torin doesn't look convinced, but nods. "Aye, see you later."

I walk through the front door, knowing that if I don't figure out my angle with Viktoria soon, my family will take it upon themselves to find creative ways to use her.

SEAMUS IS ALREADY WAITING in the reception for me when I make it to the headquarters.

I give him a nod as a signal to follow me inside. He's got more sense than Cormac did and is dressed better than I've ever seen him dressed. A tailored suit and black dress shirt beneath it, paired with a pale gray tie. Anyone would believe he is merely a business associate.

"Jenny, can you clear my morning, please? You can reschedule the meeting with management for tomorrow."

"Of course, sir," she replies, tapping frantically at her keyboard.

I don't have the time to deal with the bullshit CEO responsibilities right now. The entire setup doesn't suit my life as the boss of a criminal organization. I can't understand how Father juggled it all, as he rarely showed me this side of the business. It's the part I'm not prepared for, and it wouldn't surprise me if management got twitchy about my lack of experience and the stock prices taking a hit.

I enter my office, followed by Seamus. Once the door shuts, I spin to face him. "What have you got for me?"

"The rat, I'm pretty certain."

Finally, some good news. "Aye, who is it?"

"As we suspected, Darragh is meeting once a week with a Russian informant." He cracks his neck. "I had him tailed."

"That slimy son of a bitch." I loosen my tie, finding it constricting. "Who knows?"

His brows pinch together as he shakes his head. "Only the two of us."

"Good, keep it that way." I level my gaze at him, narrowing my eyes. "I don't want anyone to know, not even my family. Do you hear me?"

Seamus looks puzzled by my request but doesn't question me. "Got it, boss." He steps closer, lowering his voice. "Do you want me to off him?"

I drum my fingers on the table. "No, I'm going to hold off for now. I need to make an example out of Darragh in front of the clan." I sigh heavily, glancing at the calendar. "Don't give him any of the locations for the next drops. Next week I'll make him pay at the sitdown, but it will need to be at the docks, not the house."

Seamus nods. "Sounds like a good plan." He glances at the door and back at me. "Another matter while I'm here. Axel has refused our last shipment and is stating our contract is void because we missed a few of his drops." His eyes narrow. "How do you want me to handle it?"

"Fuck's sake." The bikers are gunning for us at the moment, and it's clear they want to hit us while we're down. "Where is he getting his product?" I ask, even though I know the answer.

The Italians.

"Morrone. He's struck a deal with him." Seamus

looks uncertain about his next words. "A deal for double what he was taking from us."

"Axel has always been a backstabbing snake." I run a hand across the back of my neck. "Killian is meeting with the Estrada Cartel this week. Hopefully, they can find common ground, and they'll open more doors for us to push our product."

"Aye, sir." He pales slightly. "Shall I contact the Vasquez Cartel and confirm we need to reduce our numbers for the next few weeks?"

I shake my head. "No, keep the product coming in. We can afford it." I tap my fingers on my hardwood desk. "The last thing we need is to piss off the Vasquez Cartel. They're already anxious about this war, so we don't want to give them any reason to pull the plug, or we really will be fucked."

Seamus looks uncertain about purchasing more product when sales are down, but we can't rattle our supplier. If they decide not to supply us anymore, we will well and truly be up the creek without a paddle. "Sure, boss. Do you want me to get the men to search for alternative clients?" He rubs a hand across his beard. "Perhaps we can drop the prices and get the stock moving?"

I nod in response. "Arrange it, but only ten percent."

"Aye, I'll set it in motion." He stands and folds his arms over his chest. "Is there anything else?"

"No, just keep me informed." I wave my hand toward the door in dismissal.

He walks away without a word, leaving me alone in the corporate office. I glance around, wondering why Father wanted to reduce our illegal activity and focus on the legitimate side of the business. It's stuffy and irritating, and I've no intention of making this my primary focus.

The problem is that my primary focus is the beautiful piece of temptation stowed away in a room in my house. I open the surveillance software and she appears on the screen.

I need to go to rehab any method to stop her from consuming my every waking thought.

16

VIKTORIA

*R*ourke hasn't returned since the night of the clan charity event he took me to. The event where he crossed my father and almost got us both killed. That was over a week ago now.

Every day I remain locked in my ivory tower, waiting for him to visit me. Each day, he disappoints me, and the deep hole in my gut widens. I made a mistake, letting him take the one thing I'd been guarding.

I may be paranoid, but my father barely looked at me at the charity event. Something tells me he knows I'm no longer a virgin, and I'm useless now to the Volkov Bratva, which makes me discardable. I'd saved myself for marriage, and all it took was a Callaghan to touch me, and I forgot about it entirely.

The man's touch turns me into liquid fire,

burning for him so brightly it feels like I'll die if I don't feel him again. I hate him passionately and want him with all that I am, which is more confusing than I can explain. I hate him for making me feel this way.

It's almost midday, so I know no one will visit me until later. Every day I check the door if some idiot might forget to lock it after bringing me my food. It's pathetic, as I'm always disappointed. I walk to the door and try the handle, finding it locked as always.

Surely Rourke can't leave me locked in here forever. What good is it achieving other than angering my father?

As I walk back to the bed, the jangling of keys outside catches my attention. No one comes by at this time of day. It is like clockwork; the maid enters in the morning with food at ten o'clock and again at seven o'clock in the evening. I rush to the bed and fling myself on it, staring at the ceiling.

The lock turns over, and the door swings open, revealing the very man who has imprinted himself on me. His huge, imposing frame fills the doorway as he fixes his brilliant blue stare on me. My stomach somersaults, and my heart pitter-patters faster in my chest at the mere sight of him. It's pathetic but true.

Rourke stalks into the room with his eyes fixed on me. I notice his shoulders are tense, as if he's preparing for a fight, moving toward me. "Get up," he barks.

Are those seriously the first two words he's going to say to me after a week of nothing?

This asshole took my virginity as if it was his goddamn right, fucks me and leaves without a word for days, and then barges in here acting like an absolute prick.

"Fuck you," I growl, knowing that since I've been his captive, I've sworn more than I have in my entire life. He makes me so mad that I can't help it. My father would be ashamed if he could hear me, as it's not how the princess of the bratva should speak. Right now, I don't give a damn.

He growls, eyes wide as he grabs hold of my wrist and yanks me off the bed with all his strength. "Don't push me." His eyes narrow as he moves his attention to my lips, lingering there. "I'm not in a good mood."

"Does it look like I give a shit what mood you're in?" I ask, glaring at him as the fire of passion burns into hatred so fast that it becomes one. The fine line between hate and lust continually blurring.

He moves his palm to my throat, squeezing hard as he pushes me against the bed, the back of my knees hitting it. "Tell me who your fiance is."

I stare at him, dumbfounded by his demand.

Fiance.

"I don't have a damn fiance. Asshole."

His nostrils flare as his grip tightens, blocking my airways. "Don't lie to me, Viktoria," he growls.

Adrenaline spikes through my veins as I lift my hands and place them on his hard chest, shoving him backward with all the strength I possess. "I'm not lying, you bastard."

He frees me from his grasp, stumbling back.

"I don't have a fiance," I repeat. It hurts me he's being so cold after how intimate we've been. Perhaps it hurts because this man was my first, and I expected him to treat me differently after we slept together for some silly reason.

Rourke's eyes scream bloody murder as he stares at me. "I've had it under good fucking authority that you are lying. Your daddy has chosen your suitor."

This man is an entitled piece of shit for the way he is treating me. "If that is true, I haven't been told about it." I'm not sure why my father would keep that information from me. He knows I'll accept whoever he promises my hand in marriage to, or I would have. Now that I'm not a virgin, I know everything has changed. Unfortunately, the bratva insists on a procedure to check that the bride is indeed virginal.

His eyes narrow. "Are you saying your father has mentioned no one?"

I consider his question. Over the past couple of

years, he's mentioned a few Bratva families that he spoke with and considered potential suitors from those families. "No, only a few families that he was in talks with."

"Tell me what ones."

I glare at him. "Why should I?"

He grabs my hips and drags me against his hard body, squeezing. "Don't push me, Viktoria." His eyes narrow. "I need to know the names." His palm clasps around my throat again, blocking my airways for the second time. This man is the most irritating man I've met.

I struggle against him, trying to draw air into my lungs. "Fine," I spit.

He releases me. "Talk."

"Three names I remember. Abramov Bratva, Golubev Bratva." I squint, trying to remember the name of the other family. "I think it was Morozov Bratva."

"Fuck," Rourke growls the moment I mention the Morozov Bratva. "So it's true." He paces the width of the room.

"What's true?" I ask.

He doesn't speak, continuing to pace.

"Rourke?"

He stops and glances at me, heat in his gaze. "Your father has picked your suitor. Luka Morozov."

My stomach churns as I'm no longer untouched. Rourke ensured that the other night, and now Morozov will probably refuse me after I'm forced to be examined to ensure my virginity is intact. Father will murder me the moment he learns the truth. "I'm dead," I murmur, hugging my arms around myself.

"What do you mean?" He asks, his countenance changing.

I search his brilliant blue eyes, wishing he would save me from my grave fate. He won't. He is a Callaghan and only cares about himself. "The bratva insist on a procedure to ensure that my virginity is intact before the marriage." My brow pulls together, as I'm not sure why I'm telling him this. "The moment my father finds out, he'll kill me."

Rourke's expression hardens, and he clenches his fists by his side. "Your father is a piece of shit that needs teaching a lesson."

I glare at him, wondering if he can blame my father for any of this. I'm here because of him, and I'm no longer a virgin because of him. The only villain here I see is the man standing in front of me. "You're the one who kidnapped me and then took my virginity." I step forward and shove him. "My father is a better man than you'll ever be."

Rourke's expression turns wounded as he searches my eyes. "You believe that a man who would murder his daughter for no longer being a virgin is a better man than me?" He asks, as if unable to believe that's how I feel.

I'm not sure it is how I feel. I'm so angry right now. Angry at Rourke and my father. I don't know if he wants an answer, but I don't reply.

"Let me be clear," Rourke says, moving toward me.

I take a step back, out of instinct.

He continues to move toward me, forcing me to move backward. "Family is the most important thing to me in this world. I would never hurt them, no matter what." He backs me against the wall, closing me in. I always protect the people I love, princess." His hands land on my hips tenderly, his touch gentle. "Always," he murmurs.

I shiver, feeling his words penetrate my soul. Is he suggesting that I am one of those people?

No, don't be ridiculous.

There is no way that Rourke Callaghan is saying he loves me, as he hardly knows me. It's hard to know what he is saying because he speaks in riddles. "What do you mean?"

There's a thick tension in the air as he stares into my eyes, making goosebumps prickle across the back of my neck.

He doesn't answer me, pressing his lips to mine.

The passion of his kiss knocks the air from my lungs. When he breaks away, he murmurs, "I will not let your father kill you, I promise." A lump forms in my throat at his promise, wondering why he would care. Wasn't this exactly what he wanted when he took me? To hurt my father and tear our family apart for ruining his.

"Rourke, I don't understand." I shake my head. "Isn't that why you have me here?"

Instead of answering me, he presses his lips to mine again. I accept I will not get any answers from him, allowing him to distract me. His tongue delves inside my mouth, stoking that flaming desire to life in a heartbeat. I lose myself to the man that captured me intending to harm my family. There's been a shift in the relationship between us. A palpable change that I can't understand.

If Rourke can stop my arranged marriage, he would deal a tremendous blow to my father and the bratva. He has been counting on increasing his power and wealth with an alliance with another organization once I was old enough. It's what he had intended to do with Maxim and Maeve until Maeve ran away, voiding the agreement Rourke's father had with mine.

Rourke's hand moves to my breast as he squeezes my already puckered nipples through the fabric of my nightgown. "I can't get enough of you," he breathes.

I can't believe how much I long for him, too, especially since I still hate how arrogant he is. I wrap my arms around him and press my lips to his, allowing him to feel how badly I need him. My legs wrap around his waist as he lifts me, pressing me harder against the wall. I feel the heavy length of his cock against my center, and it is enough to turn me into a pool of molten desire.

Rourke groans against my mouth, his cock hard. "I want you so bad, but we haven't got time," he breathes, forcing me away from him. "I need to figure this out now." He moves his lips over mine again in a quick, chaste kiss that doesn't quench the burning desire.

I whimper in protest as his lips part from mine, and he drops me back to my feet. He presses his forehead to mine tenderly. It makes little sense but pierces my heart and floods it with hope. Hope that perhaps the man I gave my virginity to can save me from a fate I've always believed I was okay with. A loveless marriage with a guaranteed barbaric man. Every Bratva leader and heir is brutal, and so is Rourke, but we have this undeniable chemistry. Is it possible there is a chance for us?

He kisses me again, deeper this time.

"What are you going to do?" I ask.

The conflict blazing in his eyes scares me. "I'm not sure yet." He squeezes my hand and then turns his back on me, walking toward the door. "All I know is that hell will freeze over before he harms a hair on your head. I'll kill him with my bare hands before that happens."

A shudder races down my spine as he storms out of the room, locking the door behind him.

Rourke is capable of murder, but why would he kill my father? I may not know a lot about the underworld that I'm entangled in, but I know that killing my father would only rock an already unstable Chicago. Not to mention, my father would probably end up killing him instead.

17

ROURKE

I pop my knuckles, glaring at my reflection in the mirror. I'm in too deep, and I know there's no way out. A leap of faith is all I've got left.

"What is this all about at this time of night?" Torin asks as he walks into the library.

Blaine, Kieran, and Killian are already here, waiting for me to tell them why I called them here in the middle of the night. The last time all five of us gathered here was after we learned of Father's murder. It's two o'clock in the morning, but I didn't have a choice. The Bratva has sent us a serious message, one we can't ignore. I had to verify the possibility that the claims Spartak made in the letter were true, running them by Viktoria, and it's clear that they are.

"This," I say, lifting the box toward him.

His brow furrows as he steps forward, opening it. He grimaces at the decapitated head in the box. "What the fuck?" The poor bastard, whose head it is, Jerry, was one of our low-level soldiers for the clan. It's a warning and a threat. They can get to us and wipe out our numbers faster than we can take out theirs.

"They're taking this too far," Killian growls. His eyes are wild as he glares at the box. "We need to hit them again and hit them fucking hard."

Torin's brow furrows. "Already arranged that. Men are hitting them this morning." He glances at his watch. "As we speak. A shipment is arriving at a private airstrip on the outskirts of Chicago, and we believe they are bringing approximately ten tons on a cargo plane."

Ten tons would go a long way to replacing over half of what they've stolen from us in the past few weeks. "Good," I respond, clutching onto the letter Spartak wrote. "There's a letter, though." I hold it out.

Killian steps forward and takes it from my hand.

"Read it out loud," Blaine suggests.

"Viktoria Volkov is to be married to Luka Morozov of the Morozov Bratva. If you don't return her before he arrives by next Friday, the Callaghan Clan will feel the wrath of both Bratvas," Killian reads, eyes widening. "The Morozov Bratva has more power than any of us."

"Shit," Torin roars, pacing the floor. "If we give her back, then we're admitting defeat." Tension coils through his shoulders. "We can't give him what he wants."

Kieran shakes his head. "What choice do we have? They'll blow us out of Chicago if we don't."

I already know what I intend to do, but I fear my family will think I'm insane. "She can't marry Luka Morozov if she's already married," I say calmly.

Everyone's attention moves to me. "What the fuck is that supposed to mean?" Killian asks.

I shrug. "I will marry Viktoria Volkov, stopping his deal dead in its tracks."

Everyone stares at me in stunned silence.

It's Blaine that finally breaks it, "Are you fucking insane?"

"Yeah, that's ridiculous. She's a Volkov, brother," Kieran says, standing and pacing the room.

Killian says nothing, staring at me pensively. I'm surprised by his silence, but perhaps he doesn't think it's such a crazy idea.

Torin shrugs. "I mean, it solves the Morozov problem." He narrows his eyes at me. "Although, you'll hitch yourself to a fucking Volkov for life." He tilts his head. "Unless you divorce her."

"Or kill her?" Kieran suggests.

My blood boils at the suggestion of harming my princess. "No, I can think of worse things than being married to a beautiful woman." I narrow my eyes. "Even if she's a Volkov."

There isn't a part of me that wants to rid myself of her. She's mine. A part of me now, even if it won't make sense to my family.

"Spartak will probably find out and stop it, Rourke. It's not a good idea," Blaine says.

I shake my head. "Impossible. I'm marrying her tonight."

"What?" Kieran scoffs, walking up to me and placing a hand on my shoulder. "You can't be serious. Are you sick or something?" He moves his hand to my forehead, which I swat away.

"I'm deadly serious." I pace the floor in front of the enormous fireplace. "If I do it tonight, there's no chance of him finding out. We'll send the video of the wedding to Spartak and the Morozov Bratva in Moscow."

"Genius," Torin muses, looking at me with an appreciation I've rarely seen him give anyone, except for his brother. "It's an excellent plan."

The squeeze of the door opening draws my attention. Maeve slips inside. "I got your message. What is this about?"

Maeve has frequently stayed at Gael's home in the city, and she's rarely around. It almost feels like she is avoiding us.

Kieran shakes his head. "Our eldest brother has lost his mind. Maybe you can talk some sense into him, sis."

She glances between Kieran and me. "What is going on?"

"Short story is I'm getting married tonight."

Maeve's eyes widen. "What? To who?"

"Viktoria Volkov," I announce.

She walks over to me and stops in front of me, regarding me with a strange pensiveness. "I assume this has something to do with the war?"

I nod in reply.

"Why you?" She asks.

I raise a brow. "What?"

Maeve plays with a lock of her golden hair. "Why are you the man marrying her? As the leader of the Callaghan clan, surely you could force someone else to."

Rage slams into me hard. "Because I am," I snap.

A whisper of a smile flits onto my sister's lips. She's not stupid, and she knows how I feel about her. Maeve has always been so wise, and I struggle to keep my true feelings at bay for Viktoria. "Fair enough. I support it."

Killian moves forward. "It makes sense, aye." His eyes narrow. "You're taking one for the team. Maeve's right that it doesn't have to be you."

The idea of another man so much as looking at her makes my blood boil in my veins. "It does," I say. "Who is marrying Viktoria isn't up for discussion." I glance at Blaine, who doesn't look convinced.

Kieran steps forward, eyeing me warily. "Marrying her brings a Volkov into the Callaghan family. Are you prepared to welcome a woman into our family who is related to the people who killed our father?"

I search my little brother's eyes, knowing that he hasn't been the same since Father died. Not because of the loss, but because he learned he was one of two people totally in the dark about Shane, our deadbeat uncle who Father murdered. "Aye. It's for the good of the clan. She will become a Callaghan before morning, Kieran, whether or not you are on board." I step toward him and ruffle his hair.

He shoves me. "Get off."

Blaine has said nothing else, so I turn my attention to him. "Uncle, if you have a better plan, tell me now." I glance at Kieran. "Or you."

I pray that none of them come up with a plan, as

there is no way I'm ever letting Viki go. She's mine, and I intend to cement that with the ceremony tonight.

Blaine shakes his head, taking a seat and resting a foot over his knee. "No, it's a good plan. As long as you can live with a Volkov as your wife."

I don't say what I truly feel. I can't live without Viki, as she's everything to me. Ever since I had my first taste of her in the back of that van, I knew I was in trouble. I intended to defile Viktoria Volkov, sending her back as used goods.

I now know that there is no sending her back. If she were to return to her father, he would kill her for no longer being a virgin. "I'll make it work."

Torin smirks. "He likes unwilling women. She won't be too pleased."

I glare at my uncle. "I beg to differ."

Killian's brow furrows. "Is there something going on between you two?"

I clap my hands. "Enough chitchat." I fix my attention on Torin. "Can you arrange for the priest to meet us at the chapel in two hours?"

Torin nods. "I'll do my best."

"Good." I turn my attention to my sister. "Maeve, I need you to find me a dress. Size eight."

Maeve jumps to her feet. "On it." Her brow furrows. "What about rings?"

I glance at Killian. "Does that jeweler still owe you a favor?"

He smirks. "Aye, a couple."

"Good, I need you to get the rings."

Killian tilts his head. "Size?"

Shit.

To say that I am out of my depth is an understatement. I can hear my father scolding me now.

Always have a plan and do nothing on impulse.

Sorry, pops, but I can't help myself with her. She drives my impulses wild, and this may well be the craziest thing I've ever done, but it seems to make sense because she's everything to me.

"Fuck knows. Just get two rings. If they don't fit, then we'll have them resized."

He salutes me and then heads for the door. "See you on the other side."

Kieran's eyes narrow. "What should I do?"

I clap him on the shoulder. "Nothing before the wedding ceremony, little bro, but bring your video camera." I give him a pointed look. "We need evidence to send to Spartak and the Morozov family. Meet me at the chapel in two hours."

He nods, but looks a irritated that I didn't give him a job to do before the wedding.

"See you all in two hours." I head straight down

the corridor and up the stairs, the keys to her room in my jacket pocket.

Viktoria Volkov will be my bride tonight, but I'm not sure how she's going to take it. My princess has fought me tooth and nail every step of the way, so this will likely be the same In time, she'll realize everything I'm doing is for her. There was a change in my goal somewhere along the way.

I took her to avenge my father's death and make her pay for Spartak's sin, but she soon became my aim. All I want is to claim her, own her. Luka Morozov can kiss my Irish ass if he thinks he's ever getting his hands on her.

Tonight I make it official. Once morning arrives, everyone will know that Viktoria Volkov belongs to me.

To death do us part.

18

VIKTORIA

Someone yanks me out of bed, rudely startling me awake.

I try to pull my wrist away, but whoever is holding me is too strong.

"What the hell?" I say into the darkness, blinking to see who is dragging me toward the door.

Rourke.

He drags me out of the bedroom and into the brightly lit corridor, making me shriek like a vampire who shouldn't go into the sun.

"What are you doing?" I snarl, feeling irritated by this son of a bitch waking me up so suddenly in the middle of the night. I'm seriously grumpy when I first wake up.

"You are coming with me, princess. There's something we need to do." He softens his touch, pulling my hips toward him.

I shake my head. "I'm tired and hate being wakened at—" I glance at my watch. "Three o'clock in the morning, and does it look like I'm ready to go anywhere?"

Rourke smirks, glancing down at my nightgown. His eyes linger on the visible outline of my nipples through the thin fabric. "Does it look like I care?"

It appears the arrogant bastard who I can't stand has made an reappearance. He was tender, almost sweet, when we spoke earlier today. It gave me some hope, but now he's acting like the same irritating asshole he's been most of the time since I've been here. "No, because you're like Jekyll and fucking Hyde. A monster who cares about nothing but yourself."

His jaw tightens, and he narrows his eyes at me. "I'm a monster?" He asks, moving his hand to my throat and squeezing. "Tell me what exactly I've done that's so monstrous to you."

Hatred is such an intense and confusing emotion. An emotion I don't think I had ever experienced until I met this man. "You kidnapped me for a start. A woman who had nothing to do with your father's death." I reach up to my neck, prizing his fingers from my throat. "You chased me while I tried to escape and then took my virginity as if it was your right, like an animal."

Rourke's anger is clearer with each word I say.

"You've spanked me until I'm bruised countless times." I set my hands on my hips, staring at him. "If that doesn't make you a monster, I don't know what would."

His jaw is tight, and his breathing labors as he narrows his eyes. "I kidnapped you because your father is a psychopath who killed mine." He steps closer to me, holding my gaze. "Regarding your virginity, you didn't tell me no." He tilts his head. "If I remember right, you asked me to fuck you," he growls.

My stomach dips as it's true. I asked this bastard to fuck me because he turned me into a mindless mess with his touch. I'd wanted him so badly it hurt.

"That's because deep down under all this guise of fighting, you've wanted me ever since we danced." His nostrils flare as he holds my gaze, forcing my fight to wither away.

"Regarding your punishments, you deserved every single one." He moves closer to me, his fingers returning to my throat. "Not to mention, you loved every second."

I hate that everything he's saying is true. I may not have admitted it to myself, but ever since the moment I bumped into him in that club, I've wanted him on a visceral level. No matter who he was and what he did to me, that desire for him won't die.

"Tell me I'm wrong," he murmurs, his lips inches from mine. "Maybe I'm a monster, but it seems like you like being taken by one. So, what does that make you?"

I feel numbness spread through me. Rourke's words are cold and vicious, and they hurt more than I want him to know. The warmth of his hand wrapped around my throat is the only thing grounding me.

He glares at me with such an intense stare it feels like he's looking right past my mask and into my soul. Rourke knows I want him; he knows I didn't tell him to stop for exactly that reason. He finally releases my throat. "You and I have a date in a church in exactly." He pauses, glancing at his chunky Rolex. "Thirty minutes."

"A church?" I ask, my hands shaking.

Rourke clicks his tongue, looming over me. "Tonight, princess, you are going to become a Callaghan."

"Over my dead body," I scoff.

His body turns rigid. "That could be arranged."

"I don't know who the fuck you think you are, but I won't marry you."

He raises a brow. "You will marry me whether or

not you like it, princess." Rourke moves closer, his lips inches from mine. "Your father has agreed on a deal for your hand to Luka Morozov."

My stomach churns at the mention of Luka, as he's a spoiled brat and the biggest asshole I've ever met. We met last year on our family vacation in Moscow, and the mere thought of marrying him makes my skin crawl. Rourke isn't exactly any better, though. At least, that's what I tell myself.

"Why would you marry me, anyway?" I shake my head, searching his stunning eyes. "If you marry me, then you are stuck with me."

His eyes narrow. "There's always divorce."

My chest aches at his bitter words, and I can't understand why. Maybe it is because he took my virginity, which, for some warped reason, makes me feel connected to him. Our conversation earlier today replays in my mind.

I will not let your father kill you, I promise.

Is this his solution? Rourke's fucked up way of protecting me from a grave fate, and I yank him to a stop. "Are you going to make me get married in a fucking nightgown?"

His nostrils flare as his eyes dip down the length of my body, and heat ignites in them as it is see-through. "I have a dress for you in the car."

"Why do we have to do it in the middle of the night?"

Rourke growls and yanks me against him, digging his fingers into my hips hard enough to bruise. "Because I won't risk your father finding out and stopping it." He moves his lips close to mine. "Your father has gone too far, and this is payback, princess."

I narrow my eyes at him, clenching my fists by my side. "Why do I have to pay for something my father has done?"

He yanks me down the corridor without answering me.

I almost trip over my feet at the speed he walks. "Would you slow down?" I say, trying to yank my hand out of his.

He doesn't. As always, he is acting like a self-centered prick. The limousine we took to the charity event is waiting for us both. "In."

I slide in and level my gaze at him. "Where is this dress, then?"

He nods toward a bag on the seat.

I grab it, pulling out a cream satin gown. "Great. My dress wedding dress."

He rolls his eyes at me. "It's the best Maeve could do at such short notice. It's not about the wedding, Viki, as I need to stop your father and The Morozov

Bratva in their tracks."

"What exactly happened?" I ask.

His eyes narrow, as if weighing up whether to tell me. "Your father sent a letter along with the head of one of our men." He glances out of the window, avoiding my gaze. "It said if I don't give you back by next Friday, when Luka Morozov arrives, we'll feel the wrath of both families."

"So you want to marry me instead?" I confirm.

His brow furrows as he turns his attention to me. "Yes."

I shake my head. "He will kill you."

My declaration only seems to enrage him. "I'd like to see him try. If your father comes for me, I'll kill him first."

He doesn't understand. "Not my father. Luka Morozov."

"Bullshit. There's no reason for Luka to kill me." Rourke cracks his knuckles, which he often does. "He should kill your father for losing you."

"If the Morozov family have announced our engagement, then they will not sit back while you marry me despite it." I keep my gaze firm, despite preferring the prospect of marrying Rourke over Luka. "They won't rest until they make you pay for that." Rourke may view me as a spoiled Bratva princess, but I know how the

Bratva works. It's archaic and built on years of tradition.

"Don't worry about it." He waves his hand dismissively, clearly not taking me seriously. "I can handle the Morozov family." A dark, slow smirk spreads onto his lips. "It's clear you are concerned about my welfare suddenly." He taps a finger on his chin. "I wonder why that is."

I shake my head, wishing that I didn't, on some level, care for this jerk. The intimate connection we share makes it impossible. At that charity event, I was fearful of my father getting me back from Rourke, as he changed from my kidnapper to my protector, and now he's my fiance. "Don't get ahead of yourself. I'm thinking of my life here. If you die, then I'll be next on my father's hit list, especially once I'm a Callaghan."

He straightens, the silly smirk on his face vanishing as if I slapped him. "Well, let us hope for both our sakes that I can handle whatever Morozov might throw at me." There's a sudden cold detachment in his voice that wasn't there before as he sits back and stares out of the window.

I can't understand what he expected me to tell him. That I care for him on some level? I do, but I won't give him the satisfaction. He's too much of an arrogant asshole to take that information and not use it against me.

I refuse to give him that power over me. The limousine comes to a stop suddenly, and he glances at me with those ice-blue eyes, devoid of any emotion.

"We're here, princess. Let's make you a queen."

Anticipation prickles over my skin at his words. The queen of the Callaghan Clan. Number one enemy to my family. By standing by and allowing Rourke to rush this wedding, I'm screwing my family over.

I guess I have little choice now that Rourke owns my virginity and a part of my heart. Slowly, I'm falling for the man I should hate, and him forcing me to marry him doesn't seem as bad a prospect as it should.

It gives me hope that somehow I can break the ice-cold exterior around his heart and pierce it, claiming Rourke for myself.

The door opens to the limousine, and a girl not much older than me is standing there. "Come on, let's get you ready," she says, practically pulling me out of the car and grabbing the dress at the same time. "I'm Maeve, by the way. Your soon-to-be sister-in-law, it would seem."

I swallow hard, resisting the urge to glance back at my groom-to-be. "Nice to meet you." I side glance at her as she ushers me into the chapel. "This is all unconventional, isn't it?"

She gives me a wistful smile. "Yes, I'm sorry you got caught up in this." Maeve opens the door to a back room. "You can change in here. The ceremony is in five minutes." She gives me a pitiful look. "Make the best of an unpleasant situation, I guess."

She shuts the door, leaving me alone with my chaotic thoughts. Somehow I have to stop this wedding, but it doesn't help that deep down I don't want to. Rourke has weaseled his way into my heart, despite his arrogance, and I can't let go of the hope that perhaps he feels the same.

It may be a naïve and futile hope, but it's all that is keeping me moving and the only thing that stops the despair from swallowing me.

19

ROURKE

I've lost my mind.

As I stand by the altar, waiting for Viktoria Volkov to walk down the aisle, I realize I lost my common sense somewhere along the line. Instead, instinct and desire have fueled my actions since I plucked her from the dance floor of the club.

Spartak's threat didn't anger me for the right reasons. I should have been angry that he killed one of the clan's members and made demands after killing my father. Instead, it sent me into an inconsolable fury at the mere thought of any other man ever touching my princess.

Luka Morozov will never come within a thousand miles of her.

Fuck Spartak and his half-assed threat. A threat,

trying to force my hand and give Viktoria back before he arrives in the city.

This midnight wedding is to stop the deal dead in its tracks. I will send the wedding video to both Spartak and the Morozov Bratva, voiding the deal. Hopefully, it will flare tensions between the Volkov Bratva and Morozov Bratva, as the last thing I need is more enemies in this fucking city. They are mounting around me everywhere we look.

Torin has paid the priest off to rush this sham of a wedding. Killian got two rings, which, despite being a little on the large side, will do for now. He, of course, is my best man, standing by my side while I make this "sacrifice" for the clan. No one realizes that this isn't a sacrifice. It's everything I want to shackle my captive to me for the rest of our lives.

Kieran is off to one side, filming the wedding so we can send the evidence back to Spartak and the Morozov family.

Acting hastily isn't part of who I am, but I can't help myself. Viktoria Volkov is mine. The last person I thought I'd want is a Volkov, but I don't just want her. I need her.

Maeve appears at the entry to the chapel, messing with a stereo for the music. It's almost time, as we had to pull out certain stops to make the wedding appear believable. The chapel is bathed in candlelight, creating a romantic atmosphere, even if this wedding is anything but romantic.

The wedding March floods the room on the tiny stereo, drawing my attention down the aisle. Viki appears in the stunning cream dress in the doorway, which may be simple, but her beauty magnifies it. I drag my eyes down her, admiring the way the fabric frames her supple curves. The most beautiful bride I've ever seen... I catch myself realizing that my feelings for this woman are problematic.

"Not too shabby, aye?" Killian asks, his eyes fixed on her intently as if he's undressing her with them.

I clench my fists by my side. "Keep your fucking eyes off of my bride," I growl.

Killian's eyes widen and move to me, brows coming together in confusion. He holds his hands up in surrender because I'm probably looking at him like I want to strangle him with my bare hands. "It looks like you have a got a thing for a Volkov after all."

I don't answer him, knowing that I'm acting like a man possessed. Instead, my eyes return to my bride, who approaches with slow, hesitant steps, her flowing hair cascading in dark waves against the light fabric.

Maeve walks behind her with flowers she cut from our garden, smiling as if this is a momentous occasion, but she's the only one. Kieran stands to one side, holding the video camera and scowling at the woman I'm about to make my bride. His hatred for the Volkov family is rooted deep in his soul, and nothing I can say will change that.

Viktoria's bright green eyes connect with mine, and they look utterly majestic in the candlelight, glowing like fireflies. I feel a nauseating tug at my gut as I realize that marrying this woman is probably a mistake.

What the hell am I doing?

Since I met her, I've known she differs from any woman I've ever met. A rare gem who has stolen her way into my ice-encrusted heart.

Viktoria comes to a stop, gazing into my eyes. There's no fear in them, as you would expect from a woman who is being forced to walk down the aisle. Instead, she looks at me with what I could only describe as admiration.

The priest clears his throat. "Am I right that you'd like the shortened version of the service?" He asks, looking irritated that he has to do this at all in the middle of the night.

"Yes," I reply, keeping my attention fixed on Viktoria.

She holds my gaze as I reach for her hands, feeling the air electrify between us the moment I touch her. Her lips part temptingly, drawing all of my attention. It's unimaginable how she can make me forget everything around me and turn me into a horny bastard in front of my family.

"We're gathered here today to witness the holy union of Rourke Ronan Callaghan and Viktoria Volkov. If there is anyone here who objects to the union, please speak now."

I stare at Viki, wondering if she might be the one to object. Even if she does, we informed the priest to marry us, anyway. Instead, she confidently holds my gaze as if she wants this, wants to be married to me.

"I'll proceed with the ceremony." He glances at me first. "Rourke Ronan Callaghan, do you take Viktoria to be your wife? Do you promise to love, honor, cherish, and protect Viktoria, from this day forward, for better, for worse, for richer, for poorer, in sickness and in health, to love and to cherish, till death do us part, according to God's holy ordinance?"

I stare into her eyes, knowing that despite everything, I already love her, which is a problem.

Never love a woman, lad. It's not worth it.

My father never really loved my mother, as their parents arranged their marriage. He always warned me against giving my heart to anyone. "I do," I say, knowing I have no choice.

The priest turns his attention to Viki. And Viktoria Volkov, do you take Rourke to be your husband? Do you promise to love, honor, cherish, and protect Rourke, from this day forward, for better, for worse, for richer, for poorer, in sickness and in health, to love and to cherish, till death do us part, according to God's holy ordinance?"

Unlike me, she doesn't hesitate. Her answer is so confident it knocks the air from my lungs. "I do." A whisper of a smile graces her angelic lips, and I know without a doubt that I'm more at risk than ever of losing my heart.

"By the power vested in me, I now pronounce you husband and wife. You may kiss the bride."

My body tingles in anticipation as this is the first time I'm going to kiss her in public. I step forward and grab her hips, moving my mouth over hers forcefully. I plunge my tongue into her mouth, feeling that all-consuming need to make my stake over her known to everyone, including my family. No one will ever touch her except for me.

When we break away, my family looks shocked by the passionate exchange. Kieran looks disgusted as he shuts off the video camera, eyes narrowing as he glares at my new wife. My youngest brother isn't taking our marriage well.

I hold Viki's hand and lead her out of the chapel. Husband and wife, which means Spartak's never getting his princess back. Now that I've sealed our fates together, the fallout will be immense.

It's EARLY MORNING, but that doesn't stop Killian and Torin from insisting on the family drinking together in the study after the wedding.

Viki appears nervous as she plays with the ends of her hair, which I've noticed is something she does whenever she's anxious. A trait that I shouldn't find so attractive, but everything she does deepens her pull on me.

Maeve approaches, a thoughtful look on her face. "Congratulations," she says, tilting her head. "Or consolations. Which is in order?"

If she's expecting me to admit that I'm happy about marrying Viki, I'll have to disappoint her. The clan can't learn the truth, which means no one can know, not even my family.

I shrug. "Neither, I'm not exactly happy about having to marry our enemy's daughter, but it was a vital move in the war."

Maeve's brow hitches up as if she doesn't believe that for one moment. "Sure. It has nothing to do with the way you look at her, then?"

Fuck.

"Not sure what you're insinuating, little sis." I fiddle with the wedding band on my finger, twirling it around. "Viktoria is nothing to me other than a means to an end and a way to make that bastard pay for taking our father."

Maeve's eyes freeze over at the mention of our father. "Tell yourself that all you want, Rourke. I see the way you look at her." She turns on her heels and saunters away, leaving me alone with my glass of whiskey and more chaotic thoughts. If my sister has noticed, who else has?

The clan members wouldn't be too pleased to hear their leader is shacking up with the enemy's daughter, especially not after what Spartak did to my father. Every man in the clan respected him.

Viktoria approaches me, her cheeks flushed pink as she meets my gaze. "I'm tired. Shall I head to my room?" She plays with her fingers in front of herself, always giving away when she's anxious.

I shake my head. "My room tonight," I murmur, feeling my cock thicken in my dress pants. "I'll show you up, but you won't be getting much sleep tonight." My hand rests on the small of her back as I lead her toward the corridor.

Viki visibly shakes at my words, the arousal practically dripping off of her. She's excited, practically buzzing with anticipation.

Killian gives me a knowing smirk as I walk out of the room.

I glare back at him, not giving him the satisfaction. Marrying Viktoria wasn't just a move to get one up. It was a deep and complicated decision that makes me wonder how and when I fell so far from my path.

Many factors fueled my decision to marry Viki tonight, but the one that didn't enter my mind was revenge over Spartak. My quest for revenge has morphed into an obsession, threatening everything I stand for.

20

VIKTORIA

I walk into the room, feeling a sudden coldness seep into my bones the moment I do. Rourke's room is devoid of light. It's the darkest room I've ever seen, with navy blue walls and dark mahogany floors. "Not into light colors?" I ask, glancing at him. It's the polar opposite of my bedroom at home.

His eyes narrow as he glances at his room and then back at me. "I never let anyone in here," Rourke replies, and I can't work out if that is a statement or an answer to my question. For the first time since he captured me, he looks uncomfortable, as if my presence in his space unnerves him.

"Right." My brow pulls together. "How is this marriage arrangement going to work?" I ask. If he expects me to sleep in this room every night, then I need to redecorate.

"Arrangement?" He asks, the well-known smirk spreading onto his lips. "This isn't an arrangement. You are my wife and will do as I say from here on in. That's the sum of it."

Rage slams into me. "Just because I'm your wife doesn't mean you can tell me what to do." I set my hands on my hips, glaring at the man I vowed to spend the rest of my life with.

He takes a few steps forward, forcing me to walk back.

I can't trust myself to allow him to touch me, as it seems I'm putty in his hands anytime that he does. A weakness I'm ashamed of as technically, after everything he has done, I should hate him, and yet with him, it appears there is something I can't resist no matter what he does or how dark he tells me his soul is.

"Stop walking away, princess. You're my wife now." My husband stands still, looming over me with his powerful stance. The power is always there, rolling off of him in waves, even now.

I swallow. "I'm wondering if I made a mistake."

He smirks. "Don't worry. You never had a choice."

I thought as much. Although the priest asked if

anyone objected at the ceremony, I was sure it wouldn't have mattered if I had. The ceremony would have been performed, even if I was kicking and screaming the entire time.

"Your father will receive our wedding tape in the morning, rendering you useless to him and breaking his pact with the Morozov Bratva." Rourke moves closer. "There's just one thing left to do." He stops within inches of me, eyes dipping to my lips.

"What's that?" I breathe, my body thrumming with need.

"Consummate the marriage," he whispers before moving his lips over mine, plunging his tongue between my lips, and forcing his way in like a thief, stealing everything from me in that instant. His demanding hands move to my buttocks as he digs his finger into them hard, making me hiss. The skin is tender from his last assault on my ass, which is nearly healed. I couldn't sit for three days afterward, forced to lie down in bed.

Rourke gobbles it up, enjoying my pain as he bites my bottom lip between his teeth and breaks open the skin violently. His tongue swipes at the bloody cut as he tastes it, savagely drinking me in. "I can't get enough of you," he breathes as if he fears saying it too loud.

"Rourke," I moan his name like a damn prayer,

clawing at him as if my life depends on it. His hot and cold attitude, keeping his distance only to ravage me every time he sees me, is driving me insane. "I need you."

A smirk spreads onto his lips. "Are you finally admitting to me you want me?"

I nod in response, staring into his icy blue eyes. "Yes, I want you so fucking bad it hurts." He smells of whiskey and musk and pure man, a fragrance I'm addicted to as my thighs clench. "Fuck me, please."

He appears pleased by my admission. "Good girl," he purrs, sending an unprecedented zing of need through me. "Why don't you suck my cock first? I love feeling your lips wrapped around it."

I narrow my eyes. "As long as you don't choke me with it again."

He laughs, but this time it's not cruel. It's a deep, genuine laugh that makes my insides turn to mush and a sound so beautiful I'm not sure what to do with myself. "Deep down, you love choking on my cock, and there's no use denying it."

I keep my mouth shut as Rourke's right. The way he took control and fucked my throat like he'd lost all control was thrilling. Instead of denying it, I drop to my knees in front of him, holding his gaze and waiting subserviently for him to pull out his cock.

His eyes dilate as he steps closer, unzipping his

pants and freeing his heavy, thick erection from them. It bobs in front of my face, smooth and beautiful, ready to be worshipped by my mouth. I wrap a hand around his shaft, but it doesn't fit around his thick girth.

He hisses at my touch as I open my mouth and slide him into it, lavishing attention on the thick tip with my tongue. A drip of cum spills onto it, making me moan at the masculine taste of him. "Wrap those pretty lips around it," he orders, his fists clenched tight at his side as if he's holding himself back.

I shake my head, holding his gaze, and pull away. "Fuck my throat like you want to, and stop trying to be the gentleman that you aren't."

His eyes flash with delight as he grabs a fistful of my hair, rendering me immobile. "As you wish. Open wide." He uses my hair to yank me forward as he thrusts his hips toward me, fucking my throat so deep I think I'm going to puke.

I focus on my breathing, accepting his assault as he uses me the way I want him to. The submissive side of me he brings out excites me, but I sense it has been there all along, lying beneath my strong exterior I'm expected to exhibit all the time, wearing it like a suit of armor.

Rourke's eyes hold mine as he forces his length down my throat, watching as my eyes prickle with tears from him blocking my airways. He delights in it, and so do I.

His hips find a steady rhythm, and I learn to relax, trusting him entirely when I shouldn't trust him at all. This monster holds my fate in the palm of his hands. A man kidnapped me from the club that night, intending to use me to make my father pay.

I gag as Rourke's cock goes too deep, making it impossible to breathe. Saliva spills down my chin and all over his cock and balls.

Rourke groans and pulls out of my mouth, leaning down and grabbing my chin between his finger and thumb. "You are such a good girl," he praises, eyes so dilated there's only a small rim of blue around them. Rourke looks otherworldly, like a violent God looming over me, ready to take what he wants. "Open wide," he orders, letting go of my chin.

I do as he says, as he slides the tip of his cock over my tongue. A drop of salty precum escapes the tip, and I lap it up, enjoying the taste.

Rourke holds my gaze as he fists his cock, pumping his hand three times before he groans.

A flood of cum leaves his cock, spurting into the back of my throat and making me choke. It's so much as I hold my mouth open, dutifully waiting for instruction.

"Swallow it all, princess. I want you to swallow it," he growls, fisting his cock with violent tugs.

I shut my eyes, moaning as I swallow his essence. For the first time, I feel utterly overcome by my hunger for this man, now I'm not fighting. It's a frantic and unexplainable desire that I'll never understand, but I've given up trying.

Rourke pulls his cock from my mouth and leans over again, grabbing the back of my neck and angling my face to him. "Lie down on the bed as it's my turn to eat you."

I swallow hard as I glance at the enormous four-poster bed pushed against the far wall. Hesitation coils through me as I know that there is no going back. This is my life now, and Rourke is my husband.

"Now, princess," he orders, the dominance dripping from his tone.

I turn and stroll over to the bed, lying down and spreading my legs wide for me. "As you wish," I say.

His eyes darken as he moves toward me, taking a few long strides to reach the bed. "Thong off," he commands, his attention fixed between my thighs.

I lick my busted bottom lip before lifting my hips and pulling my thong down.

Rourke groans and his eyes zero in on my exposed pussy, as he kneels between my spread ankles. "You're so fucking perfect, princess." His rough, large hands land on my thighs as he pushes them even further open. "A true treasure."

The way he's looking at me makes me believe him, which is foolish. Rourke isn't a man who falls for a woman like me, the daughter of his enemy. If he falls at all, that is. Men involved in the underground world we exist in don't love, as they can not feel.

His warm breath teasing against my soaking lips and throbbing clit interrupts my chaotic thoughts. "A fucking delight," he murmurs before thrusting his tongue into my center.

Stars burst behind my shut eyelids as my nipples turn painfully hard. Rourke reaches up and plays with my breasts, cupping and squeezing at the sensitive flesh as he teases my pussy with his tongue. "Rourke," I hiss his name, my hips bucking upward toward his face.

It's unbelievable how incredible he makes me feel. A man who I swore I hated and at the same breath want with all that I am. My body responds to the way he handles me, playing with my clit until I feel like I'm going to combust, only to back off and move his attention to my center. The flat of his thick tongue spreads me apart, driving me wild.

I reach for him, dragging my fingers through his golden hair. "Fuck, yes," I cry, my thighs shaking with the intensity of the climax he's building me toward. I whimper when he stops, smirking up at me with that handsome, almost irritating smile. "Don't stop," I pant.

He doesn't listen to me, kneeling between my legs and shaking his head. "You don't get to come yet, Mrs. Callaghan."

My stomach flips at hearing him call me that.

"I don't want you to come until I say so."

My nipples tighten as he denies me what I want, making me sure that this consummation of our marriage is going to be more like torture than pleasure. "But, I—"

He spanks my bare thigh hard, making me gasp. "Do as your husband says," he murmurs darkly before positioning the thick head of his cock between my thighs.

Anticipation and electric desire swirl in the air between us, lighting me on fire before he's entered me. With one stroke, he buries his enormous length inside of me, completing me and tearing me apart all at once. It feels like I'm free falling as my body accepts the invasion, loving every second despite my husband's wicked ways.

21

ROURKE

I'm ruined.

Viktoria Volkov has destroyed me, poisoned me into this man that feels. My father taught me to feel nothing, yet as I plow into my princess, I feel so many emotions that it's hard to keep track.

She is the epitome of beauty and everything good with this dark and sordid world in which we both exist.

Somehow, she has become the reason I exist. Everything to me in one quick stroke, yet I feel more out of control than I've ever felt.

Feelings cloud your judgment. Never fall prey to them unless you want to die an untimely death.

It was one of my father's most important lessons, and yet I've forsaken it within weeks after his death.

Viki moans as her body is on the edge of unraveling, muscles clenching around my cock like a vise. She claws herself back from the edge, clenching her jaw tightly as she submits to my command, obeying my order not to come apart until I say. Her submission is erotic as it feels almost impossible not to explode, forcing me to hold on, too.

I hold out, a tenderness creeping into my veins as I kiss her lips, thrusting my tongue between hers and deepening it.

My wife.

Marriage hadn't even been on my radar a couple of months ago. Now, I'm married to the most beautiful woman in Chicago. A woman who threatens to undo all my father's hard work. I know that taking what I want will come at a hefty cost. The war will rage in an even more violent sweep, driving a deeper wedge between our families.

"Rourke," Viki breathes my name against my lips, her eyes dilated and dreamy. "I need to come," she breathes.

I smirk, which ignites that flash of anger in her eyes. "Only when I say."

She groans, her eyes rolling back in the sockets as I fuck her harder, making her hold on with all the strength she possesses.

"You take my cock so well, princess," I murmur,

biting her neck hard enough to leave marks. "Your tight little cunt is my addiction."

Viki releases an exasperated moan, which sounds like a mix of torture and pleasure as I continue to fuck her without mercy, pushing her toward her climax and forcing her to remain in control of it. The power it gives me is enjoyable, but I love watching my princess squirm most of all.

"Fuck," she cries, her teeth sinking into that luscious bottom lip she loves to bite. "How much longer?" She whines.

"Not too long, you're doing well," I breathe, feeling my balls ache with the need to explode, too. "Only when I come can you come too," I instruct.

Her muscles tremble under me as our bodies come together in a violent clash of skin against skin. "Harder," she pleads, her breathing becoming more erratic by the second. "Fuck me harder, please."

I growl as I lift her legs onto my shoulders, pounding with so much force I worry I might break my princess in two.

She moans deeper and louder and intensely, calling to the most primal side of me. I love that she enjoys my dark side, and I sense she has a dark side, which is why we fit so well.

"Fuck, princess." I pound into her three more times with all the strength I can muster before roaring against her skin. "Come for me," I pant as I unleash my seed into my wife.

Viktoria screams my name as she tumbles over the edge, clawing her nails into my back so hard it's as if she's trying to peel it away from me. I enjoy the pain, basking in it as we both radiate together.

We collapse in a sweaty heap of tangled limbs. Viki is the first to move, rearranging herself on her back and staring up at the ceiling, her brow pinched together. "Fuck me, that was…."

"World altering?" I offer.

She meets my gaze and nods.

I position myself next to her, trying to ignore the fact she's on my side of the bed. An error that I must put right, but not at this moment. "Now it's official."

She looks at me with confusion. "What is?"

I smirk at her. "You're Mrs. Callaghan."

Her expression turns stern, and she shakes her head. "I don't believe it."

I move closer to her, propping myself up on one arm. "Well, you'd better let it sink in, as you're mine now, Viki."

She sighs and moves toward me, pushing at my chest, so I lie down. "Hold me," she murmurs.

I feel a twinge in my chest as I wrap an arm around her dainty form. My cock instantly reacts to her touch. "Are you okay?" I ask, hardly recognizing my voice, as I don't care about other people's feelings. My father warned me, but I'm falling into her trap.

A dark and deeply disturbing thought crosses my mind.

What if this was Spartak's plan all along?

Force my hand and leave me no choice to take something important to him; his daughter. Then, get her to seduce me so that she can ruin me from the inside out. My stomach churns as I know I'm being paranoid. Spartak couldn't have expected what I'd do. Not to mention, he almost shot Viktoria at the charity event.

"I think so." Her brow pinches together. "This all happened so fast. What next?" She asks, glancing at me questioningly.

It's a good question, and one I don't have the answer to.

All I know is that this beautiful creature who I've made my wife is turning me weak. I need to distance myself from her if we stand a chance of beating the Bratva. First, I'll spend the rest of this night fucking her out of my system.

"Welcome, lads," I say, once all the men invited have arrived. "I've got important business to talk about today."

I pace up and down, feeling the violence building beneath the surface, anticipating the bloodbath to come. It's part of who I am. The darkness and the violence and the chaos, all of them define me.

There's one thing I hate more than our enemies: a snitch who informs from the inside. It sickens me that anyone would turn on their people for money, but I've always known Darragh is as unloyal as they come.

He stands near the front with his arms crossed over his chest, looking confident, although he's been selling us out to the Russians. As the new leader, this is an opportunity to send a message to the rest of the clan.

"We have a leak in our organization," I announce, observing the men.

Seamus is on standby at the door to ensure that Darragh doesn't make a run for it. He's not going anywhere, at least not alive. I notice him pale while chattering breaks out amongst the men.

"Silence," I bark, forcing everyone to fall quiet. "We're fighting a war and can't afford to have unloyal soldiers on our side." I am acutely aware of my Glock nestled in the back of my belt, which I intend to pull out. "The person is in this room, so if they want to come clean, I'll make their death easier and quicker."

I don't focus my attention on one person, allowing my eyes to linger on each man in the room. Darragh's throat bobs as my eyes land on him. After a minute or more of tense silence, I accept he doesn't have the balls to tell the truth. "It looks like you will receive a painful death, Darragh." I glare at him as his mouth falls open.

He shakes his head. "Boss, I didn't—"

I pull my Glock and shoot him in the leg, shutting him up. "We have hard evidence, so there's no getting out of this."

He squeals on the floor, blood running from the wound onto the concrete of the warehouse. "I promise, I didn't—"

I shoot his other leg, making him scream.

The other men at the meeting step away, shocked at seeing this side of me. If they thought I'd be less violent than my father, they were wrong. The only thing worse than a snitch is a coward who won't own up to what he did.

I don't want to hear excuses or denial. "You're making this harder on yourself by opening your mouth."

Darragh turns silent and pale, trying to stem the bleeding with his hands and failing.

"You cost us millions of dollars by feeding our drop locations to the Russians." I run a hand across the back of my neck. "Not to mention, lost us our contract with Axel to the fucking Morrone family." I pace closer to him and loom over his pathetic body on the floor, delighting in the way he shakes. "The only thing I want to hear from your mouth is an explanation."

Darragh's Adam's apple bobs as he swallows, glancing at the terrified faces watching this bloody and violent exchange. The only people who don't look shocked are my family. Blaine, Torin, Kieran, and Killian. It's because they know me and the violence that rules me. "They had leverage over me." He glares down at the floor, knowing that no matter what sob story comes out of his mouth, he only has minutes to live. "A video of me cheating on my wife and threatened to send it to her if I didn't comply." He shrugs. "That's my reason."

Pathetic.

Darragh is a weak, spineless man that we need to exterminate from the clan. Men like him need to be removed, as they'll cost us this war.

I laugh darkly, making some men around us step further back. None of them knows the insanity I possess and the proclivity I have for violence. They haven't met their leader, not yet.

I turn my attention to the rest of the clan to address them, knowing that this will be a defining moment in my leadership.

Rule with fear.

It was my father's motto and one I intend to adopt wholeheartedly. I gate at the pale men surrounding me, observing their faces and reaction to my actions. "Let this be a lesson to you all, lads." I wave my gun across the warehouse. "We don't accept disloyalty of any form." I narrow my eyes. "I will carve any rat in our ranks out like rotting wood, poisoned and discarded of before they can make amends."

Darragh shakes violently, fear constricting his pupils as he stares at me.

"You made a big fucking mistake," I say simply before shooting him dead between the eyes.

Blood splatters the floor and some men nearby, forcing them to recoil. I notice the look on some of my men's faces; pure shock. "James, Patrick, and Cormac clear this up," I say, looking at the three most ruthless men that aren't family in the room. "The rest of you are dismissed, except for Blaine, Torin, Kieran, and Killian.

The men scatter, most of them now fearing me

for the violent scene they just witnessed. That's how I want it. My clan needs to fear me if they are going to learn to respect me.

Killian approaches, brow raised. "Nice way to set the tone."

I squint at him. "We've got nothing if we can force our men's loyalty, Kill."

"Aye, it was the right move," Torin agrees, clapping me on the shoulder. "You're shaping up to be a worthy captain. Your father would've been proud."

I'm not sure that's true, as my father wasn't one to commend any of his sons, as he wasn't the sentimental type. How he taught Killian and me to be.

Blaine clears his throat. "I've a matter to address."

My brow furrows as I glance at my uncle. "What is it?"

"Spartak is making a few waves in political circles in the city. We need to make ground there, as we don't have the same sway as he does politically."

If it's not one thing, it's another. My father was captain of the clan for thirty years, dealing with this shit. It's only been a little over two months, and I'm already tired. "Great." I sigh heavily.

Torin steps forward. "You can't do this alone, lad." He glances at Killian. "Kill is monitoring the Italians. Delegate to the rest of us."

I nod, as it's a good idea. The family is reliable.

"Okay, Blaine, you find an angle politically where we can make headway." I glance at Torin. "You take over the meeting with the Cartel." I glance at Killian. "That's next week, isn't it?" I ask.

Killian nods. "Aye, next Tuesday."

Torin cracks his knuckles. "Okay, I'll handle them."

I glance at Kieran, my youngest brother. "Kier, can you try to bring the bikers in line?" I run a hand across the back of my neck. "It's a dangerous job, but Axel is disrespecting a decade-old pact."

He looks pleased with being tasked with such an important job. "You can count on me."

I nod. "And, I'll remain vigilante keeping tabs on the Russians."

Torin smiles. "It'll run like clockwork, Rourke. You'll see."

I find it hard to believe that anything will ever run like clockwork, especially since I married my enemy's daughter without his blessing. Things can only get worse from here on out.

22

VIKTORIA

*E*verything has changed now that I'm no longer Viktoria Volkov, captive and enemy number one, but Viktoria Callaghan, the wife of the clan's leader. The staff treats me with respect I'm used to at home, and I'm allowed a certain amount of freedom, even if I'm not allowed off the property without my husband's permission.

I sigh as I lean back in the limo's seat, waiting for my husband to join me. The fourth event this week that Rourke has forced me to accompany him. Ever since we married, he's been parading me around like I'm a fucking prize horse. It's almost as infuriating as his arrogant attitude that hasn't changed since we married.

He's rubbing it in my father's face despite the danger of doing so. I'm not sure why he thinks it's sensible to go anywhere in public at the moment. My father isn't a lenient man, and he'll be angry about Rourke's clear lack of respect for him.

The driver opens the door, and Rourke slips in the side, barely glancing at me. He's been as cold as ever since the wedding night when it felt like his walls were falling. He rarely says a word to me in private for the two weeks since.

"What event are we attending tonight?" I ask as the car moves.

Rourke doesn't look up from his cell phone. "It's an event raising money for homeless people in Chicago."

I sigh heavily, shaking my head. "Are you ever going to look at me again?"

His brilliant blue eyes connect with mine, devoid of any emotion. "There, is that better?"

I clench my jaw. "Why are you acting like this?"

"Acting like what, princess? Did you expect me to be a doting husband once we got married?" A wicked smirk spreads onto his face as if he enjoys inflicting pain on me. "Our marriage is a means to an end, don't forget that." He returns his attention to his cell phone.

I know that's not true. Rourke fears getting too close to me, and that's why when it got too real, he's pulled away. "You are a coward."

His eyes snap up, and rage infects them. "Say that again."

I hold eye contact with him, smiling as I know my nonchalance will anger him more. "I said you're a coward."

He moves toward me like a viper snapping at its prey in one swift motion. Before I can move away, he wraps his fingers around my neck, pressing hard as his lips tease against mine. "You don't want to push me, Viki," he murmurs, eyes flaring with a dark rage that both excites and frightens me.

"You don't scare me, Rourke," I breathe, feeling him increase the pressure on my windpipe. "You are just a scared boy who can't face his emotions, pushing me away because I got too close."

He releases me, shoving me against the seat. "You don't know what you are talking about. I am not scared of you getting too close because you mean nothing to me."

Pain constricts around my chest as I stare into his cold eyes, wondering if he means that. "Why did you marry me, then?"

A cruel smirk spreads onto his lips. "To stop the Morozov Bratva giving your father power."

My brow pulls together, as I know it is not the only reason. I shake my head. "That's not the only reason, as you made a promise to protect me from my father," I point out.

He chuckles, and it's the coldest sound I've ever heard. "I had to find some way to convince you to walk down the aisle with me."

It feels like he's punched me in the chest. A burst of pain explodes behind my rib cage as I struggle to draw air into my lungs, feeling wounded by his indifference. I don't believe it, as I know what I felt. Rourke feels something for me just as I feel something for him. The leader of the Callaghan Clan is too scared to face his emotions and what they mean.

We're from two sides of the war. Star-crossed and forbidden, even if we're married.

"I don't believe that," I mutter, glancing out of the window.

From the corner of my eye, I notice him clench his fists and his body turns rigid. Rourke may act cool and collected, but under it all, he's feeling as chaotic as I am.

The rest of the journey to the Charity Event is spent in awkward silence as Rourke focuses on his phone as if it is the most interesting thing he's ever set his eyes on. I can't understand how he can go from so intimate on our wedding night to distant ever since.

When the vehicle stops, the driver opens it, and I slip out, followed by my husband, who places a hand on the small on my back the moment we're in public. I tense and glare at him, knowing it's all for the show when we're around others.

"Smile and be a dutiful wife, Viki," he murmurs in my ear.

I wish that his deep voice and touch didn't make me shudder, but it does. The proximity of him infuses my nostrils with that heady, masculine musk. "How about I kick you in the balls for being a cold, condescending bastard?" I whisper back.

His eyes flash with murderous rage, and nostrils flare, but he plasters on a fake smile as we walk through the crowd to the entrance. "Don't make me punish you in front of all these people."

I tense at the indifferent tone of his voice. He isn't bluffing, which is rather disturbing. There are hundreds of people in attendance at this event, including the media. I can't imagine Rourke Callaghan, CEO of Callaghan Enterprises, would be stupid enough to stir up a shit storm by punishing me in public.

"You wouldn't dare," I reply, not wanting to give him the satisfaction of my silence.

Rourke growls softly in my ear, pressing what would look like a chaste kiss to my neck to onlookers as he sinks his teeth into my skin. "Try me, princess."

I tense, realizing that perhaps he *really* is that

insane. It's best not to push a monster on edge, as the last thing I want is to be bent over and humiliated in front of hundreds of strangers. Instead, I sink my teeth into my eternally busted lip, glaring at him in silence.

"That's what I thought." He stops suddenly, glancing at the table in front of us. "This is us." He pulls my seat out for me, faking the role of an attentive husband and gentleman, which couldn't be further from what he truly is. A monster dressed as a man, hiding in plain sight.

I take the seat and glance around the room, observing all the elegant women and dapper men attending this event. All of them mix with a murderous criminal, accepting him as one of their own. I don't understand the Callaghan Clan's structure, but in the public eye, Rourke acts as CEO of the Callaghan Enterprise, despite the underground workings of the clan.

"Oh, Viki, I'm so glad you are here," Jane Morgan, a politician's wife, calls, taking her seat opposite me. Her bad-tempered husband trails behind her as he takes a seat opposite Rourke. "What are the odds we'd be together at this event, too?"

I glance at Rourke, as this is the third event this week that we've been seated with Jane and Henry

Morgan. Something tells me that isn't a coincidence, and he wants something from her husband.

"Hi Jane, it's lovely to see you again," I say, despite dreading an entire night talking about her mundane life.

Rourke's hand slides to my thigh, sending shivers down my spine. He squeezes firmly, making my stomach churn.

"How are you?" I ask.

She launches into telling me about her new stylist, who I have to book in with so we can have a makeover together. I pretend to be listening, but all of my attention is on my husband's hand, softly stroking my inner thigh.

He moves it with slow, lazy strokes closer to my pussy, leaning toward me. "I told you I'd punish you, but I didn't say how."

Considering he hasn't touched me in two weeks since our wedding night, I feel like I'm burning from the inside out, ready to explode. Blood rushes in my ears, deafening me as Jane prattles on about something or other.

Rourke pushes the string of my thong aside and dips a finger inside of me, eliciting a shocked gasp.

"Are you okay?" Jane asks, her brow furrowing.

I nod in response, perhaps a little too eagerly.

"Never better," I lie through gritted teeth, glancing sideways at Rourke.

He holds a conversation with Henry, but there's a whisper of a smirk on his lips. The bastard is enjoying this. As always, he loves to humiliate me, and if I can't hold it together, this could get very embarrassing.

My breathing deepens as I try to focus solely on Jane fucking Morgan, now blabbing on about some spa she loves to go to. I couldn't care less about attending with her, as I'm not into that kind of bonding.

Rourke continues his assault, pushing his finger deeper inside, curling his finger in the exact spot to make me groan.

"How about next Thursday?" Jane asks.

I swallow hard. "I'll check my diary and get back to yo—" My voice cracks at the end as Rourke lazily thumbs my clit, making the torture excruciatingly difficult to withstand.

It's been two weeks since he touched me like this. Our wedding night when he fucked me like an animal until the sun rose, exhausting me until I could no longer keep my eyes open. Once I woke, he was gone. Since then, he's kept his distance from me as if I'm sick with the plague and going to drag him down with it.

It doesn't surprise me in the slightest that this is the moment he touches me again. The man is infuriating.

"Are you sure you are okay, Viktoria?" Jane leans forward, lowering her voice. "You look flushed. Are you coming down with something?"

I shake my head and plaster on my fakest smile. "No, I'm fine. It's just rather hot in here, don't you think?" When the first course arrives, I'm saved by the bell, as the servers take everyone's attention.

Rourke doesn't stop touching me. He merely picks up his fork and lazily eats the salmon on his plate with his free hand, tasting it. His other hand plays me like an instrument under my table, driving me wild. I'm practically riding his hand, demanding release from him like a sex-starved nymph.

Jane is oblivious, talking to me about God knows what while my husband finger fucks me under the table. Rourke nonchalantly continues to talk about stocks and shares with Henry, appearing calm and collected, while I can't even consider eating right now.

Jane's brow furrows. "The salmon is delicious. Aren't you hungry?"

I can hardly speak as Rourke pushes me toward the edge of no return, his fingers finding a harsh and rhythmic pace. Instead of replying, I take my fork and taste the salmon, nodding. "Delicious," I bite out, knowing I'll come undone in front of a table of people any minute.

Rourke's smirk widens as he hears the tightness in my voice, increasing the pressure as he shifts the angle of his hand, thumbing my clit as his fingers continue to delve in and out of me. I'm almost certain I can hear the wet plunging sound as my muscles clench around his fingers, and I come apart. I focus on my breathing, struggling to keep silent. I bite my lip so hard my teeth break the skin, and blood trickles down my chin.

Jane gasps, eyes wide as she looks up from her salmon. "You are bleeding," she exclaims.

I reach up to my lip and press a finger to it, finding it's coated in blood. "Oops, I must have bitten myself while eating." I glance at Rourke, who is still smirking as he pulls his finger from me, wiping it on his suit pants, before resting back in his seat as if nothing happened.

I do the same, adjusting myself before finishing my salmon. Jane seems unfazed as she carries on talking about something or other. I hate having to play this part, pretending I'm the doting wife of a man who is as cold as ice one minute and hot the next.

23

ROURKE

The soft purr of the limousine's engine is all that falls between us as the driver takes us home away from the hustle of the city.

Viki is silent, her eyes fixed intently on the world rushing by the window. Her dark hair falls in waves over her powder blue dress, and her hands remain clenched in fists in her lap. She's angry at me.

"You look beautiful tonight," I murmur.

Her emerald eyes meet mine, and she glares at me with passionate hatred. "Fuck you."

I chuckle at her crass retort. "Is that the way a princess should talk to her king?"

She crosses her arms over her chest. "If you are the king, that makes me the queen."

I raise a brow. "Semantics."

Viki huffs and returns her attention to the world

rushing by the window. "You're the most infuriating person I know."

I move from my side to hers, placing a hand on her thigh and making her tense. "Is that right?" My lips tease the shell of her ear. "You also love me touching you, Viki."

I feel her shudder violently against me.

Damn it.

I can't keep my hands off my wife, no matter how hard I try. The other three events this week were torture. Now that I've finally cracked and touched her, I can't stop. "Do you deny it?" I ask, knowing it will irritate her further.

Her eyes meet mine, blazing with a mix of lust and rage. "No, but it doesn't mean I don't hate you as a person. You're just very good with your hands."

I chuckle, even though a twinge ignites in my chest at hearing her tell me she hates me. "Hmm, perhaps I should have my way with you right here."

She glances forward, eyes wide.

The privacy screen between the driver and us isn't up, but I don't give a shit. All I care about is making sure she remembers this moment vividly.

I inch my hand up the skirt of her dress, but she grabs it harder than I'd expect, stopping me. "Don't you fucking dare." She shakes her head. "I've had enough humiliation tonight." Her eyes narrow as she tilts her chin upward, feigning confidence. "You can wait until we get home or stuff it up your ass."

I wrap my fingers around her throat, making her nostrils flare. "I have something I want to stuff up your ass," I purr, my cock throbbing in the confines of my tight briefs. "I think I'll take that tight little ass of yours tonight and make you scream."

Viki shudders, her breathing becoming labored as I tease my hand lower from her neck, pulling down the front of her dress and teasing her nipples with my fingers. "You're the biggest asshole I know."

I smirk. "Your asshole will be bigger once I stretch it with my cock."

She may tell herself she hates me, but her pupils dilate at my words. "In your dreams."

I release her throat, moving to the other side of the limo. My intense gaze is intended to intimidate her as I stare at her.

She stares right back as we enter a electric staring contest.

The ride back home is excruciating, as it feels like it takes forever. Finally, when we stop outside the gates, which electronically open, I can feel the promise of release. I need to get this woman out of this limo and into my bed as fast as physically possible.

The driver opens the door and helps Viki out. I

get out myself, coming around to meet her on the other side of the car.

"Good night, husband," she says before trying to walk away from me.

We've not shared a bed since our wedding night. "Not so fast." I grab her wrist, yanking her soft, dainty body against mine. "You are spending the night with me."

Her eyes narrow. "No, thanks." She tries to pull away from me, but I hold her firm.

"It wasn't a request," I murmur, digging my fingertips into her hips hard. "You are mine, and if I want you, then I'll have you." I wrap my hand around her wrist as we walk toward the house, my dick ruling my actions right now.

The more I try to stay away from her, the more I want her. It's a sickness I can shake. Watching her on the surveillance cameras isn't enough. I need her in my bed every night, waking with her by my side every morning.

"Rourke, you're being an asshole," she spits, a feeble attempt to stop what's about to happen. I know she wants me, and it's futile for her to deny it.

"And you, princess, keep lying to yourself about what you want." I march her up the stairs, coming to a stop outside my room and using my thumbprint to open the biometric lock. "Inside," I order.

She glances between me and the door as if trying to weigh up her options. She doesn't have any.

Viki accepts her fate and steps into my room, walking toward the bed. She sits down and takes off her heels, rubbing her feet with her hands and ignoring me entirely.

I shut the door, approaching her as all my blood now south as my cock demands her naked and writhing beneath me. It's all I have been able to think about for two fucking weeks, despite being enthralled in a tit for tat war with the Bratva.

Spartak is furious about my marriage to his daughter. The Morozov Bratva accepted that Spartak fucked them over, and they've now cut ties with the Volkov Bratva, staying far away in Moscow.

"You never told me what my father's reaction was to the news," she says, not looking up at me.

I lean my shoulder against the wall and watch her. "Your father wasn't pleased."

"Did he retaliate?" She asks, still focused on massaging her feet.

I walk toward her. "Of course. The bastard blew up one of our safe houses."

Viki's eyes shoot up. "Was anyone hurt?"

Sweet and innocent Viktoria. "Hurt yes, dead no." I shrug. "It's a miracle. The place is a pile of rubble now." I sigh heavily, rubbing a hand across the back of my neck. "I don't want to talk about work." I sit next to her, placing a hand on her thigh, leaning forward, and placing kisses on her exposed shoulders. "I just want to fuck my wife."

Viki shivers, clenching her thighs together as her nipples harden beneath the soft satin of her dress.

I groan, playing with them lazily. "So beautiful," I murmur, moving my lips to Viki's neck and nibbling at the sensitive skin where it meets her shoulders.

Goosebumps rise over her exposed flesh as I continue to break her resolve with soft kisses and hard bites to her body, claiming her like the violent savage I am. "Lie down for me, princess," I murmur.

As always, my Viki is submissive and lies on her back. Her legs eagerly spread open, displaying her black thong wet with arousal. "Dress off," I command.

Viki does as I say, releasing the side zip and shrugging it off her shoulders. She tosses it off the bed and levels her heated gaze at me. I groan as she's not wearing a bra, which she rarely does, which I find sexy as fuck.

"Play with your nipples for me," I order, tilting my head as I watch her.

Her tempting lips part as she seductively moves her fingers up her body, pinching her puckered nipples and moaning softly. It's a vision fit for a king.

"Perfect," I murmur, rubbing a hand over my straining crotch. "Thong off for me."

She eagerly pulls her thong down her long slender legs, before flinging it on top of her dress. When she lies back down, she parts her thighs even wider. My princess is naked and willing, watching me for my next move.

Blood rushes through my ears, drowning out all other sounds as heat and lust and need swirl in the air, taking control of the situation. I feel my control snap as I move toward her, grabbing her thighs hard and pushing them as far apart as physically possible.

Viki groans as I bury my tongue in her sweet as hell pussy, feasting on her as if I'm starving. I am starving. Denying myself of my wife only seems to widen the soul-crushing hunger she elicits from me. I'm lost in my wife, licking and sucking and fingering her with one sole aim, making her feel better than she's ever felt before.

In no time, Viki is panting my name. Her body shudders and convulses as she comes undone, a flood of her juice gushing from her pussy as I lap it up.

I grab her hips without a word and flip her onto all fours, parting her ass cheeks to get a good look at her anus. Tight and never fucked and all mine to claim. I bury my tongue against it, making her squeal in surprise.

"Rourke, what—"

I spank her firm ass cheek, making her hiss. "No questions, princess. Enjoy the sensation." I continue to lick her ass, working my tongue in and out of the tight ring of muscles. As she relaxes, I grab a bottle of lube off my nightstand and lather her ass with it before working one finger in first.

Viki tenses, before accepting the truth, that it feels so good. Her deep rasping moans are a statement to that as I work two fingers inside, then three to four until she's panting and crying my name like a dirty little whore; my dirty little whore.

"Fuck," she cries, her body jerking around as she comes undone. Her tight asshole squeezes my fingers so hard it feels like she's trying to break them. "Rourke," she screams as she tumbles over the edge, coming undone from me playing with her ass.

It's the last straw. I snap as I drop my pants to the floor along with my boxer briefs. My thick erection dripping as I line it up with her ass, letting the tip rest against her stretched hole. I squirt lube all over my cock, coating it thoroughly before squirting more into her hole.

"You're ready, princess," I murmur, my cock twitching in anticipation. "Ready for my dick in that tight little ass," I rasp, the need becoming unbearable.

She moans, arching her back in invitation. My innocent Bratva princess is no longer innocent. I've corrupted her and turned her into a sex-crazed nympho who can't get enough. Slowly, I apply pressure to her well-worked sphincter, pushing in through the tight muscles as they clench around my shaft, making it hard to stop myself from shooting my load in her ass almost instantly.

I work every inch in, listening as Viki moans in a mix of pleasure and pain. Once my balls hit her clit, I groan. "Fuck, princess. Every inch is in." I lean down and place soft kisses on her back, making her shiver.

"Fuck my ass, please, Rourke," she begs, sending my blood pressure sky high.

I spank her ass, staring down at the way she looks with my thick cock buried between her cheeks. Perfect. Beautiful. Stunning. None of these words goes far enough to describe it. "Such a dirty girl, Viki, begging me to fuck your virgin asshole." Slowly, I move out of her, watching as her muscles cling to my thick shaft as if trying to stop me from retreating.

"Fuck," she hisses, pain lacing her tone. "It's so fucking good but hurts all at the same time. How is it possible, Rourke?" Her voice cracks at the end as I pull out of her again before slamming in.

"Because you are a masochist, sweetheart. My dirty little masochist." I'm so far gone, floating in fucking heaven as I take my wife's anal virginity. I keep the pace slow and deliberate, watching as my cock forces her ass open more easily with each thrust. "You are a fucking work of art with my cock in your ass," I growl, feeling my balls draw up.

"Fuck me," she begs, her voice no more than a rasp.

I spank her right ass cheek, watching as her firm buttock wobbles from the impact. "Such a naughty girl." I spank her left one before shoving every inch back inside of her in one quick stroke. My handle on the beast inside of me is slipping as I plow her relentlessly, speeding up my thrusts into her body.

"Oh fuck," she cries as she nears the edge. A flutter in her muscles warns me she's about to come undone.

I slow down my thrusts, needing to draw this moment out longer. "No coming until I say. You've already come twice tonight, greedy girl."

She whimpers as her muscles clench around me. Viki is trying to control herself, but she is so greedy it drives me crazy. Her muscles are squeezing so tightly I can hardly keep hold of the reins of control. The last thing I want is to hurt her. My body is burning with scorching heat as I finally snap, fucking her ass violently.

I can't control it any longer. My teeth sink into

Viki's shoulder as I pummel her virgin hole repeatedly, sending her spiraling off the edge despite her attempt to hold on. Her body crumples under my weight, but I don't stop fucking her harder than I've ever fucked her.

"Oh God, Rourke," she cries, still spasming with the orgasm I coaxed from her.

I spank both her ass cheeks in quick succession before grabbing her hips with so much force my nails break into her skin. "Take my load in that tight little ass," I roar, my cock releasing deep inside of her. I continue to slam into Viki until I'm sure every drop is inside of her. Only then do I pull out of her wrecked hole.

Viki doesn't move, her labored breathing the only sign she's still alive.

After an eternity, she rolls onto her back, placing the back of her wrist to her forehead. "Fuck me, that was amazing." She meets my gaze, and I can't help but smile.

"Good, because I intend to do it to you very often, Mrs. Callaghan." I press a kiss to her stomach, making her giggle with laughter. A laughter that I'm sure I can't live without hearing every day from now until I die.

24

VIKTORIA

I wake the next morning to the sound of the shower running in the adjoining bathroom. The darkness of the walls surrounding me surprises me, as this isn't my room. That is when I remember the events of the night before and notice the dull ache in my backside.

Our night spent together was so intimate, yet I know he's going to be distant today, as cold as ice. A shiver races down my spine in anticipation as I remain in his bed, basking in the scent of him as it clings to the sheets.

No matter how much I try to fight it, I know that Rourke Callaghan has become an addiction I don't want. A beautiful pain in my ass who will never look at me the way I look at him. The water shuts off in the adjoining bathroom as I sit up in bed, clinging onto the sheet around my naked body.

Rourke appears, a towel loosely hanging around his muscled hips. My mouth waters at the sight of the groves dipping from his hips lower, disappearing under the thick cotton towel. It looks like his chest is carved from stone, and this is the first I've been able to admire him and the ink scrolling over his flawless body. "Morning, beautiful," he murmurs, his Irish accent thick and delicious.

It's hard to believe this man is my husband, even if it is only for show. "Morning," I reply.

He smiles, and it is the most dazzling thing I've seen in my life. It's a genuine smile, not an irritating smirk that he constantly gives me. "How are you feeling?"

I shrug. "My ass is sore. Other than that, I'm great."

He laughs a deep, throaty laugh that makes my heart stop beating in my chest. "You don't say." He raises a brow. "Come here." He holds a hand out to me, and I eye it warily before climbing out of bed and walking toward him.

The ice-cold Rourke Callaghan is nowhere to be seen—yet.

I take his hand, and he drags me into his hard body, molding his fingers down my side.

"I've run a bath for you," he says.

My stomach churns at the gentleness in his touch as he lazily rubs his fingers in circles on my back. "That's uncharacteristically kind of you."

He smiles that warm, alluring smile that makes my chest ache. "Maybe you should get used to it." Before I can ask what he means, he pulls me into the bathroom. "Get in, princess."

I do as he says, sighing as the perfectly balmy water encases my skin. The ache of my ass eases as the water soothes me.

Rourke sits on the side behind the bath, and his hands find my shoulders as he works the knots in my muscles.

I sigh softly. "What did I do to deserve this treatment?"

He chuckles behind me, sending an unfamiliar warmth through my entire body. "You were a good wife and gave up your ass to your husband," he murmurs, pressing his lips to the sensitive flesh where he marked my skin last night, between my neck and shoulder.

It's tender in such a good way, as is my ass. Pain is my addiction, especially when it's coupled with pleasure.

"Does that hurt?" he whispers, gently stroking the mark he gave me with his fingers.

I nod. "A little, but in a good way."

He groans behind me, and I hear the towel drop to the floor as he stands next to the bath, stroking his heavy cock. My stomach tightens at the sight of him naked. It's beautiful. "I can never get enough of you, princess. But right now, I'm just going to take care of you. Move over."

I do as he says, shifting in the enormous bathtub.

Rourke slides in and then pulls me between his legs, wrapping them protectively around me. His arms wrap around mine, too, holding me.

The heavy pressure of his erection pushes against my spine, stoking need inside of me like oxygen to a fire.

Instead of touching me as I expect, he turns on the showerhead and wets my hair from behind, running his fingers through it tenderly. His touch is so gentle it's almost jarring as he reaches for a bottle of shampoo and lathers it in his hands.

I sigh as he massages the lavender-scented soap into my hair and scalp, being so thorough. "Rourke," I murmur his name, leaning against his hard, muscled body. "What are you doing?"

I feel him smile against the back of my neck. "Treating you like a princess."

My eyes flicker shut as I accept this oddly tender treatment from him, as he washes my hair thoroughly before conditioning it, too. Then he turns his attention to my body, washing my tits and upper body first with a sweet-smelling soap that smells like cotton candy. Then he washes my legs and ass cheeks with the same soap before turning his attention to between my legs without the soap. His fingers gently wash my recently fucked asshole before sliding to the apex of my thighs.

All the while, his hard, angry cock presses into my back demandingly, but he doesn't pleasure himself, focusing entirely on me.

I arch my back, moaning as he slips his fingers into my pussy, curling them to hit the perfect spot deep. He works my body masterfully, driving me toward an orgasm before I even see it coming.

I shudder as my release hits me. "Fuck, Rourke," I cry, arching my back as I feel so empty. I need to feel him filling me up and completing me.

"That's it, sweetheart, come for me," he murmurs.

I convulse in his arms long after the orgasm subsided, riding his fingers like I'm starving for me. "Fuck me," I whisper.

He groans, but I feel him release his hold on me. "Not right now, princess. This morning is all about you." He adjusts himself from under me and steps out of the bath, grabbing his towel and wrapping it around his hips. "We have somewhere to go today, so dry off and get dressed."

I stand from the warm water and step out of the bath. Rourke wraps a luxuriously soft towel around me. "Where are we going?" I ask.

He smiles, and it's the single most exquisite thing I've ever seen. "Lake Michigan. We're going out on my yacht."

I raise a brow at the thought of being alone on a yacht with this man. "Why?" I ask.

He sighs heavily, grabbing my hips. "You ask too many pointless questions, princess." His lips slant over mine in a passionate kiss, stealing the oxygen from my lungs. "Because I said so, that's why." He lets go of me. "No more questions, and dress appropriately, as we're going to the theatre tonight."

"Seriously, what are we going to watch?" Rourke doesn't strike me as a man who enjoys the theatre.

He shrugs. "Romeo and Juliet. A business associate invited me, and I thought, why not?"

I laugh this time, finding it hard to believe Rourke would even entertain the idea of going to watch Romeo and Juliet at the theatre.

"Why are you laughing?" He snaps.

"I just didn't take you for a Shakespeare kind of guy."

His eyes narrow. "Shut up and get dressed."

I can't help but smile as he walks away from me, tension coiling through his shoulders. When he's like this, I can imagine this marriage being something more than a sham. It's clear that somewhere along the way, I lost a part of my heart to the man who kidnapped me, and when he is sweet like this, I feel him stealing more of it each time he shows me this side of him—the real Rourke Callaghan.

I'VE NEVER SEEN the city from the lake, but it is beautiful to tour the water and see it from a different light. My father hates boats and never purchased one for himself, and I must admit there is something very calming about being on the water.

For the entire day, Rourke is sweet and attentive. His icy demeanor is nowhere to be found today, but if past experiences are anything to go on, it is only a matter of time until he closes me off again.

Rourke sips a glass of whiskey, leaning against the doorway onto the deck. In the little time that I've known him, it's become clear that he drinks far too much. It doesn't matter what time it is; he has a glass in his hand. "You look stunning," he murmurs, watching me with a look that makes my heart skip a beat. "How have you enjoyed the day so far?"

I smile at him, glancing back out over the expanse of water. "Very much. It's nice to Chicago from a different perspective."

He moves closer to me, every step sending prickles of awareness over my skin. "Have you never been on a cruise on Lake Michigan before?"

I shake my head, hugging my arms around myself as a cool breeze sweeps through the deck. "No, my father hates boats."

Rourke stops behind me, the warmth of his body radiating into mine from the closeness. "That's a shame. You look in your element on water." He wraps a powerful arm around my waist and tugs me against his chest. "We can do this more often if you would like. Take the boat away when things settle down," he whispers into my ear as if saying it louder might break the dream we're in.

"I'd like that," I say.

I feel him smile against my neck before peppering soft kisses along my shoulder. "We have to go if we're going to make the play."

I sigh heavily, wishing we could stay here and watch the sunset. "I was looking forward to watching the sunset."

He tugs me tighter against him. "You'll have plenty of chances to watch the sunset from this yacht, princess." He forces me to turn to face him. "We don't want to be late."

I don't reply as my stomach flutters, hearing him say that I'll have plenty of chances. I want to ask if those chances will be with him, but I know he may pull away if I ask him that.

The captain of the boat pulls toward the harbor. Rourke helps him dock and then turns to me, offering me his hand. "Ready?"

I nod and take his hand as he leads me down the steps onto the dock.

He yanks me against him, holding me close. The warmth of his body staves off the cold as the day slowly turns to dusk. We walk away from the lake, and Rourke flags down a cab.

"Can't we walk to the theatre?" I ask.

Rourke shakes his head, glancing at his watch. "Not unless you want to be late. It's about a fifty-minute walk, and the show starts in twenty minutes."

I sigh and slide into the back of the cab, smiling at the driver.

"Where are you going?" He asks.

Rourke clears his throat. "Cadillac Palace Theatre."

He nods and drives us the ten minutes to the theatre. All the while, Rourke strokes my bare leg with his fingers in a soothing motion. It's distracting and arousing, which is not ideal when we're in the back of a cab.

I glance at him and notice the whisper of a smirk on his lips. He's doing it on purpose.

"That's eighteen dollars," the driver says as he pulls up outside the theatre.

Rourke tosses him a twenty. "Keep the change." He helps me out of the back of the cab and leads me to the entrance of the theatre.

He tosses the tickets to the woman at the desk, and her eyes widen as they flick between Rourke and me. "These are Mr. Kendall's tickets, sir."

Rourke's eyes flash with anger. "Yes, he's out of town and offered me them."

"I see. He didn't forewarn us." She taps on her keyboard. "We need confirmation from him."

Rourke's eyes narrow. "I'm sure he'll be very unhappy to hear that you are not allowing his business associate in with his wife. After all, my company supplies his company." He runs a hand across the back of his neck. "Does Callaghan Enterprises ring any bells?"

Her eyes widen, and she nods. "Yes, sir. I-it's just protocol."

"Fuck protocol," he growls, sliding a hand into his pocket and pulling out a wedge of cash. "How much does the box cost for the night, then?"

She shakes her head. "It's assigned to Mr. Kendall, so I can't sell you it for the night."

Rourke's patience is wearing thin, and I can sense he's on the edge of snapping, so I grab his wrist. "Why don't you call Mr. Kendall now and clear it with him?"

Rourke's eyes narrow, and then he digs a hand into his pocket, dialing the number. "Sorry to call while you're on vacation, Robert, but I'm at the theatre, and they won't let me in." He slides the phone over to the woman. "Speak with him."

She takes the phone and stutters in response to everything Jerry says on the other end. "Of course, sir. I apologize." She cancels the call and gives Rourke back his phone. "I'm sorry, Mr. Callaghan. Please go ahead, and we'll be sending a bottle of champagne up to the box as an apology."

I notice Rourke's eyes narrowing as he glares at her. One thing I've learned about my husband is that he isn't very good at controlling his temper. "That's very kind of you," I reply, taking the tickets from the lady. "We best find out seats before the play starts." I squeeze Rourke's arm, drawing his attention to me.

He smiles and nods. "Yes, sweetheart." He takes my hand and yanks me up the stairs up to the boxes. "That bitch is lucky I didn't get her fired for that stunt." His eyes are wild.

I shake my head. "She's just following protocol. Calm down."

Rourke leads me to a box in the theatre's gallery.

My heart pounds erratically in my chest because of this sudden change in Rourke. He's giving me whiplash from this constant change from hot to cold. One minute he's keeping away from me and barely paying me any attention. The next, he's fawning over me like I'm the single most important thing to him. It's confusing and inspires that same naïve hope inside of me. Hope that perhaps this marriage can transform from a dark hatred to something beautiful and pure.

He moves closer to me, his lips skirting over my skin. "We have this box all too ourselves, you know?"

I shoot him an irritated glare. "Don't ruin this for me. I've never been to the theatre."

His brow hitches into his hairline. "Really? I thought this would be your kind of thing."

I shrug. "It might be. I've just never had the chance to find out." The curtains lift, signaling the play is about to start. Rourke inches his hand higher on my thigh, and I swat it away. "Stop it. I want to enjoy the play."

He smirks and moves his chair closer to mine, wrapping a warm arm around my shoulders. "Fine, as you command."

I let him hold me as the play starts, watching the first act unfold in his embrace, feeling safer than I've ever felt before, wrapped in the arms of a man who is enemy number one to my family. To me, he's becoming the single most important person in my world.

25

ROURKE

"You're in a good mood, brother," Killian says, walking into the family library where the rest of my family gathered the next morning, as well as Gael. "Did your wife finally suck your cock?"

I growl at his crass mention of my wife. "Killian, I'll fucking kill you the next time you talk about her like that." I crack my knuckles, rage flaring to life in the center of my chest as if it has a life of its own.

Killian smirks, holding his hands up. "Whoa, looks like you have got a hard-on for the Volkov girl."

I move toward him and grab him by the lapel of his jacket, pushing him hard against the wall. "What the fuck is your problem?"

Killian looks shocked, which is rare. Normally, he's the idiot joker who likes to anger everyone around him. "Sorry, bro. I'll lay off the Viktoria jokes."

Torin sets a hand on my shoulder. "Let him go, lad."

I narrow my eyes at Killian as he's been trying to get under my skin more than normal lately. "Shut it about my wife." I release him and turn away, walking toward the bottle of Irish whiskey which is calling to me on the dresser. "Anyone else want a drink?"

I'm met with silence.

Blaine breaks it. "Rourke, you have been drinking too much since your father died. It's nine o'clock in the morning."

I spin around with my full glass of whiskey. "Why does the time I drink matter?"

Everyone is looking at me as though this meeting is merely an intervention to call me out on my questionable drinking habits since Father's death. "It matters because you drink every day and start in the morning," Kier says, stepping forward.

I glare at my family. "Is this meeting about my drinking or an update on how everyone is getting on?" I growl.

Father always used to drink a lot, but I can't deny that I'm probably drinking more than he ever did since his death. It's not something I noticed until this moment.

I tighten my grasp on the tumbler before placing it down on the coffee table. Anger simmering beneath my skin at my family being so fucking uptight about my drinking.

What do they expect after all the shit that has happened since our dad died?

"This meeting isn't about me or my drinking. I want updates from each of you." I narrow my eyes, folding my arms over my chest.

Kieran steps forward first. "Unfortunately, Axel is still being a stubborn bastard and won't shift an inch of buying his product from the Italians." He runs a hand across the back of his neck. "I've been down to his club regularly with some men, but he's not intimidated by us. He has the Morrone family's men for protection."

"That snake deserves to die for his disloyalty," I say, clenching my fist by my side. I glance at Killian. "I'm sure you don't have any good news about the Italians."

He shakes his head. "No good news, as they're getting increasingly aggressive in our territory." Kill shakes his head. "I guess they're getting cocky since they stole the biker contract from us."

Great.

If the Bratva wasn't enough to deal with, now we've got to contend with the Morrone family, too.

I glance at Torin. "Please tell me you have better news about the cartel."

"Preliminary meeting went well with Thiago, and he is going to arrange for me to meet his father." It's an offense that they didn't grace us with that option initially, but we're struggling for allies in this war, and the Estrada family are our last chance.

"Great. Did Thiago mention how they can help us with selling our product?"

Torin nods. "The Estrada Cartel mainly deals in Heroine, and they are eager to partner up and offer cocaine to their clientele too."

At last, some good news. If the Estrada Cartel partners with the Callaghan Clan, we could easily bridge the gap Axel left five times over. They have some powerful influence in the city and run a vast and lucrative area of the city, as they've kept hold of the southwest side and far southwest side for years. Out of all the criminal organizations in the city, their territory is the largest and borders the south side and far southeast side, which we've always held. Central is free for all and almost impossible to gain a true hold on, but it may be possible to stake a claim if we team up with the Estrada family.

Axel and his bikers try to maintain the far north side as their territory, and they have to get their supply from somewhere, which in turn gives whoever supplies them access to the territory. The territory we've now lost rights to because Axel screwed us over. The Morrone Family controls the west side as it's been Italian influenced long before I was born. The Russians control the north side and northwest side.

"If we seal a deal with the Estrada Cartel, together we'll be in control of half the landmass of Chicago."

"Aye," Torin replies, nodding. "It's a lucrative deal, and maybe one you'd like to be a part of?"

"When is the meeting?" I ask.

"Next Tuesday. Shall I confirm you will attend?" Torin asks.

I nod in response. "Yes." I turn my attention to my other uncle. "How is it going with the politics?"

Blaine shrugs. "It's a slow process when politicians are involved, but I have a potential angle."

I raise a brow. "Care to elaborate?"

He shakes his head. "I need to explore it before I can reveal it."

Kier clears his throat. "Something concerning I heard is that there's a family from Sardinia in town, and they want to get a foothold in the city amongst the chaos." His brow pinches together. "I'm pretty sure they call them the Bianchi family."

"What? Why the fuck didn't you lead with that information, little bro?"

His jaw clenches at hearing me call him that. "Because you asked for an update on the bikers."

"Fuck." I shake my head. "We can't be dealing with another family on top of this." I level my gaze at Kier. "Can you put some feelers out to them and see if they'd be interested in an alliance?"

Gael, who has remained silent the entire time, steps forward. "I can handle that since I don't have a task in this. Why don't you leave it to me to agree on a deal with the Bianchi family?"

I meet the gaze of the man who has well and truly stolen my sister's heart. He hasn't been as active as he usually is in clan business, which has to do with Maeve. "Are you sure you can handle it?" I ask, a smirk tugging at my lips. "Or will be sister be too much of a distraction?"

Gael's eyes narrow. "Don't be an asshole, Rourke. I can handle it just fine. The more people on the case, the smoother things will run."

He's right. The more people we trust to monitor alliances and relations during the war, the better chance of surviving. "Fine. You handle the Bianchi family, but don't screw it up."

Gael's eyes flash with irritation, but he says nothing. I guess it's hard for him to take orders from a man who he saw grow up. A man who was beneath him at one point, but he's not a Callaghan. "Got it."

I gaze at my uncle Blaine, who looks like he wants to say something. "Is that a good idea?" He asks, folding his arms over his chest. "Who the fuck can trust the Italians?" The Italians murdered his sister, our mother, even if these people aren't related to the Morrone family.

I walk toward him and place a hand on his shoulder, forcing him to stop. "If we don't make alliances, we won't survive this war." I gaze at the faces watching me. "The Russians are angrier than ever since the wedding video hit their inboxes. It's only going to go downhill from here. The attacks are coming too frequently for us to keep up with."

My phone buzzes in my pocket as if on cue, and I pull it out to see Seamus flash up on the screen. He rarely rings me unless there's a problem or he needs to meet with me. "Hello."

"Boss, we've got a problem," He rasps, sounding out of breath.

"What is it?" I ask.

"Spartak has me and ten of us at the docks. Don't —" The crack of bone hitting bone fills the air as the phone clatters to the ground. I listen as heavy footsteps approach, and then someone fumbles with the cell phone.

"I have eleven of your men. If you want to see

them again, you will meet me at Darbazi in one hour."

Darbazi is one of Spartak's restaurants deep in the heart of his territory. "We need to meet somewhere neutral," I reply, keeping my tone steady.

"You aren't in charge of negotiations, little Callaghan. Darbazi. One hour. Don't be late." He cancels the call, leaving my mind spinning.

"What was that?" Kill asks concern in his tone. "Have they hit again?"

I nod in response. "Spartak has kidnapped Seamus and ten of our men." I walk toward the coffee table, picking up the tumbler of whiskey. "He wants me to meet him at Darbazi in one hour."

"Like hell. It's a trap," Torin growls, his muscles bunching at either side of his thick neck. "How do you know he has Seamus?"

"Seamus is the one who spoke first." I tip back the rest of the whiskey, enjoying the warm burn as it slides down my throat. "I can't leave him to die."

Kier steps forward. "Did he state you have to go alone?"

I cast my mind back to the brief conversation before shaking my head. "No, he simply said to meet him at Darbazi in one hour."

"I'm going with you then," Kier replies.

Killian steps to his side. "Aye, me too."

Torin clears his throat. "You need an army of guys to back you up, so we can all go."

"That's probably exactly what he wants. The entire Callaghan family to walk headfirst into a trap." I shake my head. "I will go alone."

Gael clears his throat. "He may want the family, but I ain't a Callaghan. You should at least have someone with you for backup."

"The way you are shacking up with our sister suggests you'll be family soon enough," Kier says, giving him an odd look.

"Okay, Gael will go with me. The rest of you fuckers can stay here."

Torin cracks his neck. "I'm coming too, and nothing you can say will stop me before you try."

I sigh heavily, running a hand across the back of my neck. "Fine. You, me, and Gael will leave in twenty minutes, so I need to get ready." I turn around and head out of the library and up the galleried stairs toward my bedroom.

There's honestly a chance I might not make it back from this meeting, and all I can think about is seeing her one last time. My Viki. Despite my efforts to distance myself from the Russian temptation that is my wife, she's captured what still beats of my stony heart, claiming it for herself.

26

VIKTORIA

*R*ourke bursts into the bedroom, making me jump.

His brow furrows when he sees me with a paint roller and his navy blue wall half coated in white primer. "What the fuck are you doing?"

I stand, placing the roller on the tray. "This place needs a makeover, and it freaks me out how dark it is."

Rourke's muscles are bunched under his shirt as he glances between me and the wall. "It's how I like it."

Oh shit. It would have been sensible to check with Rourk before painting over it, but this is my room too now. I spend as much time in here as he does, perhaps longer. "I'm sorry, I should have checked with you first, I just—"

He holds a hand up to stop me. "Quiet." He walks toward me, eyes unreadable. "This might be the last time I see you, and there is no way I want to spend it fighting." He hooks his arm around my back and drags me against his solid body.

My brow furrows. "What do you mean the last time?"

His eyes burn with what appears to be fear. Is my husband showing me his vulnerable side?

"Are you okay?" I ask, lifting a hand to cup his cheek.

He grabs it before it reaches his face. "I'm fine, Viki. Your father is demanding I meet him at Darbazi in one hour from now, or he'll kill eleven of my men who he kidnapped."

Darbazi.

I shake my head. "It's a trap."

"I know it is, princess." Rourke smiles sadly. "But I don't have a choice."

Panic grows around my heart, wrapping its constricting vines around it. "You can't. Darbazi is where my father tortures his enemies, and he has an underground basement beneath it filled with torture chambers."

Rourke's smile doesn't leave his lips. "Believe me, princess. I hate this too, but I can't abandon my men." He runs the back of his hand gently against my cheek. "I'm not going alone, and Gael and Torin are coming along as backup."

I pull away from his touch, pacing the floor of the room. "Let me come with you. If anyone should face my father, it's me." I turn around to find Rourke glaring at me with that same stony expression.

"Not over my dead body," he says slowly, each syllable stressed.

For once, I realize it is futile trying to fight him. Instead, I will sneak out after him and make my way to Darbazi. The only way Rourke survives this is if I can plead his case to my father and admit the truth, that I love the bastard, despite everything.

I walk toward him and take his hand in mine, bringing it to my chest. "Rourke, I know our marriage is anything but conventional, but…." I hesitate, fearful of his rejecting how I feel. "I love you," I say, finding the courage to spit out the words.

His eyes widen for a millisecond before he smiles that warm, kind smile I've grown to love. It's not the callous smirk he used to give me. "I love you too, princess." He brings my hand to his lip and kisses the back of it. "Unfortunately, I don't have time to show you just how much right now, but once I get back, I'm going to fuck you all night long."

I wrap my hand around the back of his neck and pull his lips to mine, knowing that no matter what happens at Darbazi, at least we've both finally told each other the truth. It feels like fate led Rourke to kidnap me, drawing me into his orbit.

Rourke grabs my waist with his large, possessive hands. His tongue demands entrance as it swipes over my lips.

I part them, allowing him inside eagerly. The kiss is full of pent-up emotion that makes my heart swell as he holds me so tight it feels like he's trying to pull me into his body.

"Be careful," I murmur against his lips as he pulls away from me. His warmth disappears as he steps away, gazing at me longingly.

"Don't worry, princess." He smirks, that cocky persona slipping into place. "I'm always careful." He turns and strides toward the door.

I roll my eyes. "My father will be out for your blood."

He stops with his hand on the door handle, his back rising and falling as he breathes deeply. "Perhaps I'm out for his." With that, he leaves me alone in his partly painted bedroom, wondering how I'm going to stop my father and my husband from tearing each other apart.

There is no way I'm just sitting here waiting to find out which of them survives. I pull my cell phone out and order an Uber to meet me on the other side of the park. I stride toward the closet and pull out a pair of jeans and sweater before grabbing a thick coat as it's dropped below freezing as fall merges into winter. I dress quickly, knowing I don't have much time. One hour, Rourke said. I need to make it to Darbazi before him and barter with my father to spare us both and Rourke's men.

Once dressed, I walk to the far window in the bedroom that looks done over the sunroom roof extended on the side.

I force open Rourke's bedroom window and slip out onto the flat roof below. His room is far easier to escape from than the guest room I'd spent most of the time locked in. Carefully, I lower myself down from the flat room and onto the ground, rushing toward the only way I know out of here. Ever since we married, I've been allowed to explore the grounds, giving me the perfect opportunity to take stock of all weak points.

There is a park near the back of the grounds where the barrier is only five feet, which is just short enough for me to climb over. At least, I hope it is.

Silently and quickly, I run, making it to the wall fast. I climb over it and head for the road, searching for my Uber, which should have already arrived.

I find it and slip inside.

"Hey," I say.

"Hi, Darbazi, right?" He asks.

"Yes, please, as fast as you can."

He smiles and pulls away from the curb, driving me toward my father. I don't know how he will react, and all I know is I can't sit by and wait for him to kill the man I love.

I KNOW the layout of Darbazi better than most.

It's easy to sneak in at the back, where I head for the room my father uses as an office. A card room, really, but he's never anywhere else. The man is addicted to gambling, but he has more money than sense.

I rest my hand on the door handle, pressing my ear to the door. There're no voices on the other side, so I push it open. Father stands at the far wall, gazing at the CCTV screen.

"Hello, Viktoria."

My heart stills in my chest.

"Father."

He turns to face me, tilting his head to the side. "Did you think you could sneak in here undetected, zolotko?" He asks, using the nickname he used to give me as a child, meaning gold.

I shake my head. "That wasn't my intention, Father, as I wanted to come to speak with you."

He taps his finger against his chin. "Do you mean you aren't here to return home?" His eyes narrow. "That display at the charity event wasn't merely for your kidnappers' amusement, was it?"

I swallow hard, realizing he won't be happy that I've fallen for a Callaghan. "No, I love him. That is why I'm here as your daughter to plead that you drop this silly vendetta—"

He laughs, cutting me off mid-sentence. "Why in the world would I drop this vendetta when the Callaghans were the ones to start it?" He steps toward me, forcing me to retreat backward.

The expression in his eyes is one I've seen too many times before growing up. It's a chaotic storm raging to life inside of him, ready to tear apart everything in its path.

"That's not true, according to the Callaghan family." My brow furrows as I hold my chin high, trying not to allow my father to intimidate me the way he has all my life. "You murdered Ronan Callaghan."

He rolls his eyes. "Not that again. The Bratva never laid a hand on that worthless piece of shit," he spits, eyes blazing with rage. "Anyone who says otherwise is an idiot. Someone who wanted to start this blood-crazed war murdered the man, and it wasn't me. Whoever did kill him framed the Bratva intentionally."

I look into my father's eyes, and at that moment, I'm sure he's telling the truth, but if he's right, who killed the leader of the Callaghan clan? "Who would do that?"

My father breaks eye contact with me, glancing at the CCTV screen as Rourke appears at the front desk. "Just on time," he murmurs.

Icy dread sweeps through me, engulfing me as I realize I was naïve to believe my father would listen to me. "Please don't hurt him."

My father grins like an evil mastermind. "Viktoria, you underestimated the man I am. Did you believe I'd listen to you?" He sneers. "You are worthless to the Bratva now and tainted goods which I can't use to further our position."

I shake my head. "That's not true. Maxim was going to marry Maeve. Surely this union between Rourke and me can bring an end to the war."

My father's eyes narrow as if he's considering it before he shakes his head. "There was a significant difference. I made a deal with Ronan for Maxim and Maeve to marry, but Rourke kidnapped you by force and then walked you down the aisle without my blessing." His fists are clenched so tightly his knuckles are turning white. I've never seen my father this angry before. "He made me look weak, and I won't stand by until he's paid for it." He inches closer to me and grabs my wrist, dragging me over to a chair. "Sit," he barks.

I do as he says, sitting in the chair. My stomach churns as he grabs some rope and ties me to it. "What are you doing?" I ask.

"You, my daughter, are bait." He smirks a wicked smile. "You should have put up more of a fight at the wedding. Perhaps then I might have forgiven you for your betrayal."

I glance at the camera, finding Rourke outside the room, ready to enter. I open my mouth to warm him, but my father slams his hand over it before I can. "There's no escape for your dear husband. Let him come, and you will feel genuine pain when I take him from you in front of your eyes."

Tears flood my eyes, but I don't allow them to fall. I can't watch while my father kills my husband. Somehow, I have to find a way out of this.

27

ROURKE

*D*arbazi is busy, and there's no space in the parking lot, meaning we have to park down a side alley to have an escape vehicle anywhere near the place. The van made sense since we're trying to save eleven of our men from this sick son of a bitch.

Torin and Gael exchange nervous glances as I slide out of the van into the alleyway. "What are you pussies waiting for?" I ask.

"Isn't it wise to go through the plan again?" Gael asks.

I shake my head. "We've been through it twice already. If you two knuckleheads haven't got it yet, then I'm afraid failure is a guarantee."

Gael cracks his knuckles, clearly irritated by my blatant disrespect of a man who has been involved in far more situations like this than I have over the years, alongside my father. "It's important to ensure we're all on the same page."

I sigh heavily. "Yes, I walk in the front entrance with you and distract Spartak while Torin breaks in the back to find Seamus and our men." I run a hand across the back of my neck. "It's not exactly rocket science."

Torin grunts. "Aye, I have to agree with Rourke. Let's get on with it and stop procrastinating, Gael."

Gael clenches his fists but nods in reluctant agreement. "Let's go then." He slides out of the van and follows me around the front to the entrance of the restaurant. He places a hand on my chest just as we're about to walk inside. "Careful, Rourke. I don't want to explain to Maeve why her brother is no longer breathing. You come out of this alive, you hear me?"

I glare at him, knowing he'd never issue a warning like that to my father. "I think it's time you accept your position as my second in command. You would never have said those words to my father, and don't pretend you would."

Gael holds my gaze, nodding. "Aye, you're right, but Maeve cares about you, and I don't want to see her hurt." He shakes his head. "All I'm saying is to be careful. We're meeting with the devil himself, lad." He removes his hand from my chest.

He's right. Spartak is certifiably insane. A law unto himself most of the time, and we're walking into the most unpredictable meeting the clan has ever faced. It's blackmail, and there will be nothing civilized about it.

I walk inside, and the hostess meets my gaze, her brow furrowing. "How may I help you, gentlemen?"

"I've got a meeting with Mr. Volkov in—" I glance at my watch. "Exactly five minutes."

Her expression turns stern. "Rourke Callaghan, I assume?" She asks.

I nod in response.

"This way." Her brow furrows. "He told me to expect one of you."

"Gael is my associate. He must be present."

She nods and leads us through the busy restaurant to the back, walking us straight through the kitchen to another door. Through this door is a dark corridor with rooms off each side, which appear to be full of men gambling. The Bratva's run gambling rings out of the back of their restaurants, bars, and clubs.

"He's waiting for you in there," she says, nodding at the last door on the right.

I glance at Gael, who looks a little unsure about this. "Thank you," I say.

She says nothing, walking away and leaving the two of us staring at the door.

"Something feels off," Gael says, voicing my concern.

"Aye, it does." I run a hand across the back of my neck. "What should we do?"

Gael raises a brow. "Now you want my opinion?"

I grit my teeth together, "Yes."

"We go in there ready to draw our guns at the first sign of any funny business." He claps me on the back. "What's the worst that can happen?"

"We die?" I reply.

He smirks. "Don't chicken out on me now, Callaghan. Eleven men's lives are at risk."

I draw in a deep breath and return my gaze to the door, nodding. "Okay, let's do this." I march toward the door and set my hand on the handle in a tight, vise-like grip. Here goes nothing. I swing the door open, and the scene in front of me almost slays me.

My heart turns to stone in my chest the moment I step foot inside.

Spartak has Viki tied to a chair, her eyes wide with shock.

How the fuck did she get here?

I shake my head, rage filtering through my bloodstream like fucking heroine. "Viki, what the hell?"

Tears prickles in her eyes. "I thought I could reason with my father." She glares at him. "It seems what I want doesn't matter. He'd rather use me as bait to kill you."

"Let your daughter go, Spartak. This is between you and me," I say, crossing my arms over my chest.

Spartak smirks, and it is horrifying. "No chance, Callaghan. You've made me look a fool, and now it's time for me to repay the favor."

Viki looks panicked as she stares at me, practically pleading with me with her eyes. When we get out of this alive, I'm going to spank her ass so fucking raw she won't be able to sit for at least a week.

I step closer, feeling the desperate urge to have her by my side clawing at me. "I'd say we're about even, wouldn't you?" I raise a brow, glaring at my arch-nemesis. "I made you look a fool, but you killed my father in cold blood because he couldn't bring my sister to you in time."

Spartak shakes his head. "All of you are fucking idiots if you believe I so much as touched your father," he hisses. He steps closer, eyes blazing with uncontrollable rage.

I recognize that look because it's one I've seen so

fucking often in the mirror. "He was found murdered in your club. If it wasn't you, who the fuck was it?"

"Someone who wants this war." He shakes his head. "I'm trying to find out. Two private investigators are working on it as we speak, but there's no getting past this bad blood between us now." He bares his teeth, the rage spilling out as he keeps himself on a tight leash. "You took my daughter and married her without my permission. I won't stand by while you continue to disrespect my family or me." He pulls a gun, but Gael is as fast.

"Not so fast, Volkov." He aims it at him while Spartak aims his handgun at me.

Spartak's eyes narrow as they land on my second in command, as if he only just noticed his presence. "Had to bring along a bodyguard, Rourke?" He shakes his head. "You always were a coward, and I don't know what my daughter sees in you."

I growl, marching toward him only to be stopped by the arming click of him cocking his gun.

"I wouldn't take another step if I were you."

Gael clears his throat. "If you shoot, you die, old man."

Spartak laughs. "We'll all die at some point. The question is, little Callaghan. Are you ready?"

I move my gaze between my wife and her father, knowing that I'm not done yet. My father died too young, but I don't intend to follow in his footsteps. "What would it take for me, my wife, and my men to walk out of here alive?" I realize how desperate I sound as Spartak's eyes light up with amusement.

Gael clears his throat, signaling I'm making a mistake trying to reason with him. What he doesn't realize is I'm stalling. If Torin has any chance of getting the eleven men out of here, he needs all the time we can offer him.

"End the war and hand over your south side territory to us. That's the only way you all walk out of here alive."

I raise a brow. "Are you insane?"

"Apparently." He shrugs. "Most of Chicago think I'm psychopathic, so it's probably true." He places a hand on Viktoria's shoulder and squeezes hard, making her squirm in pain. "Otherwise, my daughter will get to watch me kill you slowly and painfully before I lock her away for the rest of her life so she can reflect on the terrible mistake she made, falling for our enemy."

Radio interference crackles in my ear, followed by Torin's voice. "Clear, waiting for you in the van."

Spartak is so blindly cocky it makes me wonder how he is doing so well in this war. Our distraction worked. I just wish Viki hadn't taken matters into her own hands and made this harder for us.

"A written truce that states I concede to you and twenty million dollar payment."

Gael shakes his head. "Boss, what the—"

I glare at him, and he falls silent.

Spartak considers my offer before shaking his head. "No. Southside or nothing."

"Do it, Gael," I say.

Gael doesn't hesitate, shooting my enemy in the right leg quickly, followed by the left. He then shoots the handgun out of his hand before Spartak can react. Now I'm reminded why Gael was my father's second in command. No one in the United States can beat him with his gun skills.

"Bastard," he growls, eyes wide as he reaches for the panic button under his desk, hitting it before Gael can react.

"Shit," I say, rushing forward and untying Viki from the chair. "We need to get out of here fast."

Viki stands, placing a hand on my arm. "I know the best way. Follow me." She takes off toward the door when I hear a shot pierce my eardrums as the bullet flies past me and hits her right in the back.

Spartak grins, holding the gun in his bloodied hands. "No one takes what is mine and gets away with it, Callaghan. No one."

I charge toward him, disarming him in one swoop. My fist slams into his face, knocking him out cold. Killing Spartak would cause more trouble than it is worth.

Gael holds Viki in his arms as the wound gushes with blood. "She needs a hospital, fast."

"Fuck," I growl, lifting her over my shoulder and carrying her out of the door. "First, we need to get out of here."

Gael follows me as we navigate out of the building as the guards' footsteps echo in the distance.

"Hold on, princess. You are going to be okay," I murmur as she groans.

She had to be okay. Viki is my world, and if she dies, I will have to return and murder Spartak with my bare hands, even if it's the last thing I do.

What kind of man shoots his daughter?

A man without a soul. She's losing too much blood as I try desperately to block up the wound, knowing that if I don't get her help quickly, everything that matters will extinguish along with her.

I PACE up and down the hospital waiting room for what feels like hours.

No one will tell me how she is, and all they say is she's in theatre.

We didn't have time to get her to the private

underground clinic I usually use across the other side of town. I hate regular hospitals because no one can tell you shit. Viki might lose her fight while I pace up and down helplessly. There's absolutely nothing I can do.

I'm angry with her. Why she put herself in such a dangerous position, I'll never know. She knew how ruthless her father was, and she was the one who told me he'd kill her once he realized she wasn't a virgin. So I'll never understand why she thought she could reason with him for my life and hers.

The doctor, who was dealing with her case, appears in bloodied scrubs, looking utterly exhausted. "Are you the husband?" He asks.

I nod. "Viktoria made it through, but she's lost a lot of blood."

The tension from my body escapes me with the breath I was holding. "Thank God for that." I step closer to the doors. "Can I see her?"

"It's best that she rests for a few hours. You should return in the morning to see her. She's not conscious at the moment." He shakes his head. "It was touch and go, but we got the bullet out and sealed the wound."

"I need to see her. I don't care if she's not conscious." I fold my arms over my chest. "I'm her husband and want to be by her side when she wakes."

He sighs heavily. "Understood. Only one visitor, though, for the night." He glances at Gael, Maeve, Kieran, and Killian, who have been here with me in support. "The rest will have to leave. She is in recovery room twenty." Torin is dealing with the men Spartak kidnapped, as they were injured.

I nod. "Fine. Thank you." I turn to my family. "She made it, but you guys have to go. Only one visitor allowed."

Maeve's eyes well with tears as she pulls me into a tight hug. "I'm so glad she's okay."

I squeeze her, grateful that I didn't have to go through this alone, even if I'd never admit it to any of them.

Kill and Kier nod. "Aye, it's lucky," Kier says.

"I'm staying here tonight." I nod toward the door. "The rest of you can get home. I'll update you all tomorrow."

Killian and Kieran walk away while Maeve squeezes my hand once more before Gael steers her out of the hospital. I turn around and glance at the doors where she's held, almost fearing facing her after what happened. I know it's not my fault she got hurt, but I hate I failed to protect her from her father, even if she put herself in harm's way when I had a solid plan.

I walk through the double swing doors and search for recovery room number twenty. It's at the end of a long corridor, and when I see my wife, my heart squeezes in my chest. My powerful princess looks utterly broken as she lies on the hospital bed, eyes shut, sleeping like the angel she is.

I almost lost her.

It doesn't bear thinking about as her loss would cut me far deeper than either of my parents, and her loss would be like losing half of my heart. From here on in, no more games. I love her, and I intend to make sure she knows how much every day for the rest of our lives together.

28

VIKTORIA

My father is an evil son of a bitch for shooting me.

The look on his face when I told him I loved Rourke was cold. He's not the man I thought he was. A dark, vindictive man who cares more about power than his daughter.

Even though I'd told Rourke that he'd kill me if he found out I was no longer a virgin, a part of me didn't believe that. A part of me hoped that blood was more important to him than power, but it seems he cares more about the Bratva than me. I bared my soul to the man that fathered me, and he responded by laughing in my face. Even worse, he shot me in the back.

I drift in and out of consciousness, hearing voices

around me shouting medical terms as the blinding lights flicker above me. My eyes are open, and yet everything is a blur of movement.

"You better pull through this, Viki," Rourke says, his deep voice unmistakable as he moves along with the bed somewhere to my right. "Please." The vulnerability in his voice cuts me to the core as I try to keep hold of my conscioussness, fighting against the darkness trying to pull me under.

"I'll fight," I mutter, knowing he probably can't hear me. "For you, I'd do anything."

His hand remains tight around mine. "Is my wife going to be okay?" He questions.

"Sir, I'm sorry, but you can't go past this point," a male voice says.

Rourke squeezes my hand briefly before it leaves mine entirely, and all I hear is the murmur of doctors, their voices growing more distant with every second that ticks by.

I shut my eyes, blocking out the light and the flashes of movement. I groan, my body struggling to stay in the light as the darkness rushes for me.

"Prep the operation room. We've got a critical gunshot wound," I hear a man shout above me.

Critical.

The word registers but doesn't as my pulse

weakens in my chest, making it difficult to breathe. It feels like my world is crashing in around me, trying to squeeze the last ounce of life while my mind clings to hope desperately.

I have to survive for him. I hate the thought of leaving him when we have so much more to learn about each other. This can't be the end. I have to believe that I'll make it through for him, for us.

MY EYES FLUTTER open to the rhythmic beeping of a heart monitor, signaling that I'm in the hospital. Numbness spreads through my body as I try to remember why.

Then it comes back to me like a freight train slamming into me with force.

My fucking father shot me.

I sit up in bed straight, wincing at the pain radiating from my chest.

Critical gunshot wound.

That's one of the last things I remember hearing before I blacked out. A soft snore draws my attention to my right, where Rourke is slumped in a hard, uncomfortable plastic chair, sleeping.

My heart constricts in my chest at the sight of

him sleeping here because of me and my stupidity. I'm not sure what I was thinking when I headed to my father's restaurant ahead of Rourke, other than knowing I was worried my father might have killed my husband. A fate that is worse than dying myself.

Rourke stirs, his eyes flickering open and finding mine almost instantly. And then that flaring electric chemistry swirls in the air the moment our eyes meet. It's so palpable that I wonder if other people sense it when they're with the two of us.

"Hey," I say, my voice quiet.

He smiles and reaches for my hand. "Hey, princess. How are you feeling?"

I raise a brow. "Like a was hit by a bus and then reassembled."

He chuckles. "You are lucky to be alive," he says, his expression turning stern. "I can't believe you snuck out and went to Darbazi ahead of me, Viki."

I swallow hard, as it wasn't one of my best decisions. Scratch that. It was possibly one of my worst moves yet. "Sorry," I say, glancing down at my hands in my lap. "It was a stupid thing to do."

He nods. "Yes, it was. A stupid thing that I will punish you for thoroughly once you are healed." His eyes narrow. "Why did you go, Viki?"

I'm too ashamed of myself to meet his gaze. Instead, I focus on my hands in my lap. "I thought I could reason with my father." My throat closes around a lump wedged in it. "Seems I was very wrong." Tears prickle my eyes before slowly trailing their way down my cheeks. "I can't believe he shot me."

Rourke clears his throat. "You told me he would kill you for no longer being a virgin. Did you believe that?"

I meet Rourke's gaze and shake my head. "He'd always said he would, but I honestly thought my father cared about me too much to do that." I shrug, the tears rushing down my face relentlessly. "I was wrong."

A knock at the door sounds, making me glance over to see my brother, Maxim, standing outside.

Fuck.

Rourke stiffens. "What the hell is he doing here?"

He opens the door and holds his hands up to Rourke. "I don't want any trouble, Callaghan. I'm here to check on my baby sister." He meets my gaze and gives me a wistful smile. "I'm so sorry, Viki."

Maxim and I have never really been close, but he's always taken it on himself to look out for me and protect me. I'm thankful he doesn't share the same vile resentment toward me for my marriage to Rourke, which had been out of my control anyway.

"Dad is a fucking asshole," he says, shaking his head. "He never should have shot you."

I raise a brow. "You don't say."

He sighs heavily, rubbing a hand across the back of his neck. "I've wanted to check in on you ever since we got the video of the wedding." He shoots a glare at Rourke, who remains tense and on edge. "Father wouldn't let me. He said you were no longer a part of this family." Maxim sits on the edge of my hospital bed and takes my hand. "That's bullshit to me. You'll always be my little sister."

I glance at Rourke. "Can you give us a minute?"

He looks reluctant but nods. "If you so much as say a wrong word to my wife, I'll strangle you, Volkov. Do you understand?"

"Right back at you, Callaghan," he spits, eyes narrowing.

Rourke leaves the room and shuts the door behind him, heading left to give us some privacy.

"How is Father?" I ask, remembering that Gael, Rourke's right-hand man, shot him multiple times.

"Why the fuck do you care? He should be dead to you." He shakes his head. "That's always been your problem, Viki. You have too kind a heart."

I nod in agreement, as he's right. "True, but unfortunately, that son of a bitch still fathered me."

He laughs. "He will live. They were superficial

wounds, unlike the one he gave you." Maxim's expression hardens. "I've given him a piece of my mind for it, Viki. He has no fucking respect for you." He glances at the door as if checking for Rourke. "I can't say I'm happy you married a Callaghan, but are you happy?"

I nod in response. "Crazily enough, I love the cocky son of a bitch."

Maxim smiles, and it's one of the kindest smiles he's ever given me. "Then I'm happy for you. It may be difficult for us to keep in touch, though. While the Irish and Bratva are at war, but I'll try my best." He squeezes my hand. "I can't be here long, as I don't want the Bratva to think I'm colluding with the Callaghans." He gives me a serious look. "You know what happens to traitors."

I shudder as I vividly recall what happened to Jakov, one of my father's men, at a family dinner when I was only ten years old. My father chopped off his fingers one by one in front of us, and my mother, giving no mind to her pleas for him to stop. And then slit his throat, allowing us to watch him choke on his blood. He said we had to see the world for what it truly is, an abyss of darkness. After Father shot me, I have no idea what he's truly capable of with Maxim. "I do." I squeeze his hand back. "I'll miss you, Max."

He pushes a stray hair behind my ear. "I'll miss

you too, Viki, but it won't be forever." He shakes his head. "The war will subside." He stands and gives me a farewell salute. "Until then."

"Until then," I murmur, watching as he walks away and out of my life for now.

Rourke returns moments later, brows pinched together. "Are you okay?" He asks.

I shrug, feeling tears well in my eyes. "I guess. I just hate this war."

"You and me, both, princess." He sits next to me and takes my hand, giving me a pitiful look, which only makes me angry. "You'll see your brother again, that I'm sure of."

I nod as I recall something my father said. "Is it possible my father had nothing to do with your father's death?"

His brow furrows. "Surely you don't believe that crap."

"I believe it because I know my father, and when I confronted him about it, he was telling the truth. I'm sure of it."

Rourke releases a deep breath, shaking his head. "Fuck, if you're right, then we've gone to war for nothing." His brow pulls together. "The more troubling question would be who killed him if not your father or the Bratva?"

I have no clue. My knowledge of the criminal

organizations in Chicago extends to knowing that there are five main families, including my own. "Did anyone have any grievances with your father?"

He raises a brow. "Other than your father?"

I nod.

"Well, the Morrone family has been at war with mine for years. Other than that, he had a list longer than me of enemies he's made over the years."

I sigh, as I know it wouldn't matter if we solved the puzzle. My father said it himself that there's too much bad blood between the Callaghan Clan and Volkov Bratva to quit this was now. "Father wouldn't back down, even if you uncovered the actual killer. He's more stubborn than me." I glance at Rourke. "And you know how stubborn I can be."

He laughs a deep, throaty laugh, making my insides warm from the sound. "That I do, aingeal."

My brow furrows at the word as I've heard him use it before, but he's never explained the meaning. "What does that mean?"

The corner of his lips turns up into a smile. "It means angel in Gaelic."

Heat filters through my cheeks, making me feel like I'm burning from the inside. "I'm certainly no angel."

Rourke moves closer to me, perching on the edge of the bed and gazing down at me as if I'm the best thing he's ever seen. It makes goosebumps prickle over my skin, and butterflies flutter to life deep in the pit of my gut. "To me, you are," he murmurs, lacing his fingers through my hair in soothing strokes. "You're the most important in this world." Rourke bends his neck to kiss me softly and chastely, applying pressure to my lips with his and not forcing his tongue into my mouth, but it doesn't stop that heated desire from coming to life as I feel the wetness between my thighs.

"Cool it, Viki. You are in no shape for heavy petting," he murmurs, smirking against my lips.

I laugh and wince simultaneously as my wound kills. "Have the doctors given me enough pain meds?" I ask, shaking my head. "As it doesn't feel like it."

Rourke cups my face in his hands and kisses me once more. "I don't know. I'll go find a doctor and tell them you're awake." He stands and glances back as he reaches the door. "Never scare me like that again, Viki. I don't think my heart can handle it." Without another word, he walks out of the door.

I have no intention of getting myself into such a stupid position again. My father can go to hell for all I care. Gael shot him three times, but something tells me that man was shooting to maim, not kill. My father shot to kill that I do not doubt. He's one of the best marksmen in the Bratva, so I'm lucky that he missed my heart.

Maxim is right. He should be dead to me, and he is. I never want to see him again, as I've got my new family now. A family that would never hurt me the way my father has.

ROURKE

I enter the hospital for the last time. It's been two weeks since Spartak shot Viki, and they're only now releasing her. She's doing well, and the wound is healing, but they like to keep patients and monitor them for a ridiculous amount of time, which is bullshit.

It's their way of saying they want to make as much money off of her as they can, charging a ridiculous amount for each day she remains here, but her name is all they need to know she has money. Kerry, my on-site doctor, could have handled her care at home, but Viki insisted on listening to the professionals.

Spartak has ramped up his efforts to cripple us, but we've pushed back just as hard now we've worked out the kinks in his supply chain. I try not to talk about Spartak in front of Viki as I know how badly his actions hurt her. Only a psycho shoots his daughter.

"May I help you, sir?" The receptionist asks as I walk into the outpatient unit.

I nod. "Yes, my wife is being released today. Mrs. Callaghan?"

Her brow furrows. "Her father already arrived about a minute ago and took her down there."

My heart stills in my chest. "Are you fucking kidding?" I growl, eyes wide. "The man wants to harm her." I don't say another word, racing down the corridor she signaled at.

"Please let me go, Father," Viki cries up ahead, driving me insane.

This man has gone a step too fucking far. How did he even know she was here?

Who am I kidding? Spartak has eyes and ears everywhere. Her brother found her quickly enough.

"Shut up, Viktoria. You've disgraced this family." I run down the corridor, halting around the corner from them. "You'll never see that man again, do you understand?"

"That man? Do you mean my husband?" She spits.

I glance up at the ceiling, checking for surveillance cameras. There are two directly aimed at where they're stood. I pull my cell phone out and text Kieran, who is waiting outside in the car.

Code red. Spartak is here. Alert security that a man has kidnapped someone at the hospital.

I need him to know that this could go south as I step around the corner. I also know that if I'm getting Viki back from this son of a bitch, I need backup from the hospital security. "Let her go, Spartak."

His head whips around, and eyes narrow. "No fucking way," he says, clinging onto two crutches as a couple of men ahead reach for their guns, clearly with him.

"I would tell your men to back down unless you want your face plastered all over NBC news?" I nod at the cameras which he faces. "Now, give me my wife, and let us go in peace." I narrow my eyes at him. "I think you've done enough damage already."

He follows my gaze to the cameras and turns to face his men, holding a hand up and signaling for them to back down. "It appears we're at an impasse."

I shake my head. "No, you have my wife, and I want her back." I step forward, making him tense. "Give her back, and then we don't have a problem." I glance back down the corridor. "I've already raised the alert at the reception desk, confirming you shouldn't have taken her. Security will be here any minute."

He glares at me, glancing at me, and then at his daughter. "How do I know you aren't bluffing?"

I might be if Kier hasn't seen my text, and I merely told the receptions intends to harm her, but I doubt she is raising the alarm for me. "I'd love to see you dragged out by security, so I'll let you find out." I hold his gaze confidently, knowing I've got nothing to lose.

Spartak looks angrier than I've ever seen him as he glances between his daughter and me twice more before walking down the corridor without a word.

I release a breath I didn't even know I was holding, grabbing the handles of Viki's wheelchair. "Let's get you home."

Her back rises and falls as she sobs. "I thought he was going to kill me," she whispers.

"He couldn't do anything in this hospital without serious repercussions." The thud of footsteps rushing toward us draws my attention as Kieran comes flanked by two security guards.

"Where is he?" Kier asks.

I nod in the direction Spartak disappeared down. "He took off that way, but I convinced him to surrender my wife back to me."

One of the security guards looks skeptical as he

walks toward Viktoria. "Can you confirm who should collect you from the hospital?"

She nods, smiling widely. "My husband, thankfully, he got here in time before my father took me." Her expression turns stern. "This hospital needs to tighten its measures. I told the nurse I he wasn't supposed to collect me, but she ignored me."

"I'm sorry about that," he says, straightening up. "Would you like to make a formal complaint?"

She gazes at me, and I shake my head.

"No, we just want to get home. I appreciate your help," I answer.

Kieran takes the handles of her wheelchair. "Here, let me help you to the car."

I smile, watching my brother, who, since learning what she tried to do to save me, has done a one-eighty turn on his opinion of my wife.

"Thank you," Viki replies as he wheels her down the corridor.

I follow them, eager to get my princess home and safe. The city of Chicago has never been more dangerous for people like us, and I intend to protect her from the danger from here on out. I'll die before another person hurts my princess.

———

I CARRY her over the threshold into my room.

She gasps, eyes widening. "You redecorated?" She asks, gazing at the light walls and new floor. "Why?"

I smile at her and carry her to the cream four-poster bed I switched my other out for. "You didn't like it as it was, and I want you to be happy here." I raise a brow. "Is it to your satisfaction, your majesty?" I ask mockingly.

She laughs, wincing as she does as she's still in pain. "It is. I love it."

"Good," I say. Thankfully, Maeve offered to help, as I didn't know where to start. She runs her hands over the pale champagne satin bedspread, smiling softly. "I'm so glad you kidnapped me, Rourke Callaghan."

I tilt my head, as it's such an odd thing to say. "Are you?"

She meets my gaze and nods. "You saved me when I didn't even realize I needed saving."

I shake my head. "Don't get all soppy on me now, princess. Otherwise, all your work to prove you hate me is out the window."

"You know I don't hate you," she says, her eyes brimming with tears. "Do you infuriate me beyond belief? The answer is yes."

I laugh. The way I've treated her, she should hate me. "True."

"But for some ridiculous reason, I love you more than I can put into words." Her smile is angelic. "Every annoying part of you."

I laugh. "Right back at you, brat."

Her nose wrinkles. "I'm not a brat."

"I beg to differ and just know, once you are one-hundred percent healed, I'm going to give you your most intense punishment yet for putting yourself in danger." I help her onto the bed, pulling her shoes and socks off first. "But right now, I'm going to treat you like the princess you are."

I unbutton her pants and inch them down her legs, groaning as the tense desire that's been building inside of me ever since she was admitted rises to the surface. "Such a gentleman," she teases.

I pull my oversized t-shirt over her head, leaving her in nothing. My heart clenches at the sight of the fresh, freshly closed-up wound where the bullet pierced her skin. A reminder that I failed to protect her from harm, but that's not a mistake I'll ever make again.

Viki squirms under my gaze, her cheeks turning pink. "It's horrible, isn't it?" She asks.

I shake my head and gently run my finger down her cheek, hooking it under her chin and forcing her to meet my gaze. "No, everything about you is beautiful, even this wound." I kiss her lips softly. "Lie down, sweetheart."

She does as I say, lying back on the soft fabric. "I love this bedspread." Her eyes dilate in anticipation as I move my hands to her feet and slowly massage them.

"I love how you look naked on it," I reply.

Viki rolls her eyes. "You always have to be so crude."

I chuckle. "Not always." I move my attention to her legs, working out the knots.

She moans, head falling back on the pillow. "That feels good." I work out the knots from the rest of her body, taking care when I get to the sensitive flesh around her wound. Every time I see her wince, the guilt eats away at me. By the time I'm finished, she's beyond relaxed, and her eyes are so dilated it's clear she's thinking of only one thing.

I part her legs, licking her inner thighs teasingly.

Viki shudders, watching me as I tease my tongue around her pussy, but not yet giving her what she wants. She fists her hands by her side, making frustrated noises as I drag my tongue closer to her arousal. Her scent tinges my nostrils, infusing my body with a desire so intense it threatens to break me in half.

"Please, Rourke," she moans, holding my gaze intently.

"Tell me what you want," I order, continuing to tease her.

Before answering, Viki bites her thick bottom lip, "I want you to make me come."

I slide my tongue through her, parting her lips and making her shudder. Slowly, I move right through her center and then tease the tip of my tongue around her clit.

Her hips buck off the bed, arching toward my face.

I hold her down, placing a firm hand on her abdomen. "I'm in control."

She moans, her eyes rolling back in her head as she does.

There's nothing I love more than seeing my wife fall apart for me.

I slip a finger into her soaking channel, curling it in the way she always reacts to, pushing her toward the edge with vigor.

"You're already so damn wet," I murmur before circling her clit with the tip of my tongue. "Is it because you are thinking about how it will feel when I punish you?" Viki has darkness inside of her, darkness that she tries to fight, but it's a fundamental part of her. She craves the pain as badly as I enjoy inflicting it. We're two sides of the same coin, making us a perfect match.

Viki hesitates before nodding. "It's sick, isn't it?" she asks, her pink cheeks turning red.

I shake my head. "Not as sick as me enjoying inflicting it on you." I continue to devour her as she moans, releasing the hold she had on her inhibitions. "I want you to come for me, and I want to taste every drop as you come on my face."

Viki groans and her thighs are shaking in response.

My teeth graze the throbbing, sensitive nub at the apex of her thighs.

It's all it takes to send her into oblivion as she writhes beneath me, panting and moaning as her dainty fingers fist the comforter beneath her.

She's a picture of heaven. A goddess in her own fucking right, and my goddess at that.

"Fuck, you're perfect," I murmur before licking every drop of juice from her.

Her breathing is labored as she meets my gaze, those bright green eyes blazing with purpose. "Not as perfect as you."

I smile at her. "I'm many things, but perfect ain't one of them, sweetheart." I climb onto the bed next to her, pulling her gently against me careful of the wound. "I never thought I'd say it, but I'm in love with a fucking Russian," I murmur in a teasing tone.

She fakes a shocked expression. "Really? Who are you fucking behind my back?"

I roll my eyes and kiss her forehead. "Don't be an idiot."

She sighs, resting against my chest. "I love you too," she says, placing her small hand on my chest and tracing the Callaghan coat of arms. "You know, I want children." There's a hint of uncertainty in her tone.

"Aye, so do I. I can't exactly run an empire without heirs, can I?"

She tenses slightly. "Will they have a good childhood? As mine was anything but."

I lean away and tilt her chin up to me. "Of course, I had a good childhood, even if my father started my training a little young."

"How young?"

My brow furrows as I try to recall. "I was fourteen when I first got involved with the clan. Until then, I had nothing to do with it, and I was a sheltered, spoiled brat." I meet her gaze. "Why, how old were you when you knew of your father's dealings?"

She shakes her head. "I honestly can't remember the first time I knew, but I was ten when he first killed a man in front of Maxim and me."

It doesn't shock me in the slightest. Spartak has proven how little his family means to him by shooting his daughter, so it doesn't surprise me that her childhood was anything but happy. "Did he mistreat you?"

Viki gives me a blank stare. "Maybe? I'm not sure. I assumed it was normal, but he often shut me in the basement alone for hours on end as punishment for trivial things." She sighs. "He even did it to me the afternoon on the day we met. I never want to treat my children that way."

I kiss her softly, stroking her dark hair with my fingers. "Believe me, our children will be loved and cherished and protected, I can promise you that."

She smiles against my lips and then kisses me back passionately. Our tongues dance as the fire between us blazes to life like a living thing that exists between us, ever-present.

I can't believe that this war resulted in anything good. While I miss my father, I'm so thankful that Viki fell into my orbit because of my need for revenge.

My plan worked, as I've annoyed Spartak and forever stolen one of his family members, finding my soul mate and my reason for living.

VIKTORIA

*O*ne year later...

Rourke stands at the helm of his yacht, shirtless, gazing over the gleaming surface of the sea.

It's about time we took a vacation, even if the city is still in a state of chaos. Chaos has become the new normal in Chicago, and it's a place where instability reigns. So much has happened in one year, it's almost impossible to keep track.

I walk toward my husband, holding a glass of Irish whiskey in my hand. "I got you a drink, captain."

He turns around and smiles. "Thank you, sweetheart," he murmurs, taking the drink from my hand. His finger brushes mine with the lightest of touches, but it is all it takes to set me ablaze. "How is our little kicker today?" He places the drink down and moves his hand over my pregnant stomach.

"A little less feisty today, thankfully." I'm still two months away from my due date, but I can't deny I'm ready for the little one to get out of my body fast. It's exhausting carrying and nurturing another human inside of you. "Do you want to go for a swim?" I ask, noticing a small secluded cove a few hundred meters ahead. "That looks perfect." I point at the cove.

Rourke nods. "Whatever you want, princess." He leans in and kisses me softly, melting me. It's crazy how much I've fallen for the villain in my story, as the man who kidnapped me turned out to be my soul mate. "I'll drop the anchor as close as I can to shore," he says.

He's been freaking out about me swimming in the open sea while pregnant. I'm pregnant, not disabled. It's irritating how protective he's been of me ever since we found out, even more protective than when I almost died at the hands of my father. A man who is dead to me after what he pulled, heartlessly choosing his selfish pride over me.

Rourke drops the anchor about fifty meters from the shore and gets the steps set up so I can climb down into the water. "Hold my hand to get over," he says, grabbing my wrist as I reach for the ladder.

I roll my eyes but take his hand to climb over,

dropping into the warm water below. The oceans around the Caribbean are so beautiful, and it's lovely to get away from the biting cold of winter in Chicago.

Rourke jumps in off the side of the boat, making a wave next to me. "I bet you wish you could jump in, princess," he goads.

I hate not being able to do things because of my pregnancy, but I know jumping into the water from a height is dangerous while pregnant. I swim away from my husband instead of rising to his taunt, glancing over my shoulder. "Catch me if you can."

His eyes flash with determination. "Easy," he calls before ducking down under the surface.

I move my arms and legs faster, trying to speed away from him through the warm, shallow water.

I get about twenty meters before he comes up in front of me, smirking. "Never challenge a Callaghan, Viki. You'll always lose. We're fiercely competitive." He stands up in the water, which comes to his chest. "You shouldn't be exerting yourself too much in your condition."

I glare at him. "I'm pregnant, not dying."

He chuckles. "Always so feisty, princess." He wraps his arms around me and pulls me against him, supporting me in the water, since I'm still too short to stand. "It's one reason I love you so much."

I wrap my legs around his waist and pull him close, kissing him.

Rourke groans, his eyes fluttering shut as his tongue strokes against my lips, making me part them. And then he consumes me from the inside out. His tongue violently stokes to life that ever-present intoxicating need that no time can ever quench.

The heavy press of his cock in his swim shorts rests against my swollen belly. "Fuck me," I murmur, knowing we're in a deserted cove that only a boat can reach. We shouldn't be interrupted here, of all places.

He smiles against my mouth. "You've such a dirty mouth for a princess," he muses.

I glare at him. "Is that a yes to my proposal?"

He laughs that sweet, heart-wrenching laugh. "Always," he murmurs before kissing me again, more deeply. "I'd never deny you anything. You know that."

I smile against his lips as he hooks his fingers into the waistband of my bikini bottoms, pushing them off me. He moves his finger between my wet lips, groaning as he feels how wet I am. Ever since he knocked me up, I've been more insatiable than ever, which was an unexpected side effect.

Rourke's lips slide over my neck in a tender kiss as he sucks at my flesh, making me sure I'll have a love bite as a result, which since we've been away, he's made a habit of giving me.

I groan, my clit throbbing in anticipation of having my husband inside of me. "Stop teasing me and give me your cock, Mr. Callaghan."

He gasps, acting scandalized. "Mrs. Callaghan. Don't be so crass." He slips his finger inside of me, curling it to hit the spot deep inside of me that lights me on fire. "I only ever make love to my wife."

I laugh as he pulls me tighter against him. "You're many things, Rourke, but a gentleman isn't one of them."

He smirks a devilish grin that I've learned to love. "Touche." He thrust his fingers in and out of me faster, focusing all his attention on my pleasure. Rourke is the master of my body as he strokes my clit with his other hand.

My nipples pucker against the thick fabric of my bikini top as the pressure inside of me builds like a storm, threatening to tear me apart in one swoop. I moan deeply, his lips crashing against mine as he devours the sound. His tongue thrust into my mouth with violent desperation as I feel him free his thick cock, pulling his fingers from me when I'm on the edge of coming apart.

I whimper at the loss of his fingers, but he's quick to replace them with the hard length of his erection, driving in so deep that I come apart instantly. "Fuck, Rourke," I hiss, my body spasming in the water as he plows into me relentlessly, lifting me up and down his cock and building the next orgasm before I've finished my first.

"I'll never tire of watching you bounce up and down on my cock, princess," he murmurs in my ear as I meet his thrusts, grinding myself on him in desperation. At this angle, his cock rubs my clit with each stroke, forcing me toward the cliff edge too fucking fast.

"Oh, God," I claw at my husband's broad, muscular shoulders to ground myself.

He bites the shell of my ear before whispering, "God has nothing to do with it."

I groan as the palpable need heightens in the air between us, driving me closer and closer to the precipice of no return.

Rourke reaches around my back and parts my ass cheeks before sliding his finger in.

I groan, enjoying the sensation as he moves it in and out in time with his cock.

"You're such a dirty girl, Viki," he purrs, licking the column of my neck as his cock swells inside of me. "I love how you react to anything in your ass."

I want him to fuck my ass here and now in the

water, but we've never tried it without lube. "I would love your cock, but we don't have any—"

Rourke reaches into his swim shorts pocket, pulling out a small bottle of lube. "Lube?" he asks.

I shudder, realizing that he had planned this all along. "I'll never say you don't come prepared."

He chuckles and eases me closer to the shore so that I can stand with my ass out of the water. "Bend over," he commands.

I do as he says, allowing him to part my cheeks and lube my hole up. He quickly rubs it over his cock and then grabs my hips. "Are you okay in this position?"

I nod, eager to feel him in my ass out in the open like this, as it feels so naughty, which only heightens my craving.

Rourke lines the tip of his cock at my tight hole, pushing gently. He eases inside easily, stretching me around his thick shaft.

The burning pain is brief as it quickly morphs into that aching pleasure I enjoy so damn much. His fingertips dig into my hips as he draws me back against his cock, burying himself to the hilt inside of me. In this position, it drives his cock so deep his balls hit my clit with each stroke.

"Such a good girl." I feel him leaning back, sensing he's watching his cock plowing into my ass.

He loves watching. "I'll never get bored with watching you take my cock like a pro."

I moan, arching my back more as he fucks me hard, but not as hard as I'd like. Ever since I've got pregnant, he's too damn gentle for my liking.

"Harder," I pant.

Rourke grabs a fistful of my hair and yanks me upward, forcing me to arch my back more. "You know the rules, Viki. No rough play until the baby is born," he growls, proving his hold on his control is slipping.

I pant as he holds me in this position, bringing his hips to meet my ass in frantic motions. My pussy muscles tense, as do the muscles around his cock, warning him I'm close to the edge.

"I want to feel that tight little ass come on my cock," he gasps, his thrusts deeper, more impatient. He reaches down and fingers my clit gently, massaging it in a way that always blows me apart.

"Fuck," I cry, my body shuddering as he continues to touch me and fuck me, coming right along with me.

Our breathing is erratic as we both remain in that position for a while. And then Rourke wraps his arms around me and sits down in the shallow water, pulling me onto his lap. "Beautiful," he murmurs.

I smile as I gaze over the crystal blue sea, which

reminds me of the hue of his eyes. "It is." I squeeze his muscular forearm that's wrapped around me. "Thank you for bringing me here."

He chuckles. "I wasn't talking about our surroundings. They pale compared to you."

I shake my head. "Don't be silly. This place is stunning."

"I'm not being silly. You're the single most beautiful thing on this earth to me, Viki, and don't you forget it," he growls, anger lacing his tone.

I smile, leaning back against his hard, powerful chest. "I love that you're so over the top with me."

He growls softly. "I'm not over the top. If you want over the top, I'll take you back to the boat and spank your ass so red you won't be able to sit down for days."

I shiver, feeling myself dampening between my thighs, his thick cock hardening beneath me. We agreed we'd lay off any heavy flogging until after the baby's born, but I want him to spank me. A sick and dark need that lives within me craves the submission and the way it feels to give everything to him, trusting him to hurt me, but only for my pleasure. It's intoxicating.

"Don't tempt me," I reply.

I feel his lips curve into a smile against the back

of my neck. "Never," he whispers, his breath tickling me.

We remain like that for a long while in the silence, enjoying each other's embrace as the soft waves crash around us. The sound is soothing as I cast my mind to the future. A future that will be full of love and happiness as we extend our family.

The city of Chicago may still be in a state of turmoil, but I've never felt calmer, ready to tackle anything that comes my way with my husband by my side.

THANK you for reading Violent Leader, the second book in the Chicago Mafia Dons Series. I hope you enjoyed reading Rourke and Viktoria's story.

The next book in this series will release in march next year and follow Maxim Volkov as his father arranges his marriage to the Bianchi family's eldest daughter.

Evil Prince: A Dark Arranged Marriage Romance

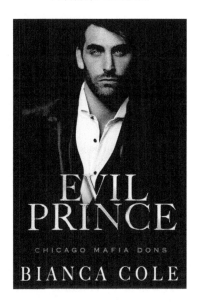

He's evil incarnate cloaked in a beautiful disguise.

My father uprooted our family, forcing me to relocate to America.

If that wasn't bad enough, he's making me marry the son of a psychopath.

Maxim Volkov.

Heir to the Volkov Bratva.

I'd rather die than be shackled to a man so evil.

A man who has no soul.

His piercing blue eyes are as cold as his stony heart.

And he's not exactly thrilled either.

My life has never felt so hopeless.

Maxim makes it clear I'm to be his slave.

A wife to tend to his every whim and desire.

The thing is, I've got darkness inside of me too.

He may think he's the monster in this union,

But violence is a part of my soul, and I won't bow down to his command.

Maxim has finally met his match.

Let chaos reign until death do us part, preferably his...

I will also be releasing a new book in January from a seperate series.

Here is the cover and blurb.

Corrupt Educator: A Dark Forbidden Mafia Academy Romance

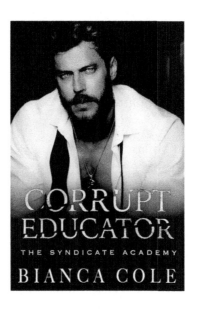

He's hiding a dark secret, one that will change my life forever.

I shouldn't be here.

Forced to move schools partway through my senior year.

The Syndicate Academy is the embodiment of everything I hate.

An academy for heirs of tyrants like my parents.

I hate it here, except for one part, Principal Oakley Byrne.

The most gorgeous man I've ever met, with piercing aquamarine eyes.

He's dark, brooding, and not your average Principal.

I'm drawn to him by a magnetic force, but I repel him.

Despite his cold treatment, I can't help but tempt the beast to come out to play.

An action I'll soon regret.

This man hides dark secrets behind his walls.

Secrets that could destroy my family and me.

They say all is fair in love and war.

I can't be a part of a war I never knew existed.

He intends to devour me whole and spit me out, leaving my world in tatters.

The question is, will I survive his wrath?

Her Mafia Daddy: A Dark Daddy Romance

Her Mafia Boss: A Dark Romance

Her Mafia King: A Dark Romance

Bratva Brotherhood Series

Bought by the Bratva: A Dark Mafia Romance

Captured by the Bratva: A Dark Mafia Romance

Claimed by the Bratva: A Dark Mafia Romance

Bound by the Bratva: A Dark Mafia Romance

Taken by the Bratva: A Dark Mafia Romance

Wynton Series

Filthy Boss: A Forbidden Office Romance

Filthy Professor: A First Time Professor And Student Romance

Filthy Lawyer: A Forbidden Hate to Love Romance

Filthy Doctor: A Fordbidden Romance

Royally Mated Series

Her Faerie King: A Faerie Royalty Paranormal Romance

Her Alpha King: A Royal Wolf Shifter Paranormal Romance

Her Dragon King: A Dragon Shifter Paranormal Romance

Her Vampire King: A Dark Vampire Romance

ABOUT THE AUTHOR

I love to write stories about over the top alpha bad boys who have heart beneath it all, fiery heroines, and happily-ever-after endings with heart and heat. My stories have twists and turns that will keep you flipping the pages and heat to set your kindle on fire.

For as long as I can remember, I've been a sucker for a good romance story. I've always loved to read. Suddenly, I realized why not combine my love of two things, books and romance?

My love of writing has grown over the past four years and I now publish on Amazon exclusively, weaving stories about dirty mafia bad boys and the women they fall head over heels in love with.

If you enjoyed this book please follow me on Amazon, Bookbub or any of the below social media platforms for alerts when more books are released.